Tainted Heart

tainted heart

MELISSA GRAVES

interlude ♦ press • new york

This book is dedicated to found family; whether stumbled upon or sought after, your unconditional love and support means the world to me.

1

THE INTERIOR OF THE JET is smaller than Kyle thought it would be. You'd think associating with the feds on this level would call for a little more legroom. Then again, there are the twice-hourly blood cocktails and heated neck pillows, so who is he to complain? Not even copious amounts of cigarette smoke—how does Elisa get away with that?—can distract him from the perks. This is the first time they've been offered the use of a private plane to travel to the federal blood distribution offices in Dallas and he'd like for it to not be the last; there's no comparing this to flying on a commercial airliner.

And it turns out that he's as comfortable at thirty thousand feet as he is at sea level.

"Can you taste the vodka?" Elisa asks. She frowns sideways at her cup. "I can't taste the vodka."

He laughs. "Brian told me that it's not actually alcohol, just some substitute that mimics the bite."

She flings her tray up in order to cross her legs. "Billions of research dollars a year and they still can't figure out how to get me drunk." Her smart, flawlessly-tailored business slacks tighten over her thighs. Kyle admires the seams. "At least they keep 'em coming."

The cocktails taste like shoe polish, but Kyle doesn't say so. He can only imagine how much they cost to serve. They aren't available to the public yet. And the blood is good. The blood is *always* good.

"Your twitching is driving me crazy," Elisa says. "Nervous?"

"Not used to the suit."

Despite the fact that this is his fourth business trip shadowing Elisa, he isn't used to the trappings. In so many ways, he still feels like that Midwestern bumpkin who passed out on her and Clara's doorstep a year ago.

"If you're gonna be a doctor's wife, you might wanna get used to formalwear and bling, *gato*," she says, a wicked smile tugging her blood-red lips wide. Unlike him, she looks at home in her business suit, from the sharp collar of her jacket to the perfect hem at her ankles.

"I wouldn't go that far, not yet."

"Trouble in paradise?"

He hesitates. It's not that. It's not that at all.

The problem is, he's not sure exactly what it is, and he doesn't want to talk about that. At the moment, his mind is a jumble of names and advice—every time they go on these trips, she coaches him so thoroughly beforehand about what to do and say and not do and say that he loses track of important details, and he wants this time to be different— and the last thing he wants to do is solicit her for relationship advice.

"You said once we reached cruising altitude that you'd answer my question," he says, evading her question in turn.

She sighs. "Refresh my memory?"

"Before we left you mentioned something about repurposing my room at the club now that I'm not using it as a bedroom. Something about putting the past in the past."

"Have we grown attached to our humble ex-abode?"

He narrows his eyes at her. In the last year, she has become one of his best friends, despite all appearances to the contrary and her protests that her "twink quota" has been full for a while. She isn't fooling him, and he no longer has to worry about pissing her off out of the blue.

"Elisa Martínez."

"All right," she says. She sips her blood, dabs her lips with a napkin and exhales. "That room? That was the room that Clara and I shared when we got to Chicago. Memories just burned into the wallpaper, you know? Some good, some bad. Sometimes I think about selling the whole building and moving on altogether."

"How did you end up there?"

"We never even graduated high school," she says. "Did I tell you that? Anyway. We were turned a year apart. After my turning and my girl taking off, I got a little clingy with Clara, you know. I knew I was being a bitch. Constantly taking her out. Teasing her with my badassness. I knew that chick she was with would run screaming if she knew about the crowd Clara was running with because of me. But Clara definitely had a taste for it. It got bad—her parents caught wind of things."

"The vamp stuff?"

"No, that was way below the radar then. But the dyke stuff. That stuff, they couldn't stand. I didn't want Clara to turn just to piss off her folks even more. But I wanted her. I—I was kind of an asshole. Selfish. She ended up sleeping with some crazy redneck vamp princess and got herself turned over a long weekend." She frowns. "I couldn't believe it. I wasn't sure whether I was upset that it wasn't me or relieved that someone else took care of it."

Kyle stares at his reflection in the little television screen that's built into the seat in front of him while Elisa talks. His reddish-brown coif has seen better days—he swears it's the altitude—and the glare created by the overhead lights hitting the screen makes indistinct, shadowy smears of his profile.

He's afraid to interrupt her with further questions, but his mind is already spinning. He thinks about what it must be like to have to hide your reality in order to survive. He thinks about having the privilege of not worrying about disappointing your parents because they aren't around to be disappointed—and then he wonders if he would have a thought that cold if he wasn't a vampire.

Elisa's eyes grow glassy. "Being a maker is complicated, you know? You can never just be with someone after that. It's a whole new level of connection. Anyway. We freaked out together. Her family figured out some serious shit was going down, but not exactly what that shit was. We couldn't stay. And things were in the air, like, what did she want? What did I want from her? I was gonna bail, just pack it up and maybe go to Canada or some-thing. Then she shows up on my doorstep covered in blood and carrying this designer bag full of whatever she could grab from her place. She'd almost killed a human feeding—her rich-bitch girlfriend. Ambulance on the way and everything. I dunno what got into us. I grabbed her, whatever I could, didn't even leave a note for my roommate. Just took her to a motel three towns over, shoved her in the shower and panicked."

Kyle can't help but sympathize with Clara. Violence takes on a whole new dimension when you're a predator in human form.

The crossover is where things get complicated. Sometimes, running is the only option.

"I knew we couldn't ever go back. There was just no way. We were too connected; too many people saw us in school, in town, at the bars together. I was gonna tell her we had to book it. She comes out of the bathroom, drops her towel, fangs out, tits in my face, pushes me onto the bed—"

"Oh, my god," he says, squinting. "How detailed is this going to get?" It's easier to make a joke than it is to acknowledge the vulnerability on Elisa's face—she doesn't often show him this side of herself, and he isn't sure if she wants him to acknowledge this or not.

She laughs. "A little pussy talk isn't going to break your gold-star gay streak, Hayes. I'll spare you the juicy and incredibly hot details because frankly, that ain't your business. Point is: amazing sex. We fed on each other, and by morning, I knew I wasn't going anywhere without her. She never got pinned for the assault on the girlfriend. I hadn't lived with my foster family for a long time and they never bothered to look for me unless they needed me to prove I still lived there. She robbed her parents blind the night before she left, which I didn't know until later— and she never got charged for that, either. Not sure why. They were probably too proud to admit how far off the rails their precious firstborn went."

All jokes about knowing way too much about their sex lives aside, Kyle wants to ask her why in the world two vampires would want to feed from each other, but he's not sure if he wants to change the direction of their conversation.

"So you had seed money and you got away relatively clean."

"Yep. Still, city life is fucking tough without a paper trail or friends. We lived on the streets and in the shelters for a while before we managed to buy the stuff that made us look legit. And finally, we managed to rent that pissy room. The whole building—the whole neighborhood—was a hellhole. But it was ours, and we kept it safe. Humans knew not to mess with us— vampires can put out a vibe that freaks them out, keeps them at bay. Clara and I were good at that."

Kyle pictures the building as it is today—still in a bad neighborhood, still shabby on the outside and down to its bones, but as safe and clean as they are able to make it. Four floors of apartment-like rooms with chairs and beds and first aid for the clients who come to experience the pleasurable pain and dangerous excitement of their blood being taken, bedrooms and communal bathrooms and kitchens for employees who have nowhere else to stay, and even a basement recreational room for those who want to socialize. He can only imagine how dilapidated and frightening the building was before Elisa and Clara renovated it. It's not exactly the Ritz now, but it seemed like heaven on earth to him when he collapsed on their doorstep. It became his home, and although he no longer lives there, he's still grateful for it.

"How did you get by?" he asks. He can't quite imagine Elisa waiting tables or filing or selling life insurance or tending bar.

"Clara's a fucking investment genius. It wasn't long before we started turning a profit. But, again, see, it's difficult to be legit on paper. It took a lot of money and time before we started to talk about moving on up. Neither of us knew what we wanted to do, really, aside from make bank and go to school so that we could make even more bank. We weren't like, married, you know, in the beginning. We fucked other girls. I could never get her out from under my skin, though. No matter what I did, it always came back to her."

Kyle loves seeing the fiercely loyal emotions that Elisa carries for Clara rise to the surface. He smiles and nudges her knee with his.

"At first, I didn't notice much about the place," she says. "We came and went real fast and quiet. You don't want to draw attention to yourself in those neighborhoods. But Clara noticed weird foot traffic at night. Unusual blends of humans and vamps. And a pretty high concentration of vamps in residence—that isn't common. We instinctively spread out, give each other a wide berth, when we have a choice. Both to hide and to protect ourselves from each other. You never can tell how strong a vamp is until you take him on. And you never know when a human might see something and fuck it all up. But even I noticed this building was different. Clara started to make small talk with our neighbors—she was better at that than me. Little by little, she heard their stories."

"What made them different?" He leans closer.

"They were blood workers," she says, turning her cup in circles between her manicured fingernails. "They bit humans for cash. Most had sex with them, too. Those two things go hand-in-hand, especially in cities. There's always a neighborhood or a block or a building you can go to for that kind of thing. Vamps get fed and fucked, humans get bled and fucked, money changes hands, everyone's happy. But it's dangerous shit. Every time someone closes that door, they risk their life. Humans risk theirs literally. Vampires risk theirs by risking exposure."

"I was freaked out by going into a room alone with a human customer when I started with you guys *last year*. I can only imagine how it was back before all the security was in place."

"It was no joke. Humans pretended we didn't exist—but shit always happened to vamps who were too open with them. Our corpses decompose so fast and in such a way that you'd never be able to find us after death unless you were right there as it happened. It's not hard to get rid of the evidence. And we aren't invulnerable. Just resilient. Harder to kill. Anyway. So Clara had this idea. I mean, these vamps were making enough money to live cheap by taking only one or two human clients a night. What if we… formalized the process?"

"You became pimps," Kyle says, laughing.

"We became pimps. These vamps were gonna do it with or without our help, and we could make it safer. Clara was as good at science as she was at business, and once she was in school, she got better every day. I recruited the vamps. Dangled promises as bait—protection, a steady cut of the profits and a share of whatever resources we had access to. She followed through. She developed the chemical spray that paralyzes vamps with a blend of household chemicals in this makeshift lab she set up in our dingy bathroom." Elisa uncrosses her legs, relaxing. She's obviously proud of this part of their story.

The small, homemade laboratory that Clara built in the subbasement of the club is still there. It's a rite of passage to be given a tour of it. Kyle remembers wondering how she managed to accomplish what she did with so little space and equipment.

"Once they realized we could offer them something no one else could, they were on us like white on rice. By the end of our second year in the city, we had the whole building locked down—security, blood workers on the payroll, blinds to keep the wrong kind of human attention away and lures to draw the johns and janes we wanted. The whole nine. It was sloppy and basic, but it worked. And once you start something like that, it's impossible to hide. Word got around." She smiles. "The neighborhood loved us."

Kyle is impressed. He also can't believe that she's giving him the story he's wanted to hear since the first night he met her and Clara Anders.

"But you asked about the room," she says. Her lips turn down. "Business was booming, but me and Clara—we sparked off of each other like hot metal. We're both stubborn and smart as fuck, but when you turn that on each other with sex and feelings in between, it's a fucking powder keg. Nothing worked. It was jagged as hell. We hurt each other. Of course, we also slept through every night clutching each other like goddamned teddy bears, but we didn't talk about that as often as we fought about everything else."

"You were young." It's a stab in the dark, but he wants her to continue.

"We were. We were pretty crazy, too. Every minute we spent cooped up in that little room, trying to keep our heads down, to do business without attracting the wrong kind of attention—it wasn't good for us. But I couldn't let go of her. I loved her as much as I needed her. I couldn't imagine living that life without her. So one day when she suggested we stop all the bullshit and make it exclusive, I said yes before I thought about what I was saying yes to."

"Things changed?"

"Sure. Shit changes when you promise someone something, even if you think you're already delivering on that promise." Her expression softens and grows distant.

Kyle swallows and looks away. The past few months, he's felt this reality keenly.

"I was never so happy and so fucking miserable in my life. I never knew if I was what she deserved. If she was what I needed. When it was good, it was good. When it was bad, it was the worst. What was hardest was that we were amazing together—the club grew every day. We paid the landlord to make changes. Converted rooms into lounges, built a lab for the experiments, made the common kitchen and bathrooms functional and clean. Installed security cameras and locks. Hired muscle to keep everyone in line. Got the vamps to stop selling sex because we wanted to go legal eventually and could never do that if word got out we were allowing that. We never had a death—neither human nor vamp. And we loved each other so fucking hard that it left bruises."

"It got bigger—everything got more serious." He can only imagine how difficult it must have been to grow not only a business but a community while trying to form a lasting relationship.

She touches his arm with the tip of one fingernail. "Precisely."

The jet's engines hum all around them. Kyle tries to absorb everything she's said so far.

"We hired people here and there, as time went on. Lawyers and accountants and phlebotomists and doctors—the science was real loose back then, but we did what we could. Our business was on the books as a spa, of course. The blood stuff was always kept under wraps. I named the club *Mi Corazón Sangrante*: My Bleeding Heart." She smiles. "Pretty catchy, if I do say so myself. And then, finally, we had enough money to lease the building from the owner. That's when the shit hit the fan." She clears her throat and pushes her hair back. She seems to set herself physically against the memory. "There was someone else. Some scientist who Clara met in class."

"Oh," Kyle says.

"Yeah. Clara was thinking about leaving me for her. Maybe even going in a different direction professionally. She could have had her pick of fields at that point. Of women, too."

"What happened?" Thinking about Clara and Elisa apart makes his heart twist.

At that moment, the pilot turns on the intercom to announce the beginning of their descent into Dallas/Fort Worth International.

Elisa smiles. She looks both grateful for the interruption and appreciative of the dramatic timing of the moment. "I think maybe that part is Clara's to tell. Buckle your seatbelt, *gato*. The landing can be rough."

ENERGY ISN'T AN ISSUE FOR Brian Preston. He's got that in spades. Nor is enthusiasm—he could corner the market. He's just weary, in a way that can't be categorized as either physical or mental, and it's making him cranky. Clara must pick up on this because she appears with a hot chocolate—his weakness—and his lab coat before he even shrugs off his clinic coat.

"Oh, god, you are an angel," he says.

She flicks her strawberry-blonde bob away from her face and shrugs. "You look like you could use it, and I was getting myself some blood from the fridge."

"I had a polio case today." He shrugs into his lab coat and begins picking through his in-tray: a stack of fresh reports and two new blank trial forms. He's more in the mood for synthetic blood testing than virus analysis and he hopes she doesn't mind. The facility is almost empty tonight—he's one of the only employees on the schedule. He volunteered for extra lab time when Kyle told him he'd be going on a business trip with Elisa.

"No," she replies, her eyes going wide.

"Symptoms, mostly. The patient was turned in 1916. Had no idea he was infected."

"What are you hitting it with?"

"OPV seems to have eliminated most of the issue, but it's strangely persistent," he says. She walks with him toward the lab, matching him stride for stride as they greet the few stragglers who are working this late. "It's strange. Usually when I find a viable solution, it sticks."

"Keep me posted," she says. "We've both had interesting experiences this week."

He stops fussing with his gloves and goggles at her. She rarely shares, at least not about facility issues—he knows he's vital to the work they are doing, but he is also by no means way up on the totem pole—and so he is immediately interested.

"We've noticed some weird background activity on the logs," she says. "Ghost user logins and deliveries keyed in new ways. And no matter what I do, I can't seem to pin down the source of the problem. I've questioned everyone. It may just be random, but keep an eye out for anything unusual when you're using the system or here at odd hours."

"Sure," he says, and then frowns. "What do you think is going on?"

"Laziness? Not sure. I'm going to see what we can do about having a trace done on the stuff that sticks out." She sits on a stool opposite him. "How are you holding up?"

He's been better. He'd like to chalk it up to a busy year, but the truth is that something feels off. He's exactly where he wants to be—working to make a difference for vampires in more ways than one—but the pieces aren't fitting together as seamlessly as he imagined they would.

He reaches up to run a hand through his wavy, dark hair and then remembers the gloves at the last second. She's watching him with eyes that miss nothing. She's going to ask, so he says, "When I graduated and you and Elisa offered me the position at the new vampire health clinic, I thought I was hallucinating. I was ready to take the slow, grinding path with the rest of the med students. Ready for rejection after rejection until I finally, somehow, got to practice vampire medicine outside of feeding them at the center. And then there you were, and here it was, this perfect little office in a not-so-perfect part of town. My name one of three on the door. That fang logo. Patients day in and day out. Adapting human treatments to accommodate vampire chemistry and physiology—and then getting to come here three days out of the week to do the research, too." He smiles, exhales and laces his fingers over his knee. "You have no idea how grateful I was. And still am."

It's been the most rewarding year of his life. Being taken out of the usual post-degree rotation to practice medicine in his field immediately *and* getting to touch the behind-the-scenes work going on at the facility seemed almost like cheating— passing go and collecting two hundred dollars and getting out of jail for free all at the same time. The training was grueling, but he managed to balance the practice and the lab, as a result of personal effort and Kyle's support.

"But?" she asks.

"I'm tired," he says. He only wishes that he were able to say this to Kyle. But Kyle has grown distant since beginning his second year of college and being taken under Elisa's wing, and Brian hasn't found the words to explain to him exactly what's wrong.

"It was a lot, what we asked of you," she says, obviously choosing her words carefully. "Three shifts at the clinic, three shifts at the facility, and you spent your post-grad downtime training."

He rearranges his stack of papers, trying to keep his fingers busy. He feels guilty, as if he's lodging a complaint—but he isn't, not really. He's just talking more to his friend than his boss right now.

"What we do here is so important," he says, his voice tense with conviction. "Adapting modern medicine to vampires. Making sure their nutritional needs are met so they can coexist with humans as peacefully as possible. Learning what we can about them so we can make humans understand that they are people, too, and not just—" He stops. Sighs. It's a speech that he's given many times, to many a bigot, and some days he gets tired of sounding like a broken record.

Clara squeezes his wrist. "Hey. What's really going on?"

"Kyle and I are both working very hard. And we're learning so much and doing so much. The new apartment feels like a rest stop instead of a home. Maybe we didn't think about what this work would do to our private life. We jumped in so fast."

And even as he says this, he's not sure what he means by it, exactly. When they're together, they are happy—they laugh and have great sex and sleep and watch television and it's all so easy. It's not as if the new-relationship shine has worn off. They are as attracted to and in love with each other as ever. It's when they're apart that the picture goes fuzzy. It's distance that allows Brian to see the cracks, and being overworked enhances that view.

"Are you guys not okay?"

"I think we haven't figured out how to combine things yet. Look—he's getting back in tonight. Do you mind if I do my sample checks and go home early?"

"Wow," she says, smiling, "changing up the schedule and everything. It must be love. Sure thing. Tash isn't on tonight and you'd be dead in the water without him anyway. When you have a minute, check your activity log, though. Let me know if there's anything unusual in there."

"Will do. Thanks."

When he gets home, the first thing he smells is Kyle's cologne—a heady mix of spice and citrus that instantly triggers a sense of warmth and excitement.

A plate of food wrapped in tinfoil is on the stove, the television in the bedroom is on and he can hear Kyle washing up at the bathroom sink. He stops in the bathroom doorway, stares at the pair of heather gray boxer-briefs hugging his boyfriend's perfect, round ass and tilts his head.

"You're on time," he says. There's no sneaking up on Kyle, but Kyle fakes surprise and then smiles at him through the mirror.

"And you are gorgeous," Kyle says, after a moment of hesitation. He drops the hand towel he's holding and settles his fingers on Brian's hips. Brian is wearing a button-up, slacks and a jacket. He looks the way he feels: like a dressed-down and very sleepy doctor who has just finished a twelve-hour day; his olive-toned skin is tinged green from too few meal breaks, and his dark brown hair is limp with product that failed him halfway through his shift.

"Mmm, is that food in the kitchen for me?" He tilts his chin up to let Kyle nuzzle against his throat. It's always the first thing Kyle does after they've been apart for more than a day or two—kisses down to the faint bruise on Brian's neck that's now permanent, the bite mark having healed over and over again, but never completely. Letting Kyle in physically is easy, and Brian latches on to this familiar foothold.

"It's just something from the store—chicken, vegetables," Kyle says. He opens his mouth over the bite mark. "Elisa reminded me that it's only fair, since you're usually my dinner."

Brian flushes to the roots of his hair. Urgency trips down his spine. "How was the meeting?"

Kyle's tongue grazes his skin. "Tense. Not sure why. Same group of people. Nothing new to talk about—just the usual argument over funding versus efficiency versus supply." He breathes out warm across Brian's jaw, laces his fingers over Brian's lower back and pulls him closer.

"Hendricks still giving you a hard time?" Brian tries to remember the names of people Kyle has mentioned working with in the recent past, but his knowledge is out of date; with every business trip Kyle has taken this year, he's shared fewer and fewer stories about them with Brian.

"Nah, she's been a sweetheart ever since we attacked Slater's love of last year's pumps."

"Sheller?"

"Still wants to get in my pants."

"And?"

Kyle laughs. "Zero success rate."

"Preston?"

Kyle goes still. "Intimacy attempted." He smiles, turns their bodies and presses Brian back into the sink until he sits on its edge. "I missed you." The tone of his voice is hesitant, as if he's worried Brian might not reciprocate the feeling.

"It was only three days."

"You made love to science, didn't you? The whole three days."

"As if it were our last time together."

How awkward this is compared to the reunions they had earlier in their relationship when they were completely sure of each another. *Why didn't I simply reply, "I missed you, too"? When did so many of our interactions become either jokes or conversational fishing?*

* * *

"I could help," Kyle says. He paces behind the glass, his voice tinny and strange over the intercom.

"Babe, I have testers lined up. It's okay, really."

The synthetic blood samples are lined up in neat, labeled rows in metal holders, and Brian is arranging them tray by tray inside the cooling unit, checking off his paperwork as he goes. He and Kyle are alone on the lab floor and have been all night. It's one of those rare evenings when Kyle isn't taking clients at *Mi Corazón Sangrante* to keep up appearances. He has no classes or rehearsals or social engagements, and Brian isn't doing anything that requires his undivided attention. It's nice to share space.

The blood is perfectly safe to ingest, but Brian doesn't *need* Kyle to test it. Still, he can tell Kyle is trying to engage him, and so he selects a vial of blood he's using as a constant, one of his own that's carrying a sample of one of the attempts at successfully integrating flavor—citrus—and presses the intercom button.

"Hey, maybe I do need your help," he says. This struggle to combine their lives is as much his responsibility as it is Kyle's. Brian is the partner with relationship experience; maybe Kyle needs him to lead.

Kyle goes through decontamination and puts on lab gear. He gets a kick out of coming inside, and Brian can't stop smiling at his wide eyes and the way his fangs press against his gums when he gets excited. Brian's sure the smell of blood is helping that along.

"Blergh," Kyle says. He smacks his lips after swallowing the blood. "That's—what is that?"

"Mango?" Brian asks.

"Er."

"Tangerine?"

"Try again."

Brian laughs. "Any change? Anything different than usual?"

"My nose is itchy, but that may be the decontamination gas."

They go through a list of checks, making each other laugh, until Brian has discovered that the citrus-flavored synthetic blood apparently tastes like floor cleaner.

"This program has a long way to go," he says.

They take off their lab gear and walk through the inter-connected chambers that separate the sterile environment of the lab from the other rooms. Kyle's hand slides into his. Brian flushes with success.

"Coming home with me?" Kyle asks. The blood has put color into his cheeks, but Brian would like to think that the idea of spending the night at home also has something to do with it.

"If you promise to keep me off the laptop."

Brian has gotten into a horrible habit of researching con-stantly now that he has access to the facility's resources and databases, and when he isn't virtually dialed in to the system, he's going over his patients' case files. Lately, in addition, he's been scouring his activity log in search of the strange activity that Clara asked him to look out for, but so far he hasn't found anything. It's weighing on his mind, and he hasn't told Kyle about it because he's sure Clara would want him to keep it quiet for now.

The apartment they've lived in together for more than a year now still feels strange around him—half his, half Kyle's, but not really *theirs*. They spend so little time at home that proj-ects never seem to come to fruition, and even though Kyle was extraordinarily picky about the furniture and décor when they moved in, school has completely dominated his time lately, and he hasn't brought up anything apartment-related since the semester started.

Still, the apartment is comfortable, and he doesn't dislike living with Kyle, which is a pleasant surprise—he's so con-trolling when it comes to space and time management that he'd worried he would be a horrible live-in boyfriend. It turns out that he's just a lackluster one. Kyle does most of the housework because it's easier for him. He also does most of the cooking because he enjoys the process. Since he doesn't eat, it's more like science to him. Brian often thinks he's a guest in his own home, and a freeloading one at that.

"Oh, god, I love this episode," Kyle says, as they settle on the couch in front of the television. "Tray is the one character on this show who doesn't make my eyes roll 360 degrees on a regular basis. He's kind of a nerd and he's shy; it's adorable. He wants to date Lori but she's like, a hardcore biker chick and human, too, and he thinks she's totally out of his league. But she likes him, too. So campy. I love it."

"That actor's social media stuff is hilarious. Have you seen it?" Brian asks. He balances a bottle of iced tea on his knee and then slides his free arm around Kyle's shoulders. He's excited that they're bantering easily about something silly.

"Yes! His tweets about being the first actual vampire to play a vampire on prime time television are both amazing and amusing."

They watch in silence. Brian is tempted to pull his laptop over from the coffee table and flick it on.

"You gave me a task," Kyle says, when he notices Brian's wandering eye, a teasing smile on his lips. "If you don't like *Dusk Until Dawn,* we can watch something else."

Brian smiles apologetically. He rubs the back of his neck. Kyle is wearing one of his oversized pajama shirts—a novelty T-shirt that says "I don't bite" on the front and "… unless you ask nicely" on the back. The television's glow makes his already pale skin light up with blue hues, his reddish-brown hair is feathering at his temples, and Brian can only stare at him. He's so gorgeous.

"Tell me about school this week," Brian says.

Kyle cuddles up to his side. "I think the shit that's going down with the vamp adaptations on campus may shut down the performing arts and sports programs."

"Is that why you aren't at rehearsal?" The question is a stab in the dark. He's lost track of Kyle's schedule this semester.

"Yeah. The school board got funding from the government to make all of the approved changes—I bugged Elisa and she let me see some of the paperwork; oh, man, zero after zero after zero—but the actual course programs need to be rewritten from the ground up. It's not enough to install physical security measures if nothing else changes. The humans are complaining that the vamps have physical advantages that require segregation to make things fair. The vamps are complaining that that would remove them from the human-dominated entertainment and sports industries they're trying to break into. Who knows what would happen if the humans ever found out some of us can read minds."

"There are definitely two sides to that issue."

"Absolutely. I just have no idea how badly it's going to shut down my track, you know?" Kyle sighs. "I have to be honest; I've been wondering if I want to continue with it, anyway."

"Is that Elisa's coaching? She has a thing for you, I swear."

Kyle smiles and shrugs. "She's kind of like my Yoda."

"I'm so glad to see my geekiness is finally rubbing off on you."

"We were having a perfectly normal conversation and now I'm thinking about rubbing off on you."

Brian kisses down the side of Kyle's neck. "Sorry. Go on. You're thinking about changing majors?"

"My Saturdays at the vamp youth shelter have been really—I dunno. I feel different when I'm there. I used to dread going. None of those kids have been vamps for more than a few years and most of them had it even worse than me. In the beginning, it was rough talking to them, especially the younger ones. But as time went by, I just—I like making them smile. I like changing their minds about the world and humans. At first I was kind of faking it until I made it. I mean, I understand the difference between reality and the kind of optimism that counseling requires, but now I'm beginning to believe things can change for the better. Sharing that with them makes me feel amazing."

Brian can't stop smiling. Kyle has come so far in only a year. "Have you told Clara and Elisa about this?"

"God, it's like they know," Kyle says. "They keep ribbing me about taking another day at the shelter and dropping my modern theater seminar."

"If you love performing, don't let anyone coerce you into stopping. But I like the way you light up when you talk about the shelter."

"I'm going to see how I feel before the enrollment deadline." Kyle draws his fingers absently along Brian's thigh.

"Just remember not to schedule anything opposite the wedding."

"How could I? Your brother calls me to talk about it three times a day. Who knew he'd be such a groomzilla, geez." Brian laughs. Michael has been a nightmare about his and Jenn's wedding. Despite Jenn's ho-hum attitude, they decided on a huge party because Michael begged for one. "I think Jenn has contemplated a name change and a plane ticket to somewhere remote. Running that veterinary hospital is the only thing keeping her from going nuts."

"She asked me if I could dig up some chemical spray to knock him out until the wedding date, then wake him up when she has him in front of the justice of the peace."

Kyle laughs. "I would pay actual money to be there for that."

"They'll be okay," Brian says, after a beat of silence. "It's more the families surviving the reception that worries me."

Brian is nervous about introducing Kyle to his father. His father is not a pleasant man. Back when he asked Kyle to the wedding, it didn't seem like a big deal.

Brian had no idea then how complicated his relationship with Kyle would become in just one year's time. He had no idea what a challenge it would be, especially regarding communication. Silence is so easy to lapse into when you're both overworked and trying to adjust to new responsibilities. Hell, they've shared more conversation tonight than they have in the last two months combined.

And god, does he miss the days when they had sex every day. It's become almost second nature to deny the urges—the sexual ones as well as the potent need to be fed off of that has only grown in Brian over time. He can never recall feeling as hungry for it as he has lately.

The fingers Kyle has folded over his thigh slide inward, trace the bare skin below the leg of his boxers, almost as if Kyle can sense what he is thinking about. Which may be because Kyle *can*.

"Honey." Kyle shifts closer. "I can smell it; you know that."

The flush on Brian's cheeks spills down the back of his neck and up along his ears. "I—I know, I just—sorry, we were talking. I didn't want to cut you off."

He can't think with Kyle's hands on him, with Kyle's lips and teeth pressing into the bend of his neck, with Kyle's hard, forever-young body against his. He can see it in his mind's eye so clearly, tight and smooth and masculine. But that's the simple part—it's the promise of being bitten that excites him. It's thinking about the pain and the way it reverberates, about what it does to him when it rips through him and then peters out into hazy warmth, about the smell of blood and the way it feels, sticky-thick-warm against his mouth when Kyle kisses him afterwards. It's overwhelming.

Kyle kisses over the marked spot where his neck and shoulder meet. "It's okay," he says, hot and sudden, against Brian's skin. "Need you. Need it. That was your blood earlier, with the flavor, wasn't it? It's been racing through my veins all night." He straddles Brian's lap. "Come on. Come on, let me, honey. Show me that beautiful throat."

Brian could never explain, even if he had a million years, what it feels like to bare his throat to a human-shaped predator whom he loves fiercely. The level of trust this requires is immense, and yet he has never, ever been afraid of Kyle, with his blown black pupils and his trembling, too-strong fingers and the sharp, curved fangs he drags along Brian's skin.

"Please," he says, finally, when he can't hold back any longer. Kyle's tongue dances over his bite mark, making it tingle with half-numbed awareness; Kyle's body presses hard against his; Kyle's fingers are closed around the back of his head and shoulders with a little too much force. An invisible power is rising beneath Kyle's skin that intends to conquer every inch of him.

"Should have moved to the bed." Kyle sucks kisses into Brian's throat. "I want to feel your skin. Want to be inside of you. It's been—weeks."

"I'm s-sorry, I know I've been logging a lot of hours."

"Shhh, don't." Brian can sense the predatory blankness taking over Kyle's thoughts. It's sluggishness with sharp edges. It's a focus leading Kyle to precisely what he requires. He's never out of control of himself when they're like this, but he is less human. Lurking beneath the surface of this young, sweet man is an animal that is constantly waiting to tear into Brian in a way that would not be enjoyable. He should be frightened. Instead he is simply in awe of Kyle's control, of the way Kyle manages to make him feel loved every time, so completely that all he ever manages to achieve is a lust so keen it takes his breath away.

Kyle's hand tightens around the back of his neck. The flick-snap of tension makes Kyle's whole body stiffen, and then the pain comes. Brian sees white. He goes rigid. It hurts, even with the numbing effect. He gasps—once, twice, three times—and Kyle's other hand holds onto his shoulder, keeping him still so that when Kyle's teeth slide out of his neck to allow the blood to gush, the tearing will be kept to a minimum.

Warmth. Light. Wave after wave after wave.

His cock tents his boxers, and Kyle's thigh pins it down. He can't get away. He can't see. He dissolves in the pleasure, letting it carry him through the pain.

He hears—feels—their hearts racing together, his a drumbeat that's one step behind Kyle's. The rush of blood and the resulting satisfaction saturate Kyle like sunlight piercing shallow water. He sobs—he can't control it, can't get around it, can't breathe through it, and Kyle is hurting him, fingers biting into his skin, mouth bruising his throat, and it's not enough and it's too much.

Kyle pulls off with a gasp, and Brian doesn't feel blood dripping; he knows Kyle is finished because the coagulant kicked in. He takes advantage of Kyle's distraction by pushing Kyle to sit down beside him and then, boneless, he sinks to his knees in front of the couch. He's in pain and dizzy but he doesn't care—he needs to give more.

Kyle is a vision of lovely lines, milky skin and blue eyes that are now almost entirely obscured by black pupils. His body is soft around his belly and hips, a visible reminder of having been turned at sixteen that he often expresses a disliking for. But all Brian sees is an opportunity to remind him how gorgeous he is. Brian himself is not a bulky guy—he's always been compact and on the wiry side—and he's glad of it now, because it's one less lopsided comparison for Kyle to make.

"Y-you don't," Kyle says, when Brian tugs his boxer-briefs down and pushes his T-shirt up, "have to—oh, god."

He knows what the sight of him, bloody and bruised and on his knees, does to Kyle. "Too late to do anything else." He licks Kyle's cock into his mouth. "Want it."

In the beginning, they stepped around each other carefully, avoiding the rougher side of things in the bedroom, but that's not a concern now—Kyle has learned what he likes and wants, and his desires have never clashed with Brian's. When he puts his fingers in Brian's wavy, dark hair and begins gently fucking Brian's mouth, it's perfect and exactly what Brian wants, too. It feels so good, to be held and used and full and wanted, to feel Kyle's hips slapping against his chin, to feel Kyle's cock edge into his throat when he stops trying to be polite.

"So good," Kyle says, broken and panting. The long column of his throat cords up visibly. "Mouth so warm and wet, oh, f-fuck, take my cock so well."

Brian thinks, *Come. Come in my mouth. Come down my throat.* He knows Kyle hears it, feels the reaction in his cock and balls when the words translate. He shivers. It's incredible, to be that connected to another person, to be as close to them mentally as physically.

He chokes a little when Kyle complies, because it's a lot and right against the back of his mouth, but he closes his lips tightly around Kyle's cock and swallows until there's nothing left. It's only when he's wiping saliva from his chin that he realizes he came in his underwear at some point during the blow job. It would hardly happen with a human partner, but when things are intense with Kyle, it's a common occurrence. Kyle helps him to his feet; peels the boxers from his sticky, spent cock; and kisses him—his lips, his cheeks, his jaw, his pronounced nose. Gratitude as pure as a child's flows from his mind into Brian's.

"Let me take care of you," Kyle says, and Brian knows that means first aid as well as a damp cloth for the mess, and probably a heavy dose of cuddling and kissing. It sounds heavenly.

"You always do."

In this way, at least, they have never failed each other.

2

THE UPROAR AT SCHOOL HAS thrown so many monkey wrenches into Kyle's schedule that he isn't surprised when, one day, he gets his wires crossed and stays late on campus when he also has clients scheduled at *Mi Corazón Sangrante*. He'd like to think that Brian's obsessive-compulsive scheduling has rubbed off on him in the same way that superhero movies have but, alas, this isn't the case.

He arrives at the club about half an hour late, changes into his company-issued black dress shirt with the reverse vampire logo etched in blood red on its breast pocket and a pair of slacks, only to find his client—a forty-something year old man named Andrew—leaving, followed by a dark-skinned female vampire with hair standing out about six inches around her head in every direction. She's wearing thick-rimmed glasses and the same uniform he is.

"Mr. Pierce?" he asks. "I'm so sorry I missed our appointment. I'm sure we can reschedule at no charge, and I will personally—"

"No problem," Andrew says, looking post-blood-drain goofy. "Lee explained that you weren't feeling well. Same time next month, perhaps?"

"Sure thing." When they're alone, he turns to this vampire, whom he has never met, feeling awkward and tense. "Uh, hi. Sorry. I'm Kyle." He frowns. "Not sure how you got the assignment—"

"He's flexible," she says, shrugging, "and I'm flexible. It worked out." Her voice is more high-pitched than he expected.

"Oh, you're…" He stops. Realizes that he's about to be rude.

"Bi? Yeah." She smiles and leads him toward one of the common rooms with a flick of her hand. "I know. It's like meeting a unicorn for you boys, isn't it?"

He laughs. "No, it's—sorry, we just usually seem to get clients who land on the more extreme ends of the Kinsey scale."

"Or so you think."

He sits down, pops the top button on his shirt and relaxes. With Andrew out of the way, he doesn't have another client for at least an hour.

"Can I ask when you were hired? I've never seen you before."

"You must be one busy blood-sucker." She smiles in a way that's almost indulgent. "I'm in your poly sci 201 course."

"Oh, god, I'm—wow, sorry. Can I be honest? I tend to nap through that one. I've never noticed you."

"I overheard you mention the club once in class, decided to look into it," she says. "It's good money, and I don't have an issue with the work the way some vamps do."

"Well, thanks for covering for me. You saved my ass."

"I need to knock off," she says, taking a light jacket from the coat rack near the door. "Why don't we get coffee before class this week? You can tell me client horror stories."

Two coffees and three weeks later, he and Lee Walker have hit it off pretty well. It's nice to be friends with someone with whom he can talk about both school and *Mi Corazón Sangrante*, although of course he can't say anything about the vampire research facility that exists behind the club's facade. She's a social work major with a sociology minor, which makes her even more interesting to him because he's been considering switching to that major all semester.

Unlike so many of the friends—acquaintances, really—that he's made at school, he finds himself wanting to truly connect with her. He's not sure what makes her different from all of the other university students he's met. She makes him feel happy and comfortable, and he's learned to go with that feeling.

He hasn't made many inroads into college social life. He isn't the party type—a party he attended at sixteen resulted in him being turned into a vampire and nearly sexually assaulted—and he doesn't find satisfaction in having vast quantities of friends rather than fewer but more intimate ones. He isn't a hermit, but he picks and chooses his nights out more carefully than most people his age. Even though he looks like a teenage boy, he comforts himself with the knowledge that he's twenty years old on paper, at least.

Of course, any outing is a good time as long as Brian is involved, but lately he and Brian haven't found the time for anything but work and early nights. He's been stuck in a rut for months now, and so when Lee invites him to a nightclub to celebrate passing a difficult exam, he happily takes her up on the offer. Brian is working the night shift at the facility. He won't mind.

"I know you're as gay as gay can be," Lee says, laughing, "I'm not asking you out or anything. Just come dance. I have friends that I want to give to you—I mean, introduce you to."

"I dunno, you're sort of my type, Walker. If you disregard certain physical attributes."

She laughs at his joke, adjusts her coat over her slender frame and swats his arm. Her wide hair bounces as she walks. "Would you believe you're the first person in this city to say that to me? Man, if bi girls are supposed to get as much play as everyone seems to think we do, I got left off a list."

"Female sexuality being a mystery to me aside, I think you're pretty awesome."

She's the first woman with whom he's had this kind of easy conversation. All the other women now in his life are much older like Erica and Jenn, and Clara and Elisa are mentors as well. His brief attempts to bond with girls in high school never felt right. Before he realized that stereotypes were relatively meaningless, at least in terms of his own personal experiences, he thought that being a teenage gay guy meant that "bestie" relationships with girls would come naturally to him. They never did. Then again, friends with guys of any orientation hadn't either, so perhaps it was more of a people failure than a sexuality-specific one.

He'd like college, Chicago, adulthood, to be different, though.

At the club, they discover that Lee's friends haven't arrived, so they settle at the bar.

The eighteen-and-over vampire nightclubs are now openly serving fresh blood—roaming volunteers who wear name tags that announce their employment, clean bill of health and blood type, troll the bar to make sure that every vampire who enters is offered roughly a finger's worth. Biting isn't permitted, but they have special tools, thimbles with a needle at the tip for discreet puncture at the wrist or throat or inner arm, and kits that hold everything they need to clean up and move on to the next vampire with little to no fuss.

It's strange to watch. Kyle has never bothered—he has access to more blood than most, between the center, *Mi Corazón Sangrante* and Brian—but it seems only polite to partake, since they are out for the night. He purchases blood from a dark-skinned young man with a beautiful smile. It tingles all the way down, and he catches a sense memory of the smell of wood smoke, and wonders about that for as long as it takes Lee to recapture his attention.

"How long have you been a vamp?" she asks.

"Four years. You?"

"Ten. Did you have a choice?"

"No," he says, and feels no shame. "You?"

"I did." She licks at the corner of her mouth. The dim bar lighting glances sideways off of her glasses, creating a glare that hides her eyes. "Was in a bad situation. My parents separated— my mother got violent after she left us, real badly, and my dad never knew what to do about it. I had little brothers and sisters who looked up to me. I wanted to protect them. And eventually I wanted things to become stable enough so that I could go to school and have a life of my own. So I turned. I did what I set out to do, and when she finally passed and the kids were old enough to do with just Dad, I left."

"I'm sorry. That's rough."

"You didn't have a choice. I assume yours wasn't a cakewalk either."

He works his lips against his teeth. "House party. I was six-teen. Some college guy wanted to get in my pants. When that didn't go as planned, he bit me. Turned me when he realized he took too much blood."

"Shit," she says, chin in hand. "Oh, man. Fuck that guy."

He feels a weight on his chest talking about it, but the feeling is nowhere near as intense as it used to be—and being forced to become a vampire was nowhere near as complicated as the night of his high school graduation. He thought he killed a peer, who forcibly took his blood in order to become a vampire, and then fled his hometown of Mansford, only to be pursued by the guy all the way to Chicago, where his misguided romantic pursuit of Kyle put both Kyle and Brian in mortal danger not long after they met and began dating.

"My life went downhill and then to hell after I was turned," he says. "My aunt and uncle never wanted anything to do with me after my parents died and they became my reluctant guardians. After I came out and then turned, they more or less decided to pretend I didn't exist. I graduated and—" He doesn't know Lee well enough to confide in her any further about the events that led to his name being cleared from the missing persons record. He avoided "murder suspect" altogether, because his attacker survived and then went catatonic shortly after Clara and Elisa helped Kyle capture him. "Came here. Found work at the club." His mouth curls into a smile. He can feel the heat on his cheeks. "Met Brian."

"Lucky you," she says, a teasing glint in her eye.

"He's practicing at the new city clinic now," Kyle says. "He's incredible."

When Lee's friends arrive, Kyle is plunged into a series of introductions that go on too long—he won't remember everyone's names. They come from a variety of majors and range in age from freshmen to graduate students, so Kyle doesn't feel awkward telling them that he's a performance major. Most of them are vampires, so when they start drinking blood and mingling around him, he feels even more at home.

There are a few latecomers. He misses out on the chance to learn their names because everyone has dispersed on the dance floor, and Lee isn't around to make introductions. He notices a tall guy talking to her, and takes the opportunity to say hello and ask her if she wants another drink.

"Hey, you," she says, dragging him close so he can hear her shout over the music. "This is Max Cumberland. He's an engineer."

Max laughs. "I guess that's all I boil down to, huh? Super-awesome intro, thanks."

"Any time," she says.

"Care to dance?" Max asks. It's only after a moment of direct eye contact that Kyle realizes Max is talking to him and not Lee.

The question throws him off. He isn't sure why. And then he hears himself saying, "Sure."

He's danced with guys before, mostly friends of friends, and sometimes friends of Brian's, but the moment Max's fingers touch his waist, he feels a rush of something distinctly not platonic. Up close, he notices that Max has short, light brown hair and eyes that are a muddled combination of blue, green and gray. He's good-looking—in a different way than most of the guys Kyle notices—if a little too skinny, with long, sharp features, and he has at least five inches of height on him.

"I have to admit, I knew you were going to be here tonight," Max says, speaking over the music. "Lee's been talking about you nonstop." Kyle is nervous. He's not sure he likes this guy knowing about him when Lee has never mentioned Max. "Hey, don't look at me like that. I just wanted to say hi." Max moves them to the beat of the music. "She keeps trying to get me to take a shift at the shelter by telling me about this cute guy who volunteers there on Saturdays."

Max's hands on his hips are making Kyle's body heat up. Being attracted to someone he has just met is unsettling. He can't decide whether he likes it or not—but, in any case, he isn't available.

"I have a boyfriend."

"Human?"

"Yep."

"Ooh la la."

Kyle laughs. "I know what you're thinking. It isn't like that." He tries not to let their bodies touch too much. "I mean, we— you know. But that's not the reason we're together."

"Hey, I didn't say that." Max smiles. "But I'm guessing it's fun for you."

"It works out pretty well for both of us." Blood pounds in Kyle's cheeks. Having this conversation is making him think about going home later to find Brian in bed, maybe even waiting for him.

"Well, Kyle Hayes, performance major slash part-time volunteer social worker, Max the engineer is pleased to meet and dance with you, boyfriend or otherwise," Max says.

Kyle relaxes. It's nice to finally be making friends.

* * *

DURING A RARE EVENING BREAK, Clara and Erica invite Brian to dinner down the street from the facility at an Ethiopian restaurant that he and Erica love. Despite his plans to work through dinner, he says yes. He's worn out and not a little starved for social interaction. He can't imagine two people—except Kyle and maybe his sister-in-law-to-be Jenn—with whom he would rather sit down for a meal.

Erica and her boyfriend John are now engaged, but they have no plans for a wedding any time soon. Brian is glad that she's happy and professionally fulfilled. She's now the full-time administrator of the downtown blood center. Still, hearing her work stories is like going back in time for Brian, who has come so far in a year that he hardly remembers what it was like to worry only about blood supplies and feeding vampires the correct type to match their nutritional needs.

Clara sips discreetly from a flask of blood that she brought for herself while Brian and Erica indulge in the spicy fare. They chat about their plans for the holidays. Brian and Kyle are having dinner with Michael and Jenn on Thanksgiving, but have no definitive plans for Christmas. With Michael and Jenn's wedding in January, their focus has shifted.

"Don't even get me started," Brian says. "She managed to get Michael to promise that it wouldn't be Christmas-themed, but he's had a big winter wedding fantasy in his head since day one and he would not budge on that. And he was desperate to book the Langham in time."

"Ergh," Erica says. She tosses her long, glossy black hair over her shoulders as if shrugging the notion off. "Sorry, I just—no. I can't even imagine. I mean, it's a beautiful venue, but thinking about a celebration that huge gives me *hives*."

Brian is more concerned about his best man duties than the venue or the size of the guest list. Michael has already vetoed a bachelor party—"That's barbaric, Brian"—but the speech, well. He was flattered when Michael asked him to fill the role, but now that the event is looming, he's getting performance jitters.

And then of course there's his father. Both he and Michael were surprised when the invitation they sent to Edwin Preston and his new wife was returned with an affirmative reply. It's been a long time since they've seen their father—outside of polite cards at the holidays and coolly penned checks on their birthdays, their interaction with him since their mother died has been limited. The thought of seeing his father for the first time in years at the same time that he watches his older brother get married *and* introduces Kyle to everyone… it's a heavy thought, especially when he considers how unsettled things have been with Kyle lately.

After a few beers, Clara manages to get him to open up.

"I feel like I'm losing him," he says, slurring his words. "You know when it starts with someone and—it's easy. It feels so right. There's a foundation, you know, and every moment after you decide to be together adds another layer to that foundation. But now it feels like we're just clinging to bricks. They're—good, those bricks, they're sweet and romantic and sexy and fun. But they aren't building anything, they're just—static, disconnected hunks of clay and rock."

"Bricks," Clara says, dry and not a little sarcastic.

Erica—her dark, almond-shaped eyes flashing—pointedly takes his beer away.

He groans. "You know what I mean!"

"Let's be real," Erica says. "Kyle is young. Inexperienced. He's growing up right in front of you. He's living his own life for the first time. He isn't going to stay the same. So, things between you aren't going to, either. If you cling to the way he was when you first met him, you'll lose the person he's becoming now."

"I get that," he says, the lines across his forehead deepening. "But aren't I entitled to some things staying the same? His commitment, his love, his interest. I mean, those things have to in some way remain stable, or how can we even try?"

Clara throws a balled up napkin at Brian. "He's a vampire, not a relationship guru. I know that sometimes we seem more mature than our years suggest because we see the darker side of life more often than humans, even as children and teenagers. But he is still just a kid. Have you thought about downgrading your relationship to a more relaxed arrangement until he graduates, at least?"

Brian frowns. The idea of sleeping with Kyle casually, loving him but letting him explore other romantic options, is devastating to Brian. He can't imagine being comfortable with that, or happy living with someone who wasn't satisfied by what he had to offer. Until this moment, he never imagined that Kyle would want that kind of arrangement, either. Is it possible that he does? Has Kyle met people at school to whom he's wanted to get close but can't because he's not single? Brian doesn't want to imagine Kyle being seriously interested other men, but he has to admit it's likely. Kyle has never been with anyone else but Brian. He is a sexually active young person with a newly stable life and a whole city at his disposal. Why wouldn't he wonder about opportunities beyond Brian?

These are the same fears Brian endured when they began to fall for each other, before he discovered Kyle's reason for fleeing to Chicago under less-than-ideal circumstances. And even without the knowledge of that complicated and dangerous history, even before Brian was attacked and kidnapped by the very person Kyle thought he had killed, things between them were not easy. Still, after the truth was revealed and their lives made safe again, he had every conviction that they could make things work.

But what if they can't?

* * *

THE LAST THING KYLE EXPECTS when he shows up for his two o'clock appointment is to see his boyfriend reclined on the tiny mattress in the client room. He stops in the doorway, his fingers twitching at his sides at the sight of Brian's dark, wavy hair, olive-toned skin and chocolate-brown eyes. The come-hither look on his face makes Kyle's belly swoop.

"Hi," Brian says, honey-sweet and eager.

"Ummm…"

He knows that an appointment was made and paid for, and he isn't sure what to think. Does Brian think he needs to schedule time with him now? Is that how off-kilter they've gone?

And then every coherent thought in his head evaporates when Brian licks his lips and says, with a deliberately innocent tilt of his head, "Sorry. This is my first time. I guess it's obvious, huh?"

Oh, my god. He wants to role-play.

If they had discussed this in advance, Kyle would have laughed and blushed and maybe put it off until he thought it to death—but like this, sprung on him out of the blue, it's like an impromptu performance, which he's quite good at.

So he smiles, broad and wicked, and closes the door behind him and leans back against it. Brian's knees are splayed wide and his posture is relaxed, but when Kyle turns the lock into place, he sits up and forward, feigning nervousness as he clasps his hands together and ducks his head.

"There's a first time for everything," Kyle says in his high-pitched, breathy tone as he closes the distance between the bed and the door. "I'm Kyle. It's nice to meet you." He steps closer. "Where did you want the bite, Mr. Preston?"

Transfixed, he watches Brian's hands run down the length of his thighs, drying his palms. His face is bright red, as if he's actually embarrassed, and something about that and the put-on fear that's radiating off of him in waves is intoxicating. Kyle feels his own pupils dilate, and when his fangs press at his gum line, he lets them descend without hesitation.

Brian's lips part. "Oh. Ummm. I—" His Adam's apple bobs as he swallows. His fingers splay open over his thighs. "They told me downstairs that you can, um, on my thigh? Inside?"

Kyle's heart slams against his chest. He's so in tune with the need thrumming beneath Brian's skin and behind Brian's conscious thoughts that he forgets they're pretending.

It's always a challenge to keep his urges in check when he bites someone in an intimate spot. His clients are all men, so each presents a potentially embarrassing scenario. It's not about looks or even sexual attraction, really. With humans, it's about the way their thoughts feel, their desires and emotions and needs all rolling up into a mental calling card that Kyle has learned to not only read but be sensitive to. When they get excited, when they want it so badly they can hardly ask him for it, he feels every bit of that, and it's thrilling.

Out of instinct, Kyle glances over at the table beside the bed to make sure all of the first aid items are present. He wants to draw this out, make it realistic, if that's what Brian wants.

Tension snaps between them, so sharp that Kyle almost chokes out, "Take off your pants for me." The pulse that began knocking against his throat and chest settles in his wrists, bleeding heat with every throb.

When Brian stands and slides one end of his belt from its loop, Kyle's cock twitches. Brian catches Kyle's eye from beneath thick, lowered lashes as the belt whispers free. He carefully undoes his fly, lowers his pants around his knees, and steps out of them.

Kyle's fangs brush his bottom lip. "The armchair would be best."

Brian lowers himself into the chair beside the window, adjusting his legs and genitals discreetly. He's getting hard, but Kyle doesn't acknowledge that. It's become second nature to make the encounter as non-sexual as possible, even when there is a visible reaction. But when he kneels between Brian's legs, it takes every bit of the actor inside of him to not lick his lips or press his face right against that gorgeous, fat bulge at the front of Brian's boxer-briefs. He can smell Brian so keenly—his skin, pubic hair and sweat, as well as his arousal and excitement.

His eyes wide and wet, Brian stares at Kyle's mouth. His bare, hairy legs are giving off heat like a furnace. He puts his fingertips just above his knee and asks, "Here?"

Kyle smiles. "A little higher." He eases Brian's bottom forward in the chair by grasping his calves and tugging. "And a little farther in." He gently lifts Brian's legs and then leans in, dragging his nose and mouth along Brian's thigh, breathing in the almost dough-sweet smell of him, masculine and unforgettable. He kisses the spot he intends to bite. His fingers begin to shake as he anticipates the blood and Brian's reaction.

"Oh," Brian says. His hands flutter over the arms of the chair. "Are you going to do it?"

Kyle stares up at Brian through his eyelashes. "Unless you need more time."

"No." Brian's cheeks darken. "N-no, do it. Please."

Kyle braces one hand beneath and around the thigh he intends to bite and the other against Brian's chest—experience has taught him how to hold men in order to control the instinctive pain reaction their bodies have. Brian is more relaxed than most. He's used to the bite, and—well. He enjoys pain, and he has learned how to take it. It makes the process much easier.

Kyle allows himself to get lost in the need for blood. That lust rages constantly, of course, to one degree or another—at its gentlest, it's like the buzz of gnats that never seem to find someone else to bother, but in the moments before feeding, it's a wild animal set loose inside of him.

He tightens his hold before he bites down, precise and fast, like a snake. The insertion is clean, salty and skin-bitter, and then he withdraws his teeth and the blood comes. The taste and texture slam into him, stealing his breath away. The blood going down his throat is like water hitting parched earth.

Inside of the drinking, it's like a wind tunnel—full of confusing, overblown rushes of intimacy, like clinging to someone during freefall. He hears Brian's mind chant gibberish, encouragement and desire and desperation. He hears Brian's heart race with fear and the stress of blood loss. He hears his own heart pound the pavement of his body, seeking the slaking of his thirst. And he feels Brian's body fall apart under the onslaught of pleasurable pain, his skin hot and his cock filling, curved thick and eager, standing up and sideways against the waistband of his underwear, its head nudging the elastic.

"Kyle." Brian rubs his cock against the cotton. A wet spot is forming there—the smell of pre-come sizzles through Kyle's senses, making the urgency burn brighter.

When he stops, the blood congeals around the bite marks and he reaches for the gauze on the table beside them, but Brian's fingers grab his wrist and hold on, surprisingly tight for someone who has just lost a lot of blood. Kyle was halfway standing, and Brian's touch, combined with his own disorientation from drinking, makes him wobble forward. He puts his free hand on the opposite arm of the chair and looks down into Brian's blown pupils.

"Don't go," Brian says. He's trembling.

"Are you okay? Do you feel like you might pass out?" Asking this is standard procedure.

Brian licks his lips. He reaches out and presses the pads of his pointer and middle finger to Kyle's pink mouth, and then to his blood-stained fangs, in some kind of wonder.

"D-don't," Kyle says. His facial muscles twitch. "Sensitive."

Brian slips his clean fingers into the hair at the nape of Kyle's neck. "Want to taste it."

Kyle moans into the kiss. This is definitely not something he would do with a client, but even though they are pretending tonight, Brian isn't actually a client, and he can't resist. His body feels like one huge gaping hole waiting to be filled—the blood satisfies his nutritional and predatory needs, but that's only part of the solution when he's this close to Brian.

Brian licks the blood residue from Kyle's mouth, tonguing his teeth and gums and the insides of his lips. Feeling the satisfaction that thrums through him at the copper-salty taste of his own blood is almost enough to have Kyle reaching for the throbbing erection that's distending his underwear. Brian whimpers against the corner of his mouth; his other hand reaches down to cup Kyle's hip and thumb the bone through Kyle's pants. Kyle straddles his thighs and sits down, wraps his arms around Brian's neck and deepens the kiss.

"We shouldn't—this is against the rules."

Brian exhales against his neck. "Do you want to stop?"

"No. I want your cock," Kyle says against the crown of Brian's head. "I want you to fuck me."

"Oh, my god." Brian whimpers, tearing the hem of Kyle's shirt from the waistband of his pants. Kyle hurriedly undoes his belt and fly. The rustle of clothing being shoved aside excites him, sends the blood—both his and Brian's—surging faster through his veins.

He feels empty. So fucking *empty*.

Brian's messenger bag is on the floor beside the bed. Kyle holds his breath as Brian reaches for the lubricant bottle he packed. He takes it as soon as it's in reach, slicking his hand while Brian shoves his pants and boxers down around his thighs. He whimpers.

"Turn around," Brian says. His voice is already raspy. "Turn around and let me see."

Kyle turns easily, flushing hot when Brian's trembling hands stroke and squeeze his bare ass. It feels so dirty, being almost fully dressed while his cheeks hang out. Brian lowers him a little, lets him feel the hot, hard curve of his erection through his underwear. Kyle makes a noise that dies halfway up his throat when Brian bites the back of his neck and slides an arm around his waist.

"Your uniform is going to get messy," Brian says. He cups Kyle's cock, pushing it down between his legs and straightening the shaft so he can tug at it.

"Oh, my god, please," Kyle says. "I don't care."

"Do you want to come with me inside of you?"

"Yeah. Fuck yeah."

"Take me out. I want to watch you do it."

Fuck, what has gotten into Brian?

Kyle fishes Brian's cock from his underwear. It feels so good, even just in his hand. His body is clenching in anticipation—the base physical desire to have his ass full is overwhelming. He holds his breath, tries to calm down.

"H-how do I know you're clean?" he asks.

"You don't." Brian spreads Kyle's cheeks apart. Kyle whimpers and arches his back. "You want it badly enough to take me bare?"

Brian knows this is one of Kyle's biggest turn-ons. Kyle still jerks off to the memory of the first time they had sex without protection. He isn't sure whether it's the predator in him that craves natural, unadorned sex acts, or simply that he gets off on the intimacy and trust that's required to let someone in like that. Either way—with Brian, it's safe.

"Yeah." Kyle rubs his ass back against Brian's cock. It's so hard and thick and *right there.*

Brian thumbs his hole, starting around the rim and dipping down into the pucker to spread the lubricant and get him to relax. He's tense with wanting it, preferably five minutes ago, but Brian knows how to get him to open up. The touch is perfect. His heartbeat slows down, and finally Brian's fingertips catch and curve forward and down.

"Please." He circles his hips. Brian's free hand grips his waist and is joined by the other when Brian lets his cock press against Kyle's cheeks. "Want it."

"Let me take your shirt off." Kyle breathes unevenly as Brian's fingers dance down his shirt front, plucking black buttons free of buttonholes. He's wearing an undershirt beneath that and this comes off too, whispering as it joins his button-down over the arm of the chair. "Pants off too?" Kyle nods.

He wants to be able to spread his legs and move. When he's naked, facing away with Brian panting against his shoulder blades, he grips the chair's arms and settles his ass back into Brian's lap. "God, you are gorgeous." Brian peppers his bare skin with kisses.

"Fuck me," he says, writhing backward until Brian's cock is slotted between his cheeks. He reaches back and grasps the shaft, guides it up and in, and when the blunt, wet head settles into the depression of his pucker he stutters out a breath. It always feels like so much in the beginning, almost too much, especially considering that Brian usually prefers to bottom and Kyle goes long enough between experiences to forget how amazing it can feel.

"Shit," Brian says, as Kyle's ass comes down around him, "shit, shit, *shit.*"

Kyle could bounce on Brian's cock for hours, but he can feel the pain that Brian is experiencing with every movement; the bite wound on his leg, though small, is still a wound, and it hasn't entirely stopped bleeding. Part of Brian enjoys that, Kyle can tell, but there is only so much pain that he can endure before pain is simply pain. Kyle takes his own pleasure, though, quickly and selfishly, enjoying every thrust of Brian's cock inside of him.

"Touch yourself," Brian says. Kyle twitches to comply. It feels good to move, to feel Brian's arms around his hips and waist, Brian's voice rumbling against his skin. When he comes, finally, his own fist around his throbbing cock, clenching up around Brian with every pulse, it's so intense that his eyes glaze over.

Brian pushes Kyle onto the floor to his hands and knees and presses back inside of him with a grunt.

"Oh, my god." Kyle moans. He steels his thighs and takes it, his fingers curling into the carpet; the fabric roughly scrapes his kneecaps as Brian fucks him.

The last few minutes are uncharacteristically silent, hot skin and the slap of their bodies and Brian's fingers wrapping possessively around the curves of his hips and ass. He goes down on his elbows right before Brian comes, presses his face into the sweaty crook of his elbow and whines, spreading himself as wide as he can go.

"Love you," he says, "love you, please, *please.*"

When Brian comes he cries out, his pelvis stuttering against Kyle's ass, and then falls forward over Kyle's back. He kisses Kyle's sweat-spiky hair. Kyle loves these moments after, when he feels the soreness in his ass because the friction is gone, when he feels their heartbeats pound where they're connected, when he feels the slick mess inside of him slide against the softening length of Brian's cock.

"God," he says. Brian's fingers trail across Kyle's heaving belly. "That was—what was that for?"

"Just missed you," Brian says. Kyle squints. He sits up on his knees, pulling Brian's arms around his waist. He tilts his head to kiss Brian and gasps sideways across Brian's mouth when three of Brian's fingers slot back inside of him. "So much." He gently corkscrews Kyle open, smearing the come that trickles out all over his crack. "Sometimes I don't think you have any idea."

"What?" Kyle asks. That statement makes him feel abruptly unsure.

"Sorry, I'm just—really needy tonight." Brian reaches for one of the moist towels that sit beside the first aid kit. "And my leg is killing me, crap; we waited too long."

"I was going to say. You must be uncomfortable."

They take care of Brian's wound and then clean up the other mess, side by side on the floor at the foot of the armchair.

Kyle wants to ask what's up, but the truth is he's not ready to know, and he isn't sure Brian is ready to share. Just knowing that there *is* something wrong is making him hurt all over and want to retreat.

In these moments, he sees the divide between them so clearly. It's easy for him to hide behind predatory walls, to see things in matter-of-fact, even distant, ways. Brian is not only unable to do that as a human, at least not all of the time and certainly not subconsciously, but he is also a very sensitive person. Kyle isn't sure if he's learned how to bridge that gap without hurting Brian.

3

"OKAY, YOU HAD TO KNOW how that was going to end," Brian says, laughing, at Beth's desk.

"Tuna and asiago salad sounded amazing this morning, though!" Beth—young, sweet, and blonde—has been the receptionist and general office guru for the vampire health clinic since it opened last year. She's just come back from medical leave herself—a bad case of the flu.

"Until the microwave started up," Brian says.

"Oh, my god, I am so sorry. The smell is horrible, I know."

"Just promise me: never again?"

"I promise. Never again will I stink up the kitchen with such a thoughtless lunch selection." She smiles. "You know what's worse? It wasn't even that good."

Brian laughs. "Okay, no, just, stop. I can't breathe."

"You had better. Your two o'clock is here."

Brian lets his assistant do the intake. When he approaches the examination room, he squares his shoulders, puts a friendly look on his face and enters smiling. His assistant remains in the corner, out of sight and mind, armed and ready with chemical spray should the patient become violent.

Early on, during negotiations about the security and layout of the clinic, the feds wanted walls in the examination rooms, the same glass-and-metal monsters as at the blood center and in most "vampire-safe" public buildings. Brian fought tooth and nail against that. How was he supposed to take care of people if he couldn't touch them, see them up close, establish some physical connection, earn their trust? The feds compromised, agreeing to drop that idea, but insisting on the employment of medical assistants who could do patient intake as well as provide physical security.

Brian hasn't had an incident yet.

He isn't sure if he will have one today. Even though his patient looks like a ten-year-old child, she is actually a thirty-two-year-old woman. It isn't rare to see child-sized vampires, but it is rare to see a case where the apparent physical age and actual age disparity is so large. The sad reality is that they don't usually last long, these kids who are turned that young. They commit suicide long before they have a chance to mentally mature. It's a difficult life to live; a part of Brian can't blame them.

"Ms. Blaylock," he says, "I'm Doctor Preston. How are you feeling today?"

"Well, you can see for yourself what it looks like, at least." Her voice is smooth and deep, a shock to hear coming out of such a tiny mouth.

He flips through her chart while pulling up a stool to sit beside her. "If I'm not mistaken, you seem to be showing symptoms of chicken pox. Is it possible you were infected before your change?"

He snaps on a pair of gloves. He takes a tongue depressor from his pocket and checks her mouth. He shines a light in her eyes and down her throat. He turns her face this way and that to look at the faint pox marks on her skin, then shifts the collar of her dressing gown to look at her shoulders and upper chest. He listens to her heart and lungs through a stethoscope.

"Of course," she says. Her flat tone shows a disinterest for details. Like so many patients, she probably just wants to receive treatment and be sent on her way. "Though I have no idea why it's taken decades to show."

Brian goes through his checklist of questions. None are specific to her case, but they allow him to learn things about her living situation when she was a child, with whom she came into contact, how long she's been a vampire and what her general health has been like since. He isn't sure whether to treat her as he would a child or an adult with chicken pox, so he orders several antibody tests and advises her on how to treat the rash itself until her next appointment. "Cool or lukewarm baths with a pat down—not a rubdown—after, calamine lotion, not warm but cold blood. No aspirin, and no scratching is very important." He tells her to avoid newborns, young children and pregnant women, if at all possible.

The test results show that she definitely has the children's kind of chicken pox. He's intrigued and not a little concerned—to show symptoms of an active viral infection left over from her human body twenty years after turning is bizarre.

"I can't give you antibiotics," he says, "because of course this is a virus. If your sores became infected, we would prescribe antibiotics, however."

Her eyes narrow with obvious suspicion. "Aren't we supposed to have this sort of thing figured out by now?"

He smiles. "We're trying, ma'am."

After Ms. Blaylock leaves, he takes her file to Beth and leans against the wall behind the front desk, out of sight of the waiting room. She gives him a look.

"Chicken pox?" she asks in a barely-audible whisper, her eyes widening. He can't quite wrap his brain around it either.

He runs the case up the facility's flagpole, and isn't surprised in the slightest when he's pulled into a private meeting with Clara and Elisa.

It's late at night, about a week after he filed his report, and he had plans to go home on time that, he supposes, he'll have to momentarily shelve, along with the sour truth that he has no idea if Kyle will be in tonight—their communication has become woefully spotty.

"No, but, like, do they *do it*?" Elisa is asking Clara as he walks in.

"Oh, for god's sake," Clara says, squeezing her eyes shut. "Mental images!"

"Can you imagine being stuck in the body of a ten-year-old but having the mind of an adult, along with all of the urges?"

"I *will* make you stand in the hall. Please."

"My curiosity: She is morbid and possibly illegal."

Brian chuckles. He isn't surprised that Elisa finds this amusing.

"So," Clara says, looking at him, obviously grateful for the chance to change the topic of conversation. "Chicken pox."

He sits down. "Yep. I took the liberty of pulling some of my 'unusual' case files from the last six months. I'm not alarmed just yet, but there has been an upward shift in the emergence of human diseases and conditions in my patients lately. It's a grab bag of things—HIV, chicken pox, polio, cancer, diabetes, heart disease, lupus. No connections or patterns in the patient pool that I can see."

"The police department has also noted a rise in aberrant and violent behavior in the last six months," Elisa says. "Interesting. Mercury in retrograde? Something in the water? Seasonal affect disorder?"

Clara's mouth twitches upward.

Brian sits back in his chair. "I don't see the connection. Could it be we're reading signs that aren't there? Or, now that we're finally compiling and cross-referencing data, we're seeing patterns that have always existed but are new to us?"

"Possibly," Clara says. Her eyes move rapidly over the papers and laptop in front of her. "The science is vague. Each one of these cases requires a completely new approach because of how variable and misunderstood vampire physiology still is. But they definitely have one thing in common: These vampires carry their conditions in stasis, similar to the way their aging is dramatically slowed down. And now, in a relatively brief span of time, they have all become *active* medical issues. What's the catalyst?"

"See again: Something in the water?" Elisa asks, in a sarcastic tone.

"Should we take this to the feds?" Brian asks.

Elisa and Clara share a look.

Brian frowns. "Look, I know I'm not in every loop here, and I'm fine with that. But these are my patients. I need to know what's happening to them."

"Understood," Clara says, her usually raspy voice softening. "But we've had security issues lately and we're not sure who is involved. The ghost activity in the system that we were tracking earlier this month has all but disappeared, and we don't know if or how we've been compromised."

"You think the security issue is related to the medical and behavioral problems we're seeing in the vamp community?" Brian asks.

"It's an odd coincidence. We're not sure. But we're trying to find out."

Elisa stands up straight. "Keep us updated, Preston. Between this, the usual day-to-day bullshit, and those anti-vampire wackos at Turn Back, we've all got full plates. Let's take care of our people and see what we can find out in the process."

* * *

"It's not silly. It's just a list!" Max says. He spreads out his hand of cards.

"It's silly," Lee says.

"Okay, so, what's on the list?" Kyle asks.

"Everything we kind of sort of don't need now that we're vamps. It's a thing I do. Every day—well, I come across something, and I add it to the list."

"It started with tire jacks," Lee says.

Kyle laughs. "Okay."

"We got a flat. We're on the highway, right, middle of the night, and like idiots, there we are, fumbling through the trunk for a jack, I mean, at least five solid minutes of searching. No lie. And I look up at her and she looks at me and we lose it, I mean we just lose it, when we realize that we could have lifted the damn car up ten minutes ago."

"You don't think about it until something new happens," she says. "That much is true."

"I don't think I've ever thought about tire jacks," Kyle admits.

"Toothpicks," Lee says.

"Corn on the cob handles."

"Anti-wrinkle cream." They stare at Kyle. "What? It's true!"

"Speaking of necessities," Max says. He stands and takes Lee by the arm. "Mr. Hayes's relief has arrived and I am famished." Kyle waves at his replacement as he, Max and Lee exit the vampire youth shelter.

"I'm good," Kyle says, when they arrive at the center. "I mean, I don't need the blood ration. Not tonight, anyway."

Max puts an arm around Kyle's waist and pulls him inside. "Aw, come on, eat with me."

The center where most of downtown Chicago's vampire population goes for its daily ration of free blood looks much as it did a year ago when Kyle stumbled through its doors starving, on the run, thinking himself a murderer and one hundred percent desperate. As he stands in line, his stomach flutters. He can still remember what it was like to see the most handsome man he'd ever laid eyes on standing on the other side of that glass. How Brian bent the rules to give him synthetic blood even though Kyle didn't have any identification. How he was drawn to Brian and the center for weeks after as he settled into life with Elisa and Clara and got back on his feet working for them.

Things were simpler then, in many ways. Falling in love was so easy. He tries not to wallow in these thoughts as they take their rations—now in recyclable bottles instead of plastic packets—and go back out onto the street.

He has to admit that human blood obtained without effort is nice. It wakes up his mind and makes him go hot and loose all over. When Max puts a hand in Kyle's hip pocket, he finds himself leaning into Max's lanky frame with a smile, feeling comfortable and eager.

"So what do you think, Kyle?" Lee asks. "This spring, you going to be joining the ranks of social services?"

"Since I was a little kid, all I ever wanted to do was perform," he says. "Be someone else and be loved for doing it well. I still get such a rush on stage. I mean, it feels right. But when I'm with the kids at the shelter, I just—it's a different kind of right, in a different place inside of me. You know?"

"You sure that was just blood?" Max waggles his eyebrows. He pokes Max's side. "Hey!"

"I'm kidding. I think it's adorable. You're into it."

"Yeah," he says. "I am."

"I can give you the inside scoop on the department," Lee says.

Even though it's late and he has homework, Kyle agrees to one club stop. Lee has a friend who wants to see her, and Max seems excited about tagging along. Kyle doesn't want to be a drag.

Inside the club, Lee disappears into a corner with her friend, leaving Max and Kyle at the bar. They chat idly for a while, but when it becomes clear that Lee's interest in her friend is more than a passing platonic fancy, Max says, "So, hey. I have a friend who works in the back here. He's a donor, if you're interested in a little nightcap."

"Oh, I don't want to step on your toes, if you wanted to do that," Kyle says. "Go ahead. I'm good here."

"Let me introduce you, at least. Lee's going to be a while."

Out back, club employees take their breaks and smoke, and Max finds his friend there. They exchange hugs and kiss each other's cheeks. His name is Kevin.

"Do you mind?" Max asks, pointing to a secluded corner.

Kevin smiles playfully when Kyle hesitates and then finally shakes his head. Kevin takes Max's hand and gives Kyle a curious look as he and Max disappear into the corner.

It's awkward. Kyle doesn't know where to look, so he turns away. This kind of exchange is common, but to him it seems weird. What he does at *Mi Corazón Sangrante* is professional—prescribed, ordered and clinical, even when it's arousing. This, on the other hand, is as casual as it gets.

He's embarrassed to admit that he's intrigued, despite his misgivings. He watches them out of the corner of his eye. Max's long body looms over Kevin's shorter, stockier one. They aren't noisy, but Kyle's hearing naturally picks up every whimper and catch of breath. The smell of human blood is overpowering and immediate. His skin goes hot when Max inserts a thigh between Kevin's legs. He licks his teeth, his gum line humming where his fangs press, wanting to drop.

Kevin opens his eyes. Kyle looks away and then back again when he realizes Kevin is smiling.

The invitation is clear, and Kyle can almost hear him think, *Come here. It's okay.*

He actually takes a step forward before stopping himself. The temptation is that strong.

When it becomes obvious that Kyle isn't going to accept the offer, Kevin smiles, shrugs and shifts his focus back to Max. Kyle isn't sure what they do after that—he turns away again—but he can smell sweat and semen. Max returns to his side after saying goodbye to Kevin; his pupils are blown black and his body is humming with blood-dizziness and sexual energy. It's intoxicating to be close to him when he's like this.

Kyle finds Lee in an intimate embrace with her friend; with a kiss to her cheek he tells her he's going to head home and leaves the club with Max.

"Hey," Max says. The sultry tone of his voice when he's full of blood and orgasm-shaky trips down Kyle's spine like fingertips. "I'm sorry. Was that weird for you?"

Kyle shrugs. "A little? I'm not judging you. The club kind of drills it into us that biting humans is a business transaction. At the center, human blood is government assistance. At home, it's Brian. I never learned how to make it—what you just made it. Maybe I should."

Max shrugs. "You don't have to. Just do whatever feels right."

"It is weird for me, I guess. But I'm not offended or anything. I don't think biting has to be—you know, a big committed deal. Doing it the way you just did is outside my realm of experience, that's all."

After a brief silence, Max says, "The night we met, you said you were turned against your will."

Kyle is quiet for a few steps. He makes an affirmative noise and then allows his arm to brush Max's. The contact is nice, comforting and immediate.

"I was, too," Max says. "I get how it feels. In the beginning, I was so hopeless, so angry." His eyes change, darken and glisten. "Then I figured—if I'm going to be this way forever, I might as well enjoy myself, you know?"

Kyle isn't prepared for Max's hand sliding down his arm or Max's fingers folding around his. Max is unavoidably strong— vampire-strong, as strong if not stronger than Kyle. It's the first time Kyle has felt that kind of strength and been drawn to it. Strength has always seemed cold and unappealing to him—a weapon used to hurt or a wall to hide behind. Max's strength, though, is very much like his own. They are made from the same stuff.

He grips Max's hand. He can't help it. Pleasure ripples through his body in uneven waves.

"I get it," he says, embarrassed when the words come out breathy.

Max squeezes back, obviously allowing Kyle to feel the power in his grip. "I thought you might."

"How did it happen for you?"

Max doesn't let go of his hand. "That's the shittiest part. I was jumped. There was this gang of vamps where I grew up that recruited by challenging potential members to turn humans. I just caught their eye one night. It was that simple. That meaningless."

"What did you do?" Kyle asks, after a moment of hesitation.

Max clears his throat, and something changes in his expression that makes Kyle's blood run cold. "Let's just say I did what I had to do. And that I—I've moved on."

"I understand. I've tried to move on, too. And I have. Mostly."

"It's not easy. You seem to be doing pretty well, from what I can see."

"I think so, too, but then I'll have a bad day. Like I'll see someone who looks like my maker and I'm right back there again, bleeding out on that bed. I go cold. I just can't feel anything."

Max's thumb sweeps across the back of his hand. "Does Brian understand?"

"Oh, yeah. Wow, he's—he's great. But he can't fix everything." Kyle smiles. "He likes to think he can. Sometimes he even convinces me it's possible."

"He sounds amazing."

Kyle allows himself to feel the cold evening air biting at his skin, and wonders why he feels such relief walking the streets of Chicago holding someone else's hand.

* * *

"'THE PRIMARY PURPOSE OF THE social work profession is to enhance human well-being.'" Clara reads from the pamphlet in her hand as she and Kyle stroll side by side across campus.

"There is something either deeply ironic or grossly meaningful about that, considering your circumstances."

Kyle laughs. "Okay, so that pamphlet should be updated to read 'human and vampire.' But, I dunno. I'm thinking about it. I'm good with the local vamps. They talk to me. I help them. Maybe that's what I should be doing with my long life." It's cold today, cold enough for even vampires like themselves to bundle up and huddle together. They bought coffee to walk with, though neither of them have any intention of drinking it. It warms their hands through their gloves nicely.

"Maybe it is," she says, and slides her arm through the crook of his elbow.

"I wanted to ask you something."

She doesn't miss a step. "Okay."

"Elisa was telling me about what happened with the building you started the club in. About how you lived there. About how you almost didn't—stay together." He can just hear the noise of her reflexive swallow, the half of a heartbeat missed before she replies.

"There was someone else, that's true," she says. "Another scientist I met at school. She was—well. She was nothing like Elisa. She was mousy and thin as a rake. Hopeless with people. But I fell for her the moment we met."

"Was she human?"

"Yes." Clara stares off into the distance. "Her sister was a vampire, though, and she knew I was one as soon as she laid eyes on me. It was the first time I'd met a human I didn't have to explain myself to or hide from. And she was smart. So smart."

"What happened?"

"Several things at once, as always. She came home with me a few times. I confessed to her what I did for a living. She was put off by it. Not in a dramatic or moralistic way—she simply never liked the idea of the business, never saw the merit in it. She had many complicated goals in the field of science, but she wasn't intrigued by the scientific application of what I did. She found it lacking, directionless. Elisa was, naturally, not impressed by her attitude."

Kyle smiles. "This is not my surprised face."

"But what really put a stop to it was the federal government showing up on our doorstep," Clara says.

This stops him dead in his tracks. He switches his coffee cup from one hand to the other, turns to face her, and asks, "How did that…?"

"It was the first time they approached us openly. Apparently word of both our financial success and the few defensive weapons we developed against vampires had finally reached the right ears." She shrugs. "Or the wrong ones, depending on your point of view."

She starts them walking again. Evening is falling all around them, a light snow flurry dusts their heads, and she turns her hood up so the dark material frames her pale face.

"We knew that vampires weren't going to stay a secret forever. Media and technology were constantly evolving—the recording and sharing of live events on a global scale was becoming more common with every passing day. Young vampires were growing restless and careless. Humans were talking. Elisa and I hoped to weather the storm in our own way, protecting who we could, but that dream was fading. The Outing was inevitable. It was only a matter of how and when."

Kyle shivers, from both the cold and her recounting. It must have been a frightening time to be on the front lines.

"Apparently, the government wanted to prepare, too," she says. "They knew exactly what we were doing. They knew that the money-for-blood exchange was just the tip of the iceberg.

We circled each other for a while. They never made an offer, per se, but they did make thinly veiled threats. We never let them push us, but we listened. Every time they showed up, they sent someone new, as if they were trying to find the one individual who could secure our cooperation. It was surprising, at first, how sharply they focused their attention on us. I suppose we thought we couldn't be the only ones doing this, so why choose us? Of course, we weren't the only ones, but we were swimming in a much smaller pool than we realized."

"You've mentioned New York before. Are they like us?"

As a small town kid with no opportunities to travel, Kyle has always been fascinated by big cities. He loved Chicago as soon as he was able to comfortably experience it. Knowing that there are other research facilities in places like New York and Los Angeles is both a glorious and frustrating tease. He knows he won't be given every detail about these operations, but a precious few facts would satisfy him for the time being. He only hopes Elisa and Clara don't ask him to keep such details from Brian; he's not sure he could resist sharing them.

She smiles, turning her head far enough to let him see the look of friendly denial on her face. "That knowledge is still far above your pay grade." She pauses. "We could tell from rumblings in Chicago that events were escalating. Finally, we decided something had to be done. We theorized that if vampires were outed, the primary thing that would make living openly alongside humans impossible would be the need to use humans as a food source.

"And second to that, what we could never hide, our strength, which would present an immediate and ever-present danger to them. We figured that if the government were to have programs set up to feed vampires and arm their law enforcers against them in advance of a public revelation, the populace might not instantly become a vigilante mob when the news broke." She exhales. Her brow furrows. "It was difficult because, in a way, I was insulting my own people; boxing them up into this little space, trying to present them as harmless freaks, in order to save them from—I don't even know what. Mass arrest? Extermination? Lives as science experiments? Elisa was furious. She didn't want to work with the government at all. But she knew the truth as well as I did. We were running out of time."

Kyle can't imagine what it must have been like to be ahead of that tidal wave—knowing what was going to happen, having ideas about what might help subvert the catastrophic results, but at the same time having limited resources, having to bargain with blank-faced suits at the federal level, scratching and clawing for every concession while knowing realistically that the cards would always be stacked against you no matter what you accomplished.

"What were they asking you for?" he asks.

"Our working weapon prototypes, our scientific research and our input on the blood distribution program. And when I say input, they basically wanted us to design it. They were especially clueless in that regard." She laughs. "Elisa had fun rubbing that one in their faces."

She no doubt did. "So you agreed to work with them."

"We had to. What was happening in Chicago was happening all over the world. Vampires showing their true natures in public. Incidents with humans." She sighs. "The ink dried on our government contract a few days before the killing spree in Las Vegas outed us to the public." Kyle watched clips of archived news coverage of the event on YouTube. A group of blood-hungry vampires rampaged through a packed casino, killing dozens of people before they were subdued. "It was a damned whirlwind after that. Months of panic and shock. Blame placed on vampires everywhere instead of on the individuals who actually committed the crimes.

"And then, finally, once the initial clamor died down, the rollback—families coming out in support of their vampire loved ones. Vampires in the media from all walks of life, from every country, race, religion, orientation and gender. Vampires are more easily accepted, for the most part, in other countries, less of a secret, but never openly acknowledged.

"What happened here changed everything. After that, national organizations were formed. Civil rights supporters became active. Scientists 'confirming' that vampires were an evolutionary offshoot of humanity, even though they had no real proof of that. The government took what we gave them, embellished it and rode it for all it was worth. In return, we managed to gain some level of acceptance, the programs that allow us to live even though we don't thrive and the power to have some say in our own affairs."

They sit on a bench, their coffee cups now as cold as their skin. She turns into him, just slightly, almost as if seeking comfort. He leans against her side.

Her version of the events of the Outing make him feel so many things: bitter that he didn't have any support at all when he was turned, while many other vampires did; regretful that he couldn't have experienced that time in their history firsthand; and somehow at the same time relieved that he became a vampire without knowing exactly how fraught things once were.

"Our situation isn't what I hoped it would be at this stage, though," she says. "Civil rights lag behind, as always. We fall into the human system justice system and don't come back out. We die and our deaths aren't investigated. We're still arguing over things like the validity of our Social Security identification, driver's licenses and medical benefits. Our citizenship is constantly threatened—the feds love throwing that one around when things don't go their way." Her upper lip curls in disgust, but there's resignation on her face, too. So much of what she did must have been out necessity instead of choice.

Kyle doesn't know what to say.

He's deeply impressed by what she and Elisa have accomplished. He's always been in awe of them, but now he finds himself hurting for her, too. She's done so much, but maybe she doesn't see that because there is still so much left to do.

He's met with the upper echelons of the blood distribution program management team many times at Elisa's side, but those people are only involved at the organizational level, and their view of these events could not be any more different than Clara's. It seems so simple when he's there, chatting with people wearing expensive suits who earn untold amounts of money every year to approve spreadsheets filled with numbers without thinking about the lives that exist behind the data. Were they ever offered knowledge of what actually happened?

"So, the Outing happened. You kept dealing with the feds. And you and Elisa and… what was her name, the scientist?"

"Amanda. Her name was Amanda." She puts her coffee cup down and rubs her fingers together. She pronounces the name with reverence, and Kyle knows immediately that she loved this person. "I had to tell her what was going on. The Outing and its aftermath scared her. Her sister was panicking, too, making it worse. I knew I was losing her, but I respected her too much to not keep her in the loop." She frowns. "The look she gave me when I told her that I was getting more involved—well. I knew it was over between us. Truthfully, I was never sure what exactly 'it' was. I was enchanted by her, and it was definitely a kind of love, but Elisa—Elisa was in my blood. My bones. I always went back to her, no matter how far I roamed."

Kyle's cheeks go warm. He can't help but think of Brian. And of Max.

"I found out a few years later she committed suicide," Clara says. "She never recovered from the imbalance I brought into her life. I blamed myself for her death."

"Oh," Kyle says, touching her arm. "Oh, god, no. You can't be held responsible for that."

"She was talented. She could have done so much good. If I'd never darkened her doorstep." Her mouth squirms, and she braces herself. Her eyes glaze over. "And I don't think Elisa has ever forgiven me for loving her."

"I think maybe she has, in her own way."

"We just keep trying. That's all we can do." After a long pause, she looks at him. "Why the sudden historical curiosity?"

He isn't sure how to answer. He's been spending a lot of time with his new friends lately, but he always seems to gravitate toward Max in particular. Their one-on-one interactions leave him flushed and wanting more. He knows he shouldn't act on these feelings, and a part of him doesn't want to. He loves Brian. But there is something there with Max that isn't with Brian—an innate understanding of their natures and what it feels like to have been turned against their wills. As a result, there's anger and defeat in them both, but also an almost defiant determination to recover and rebuild. Max understands.

"I'm trying to figure things out," he says. "My place at the facility—among other things."

She takes the social work major information pamphlet from her pocket and hands it to him. "Not a bad place to start?" She smiles. "Begin within, as they say."

"They say that?"

She laughs. "I think I might have made that up, actually." Another pause, and then, "I want to say—Kyle, you are very lucky in love. Brian is a hell of a guy. You know. For a human." She winks. "But you're just as important in that equation, you know that, right? You're entitled to feel and struggle and change and wonder, as much as he is."

She saw right through that, then. He sighs. "You make it sound easy."

"I'm not trying to. I just want you to remember that your point of view matters."

"Thanks," he says. He leans his head on her shoulder. "Really. Thanks."

4

BRIAN IS AWAKENED AT THE kitchen table by Kyle's hand on the back of his neck. His laptop keyboard is imprinted on his cheek. He wipes drool off of his mouth as he sits up.

"Crap," he says. He pushes a hand through his hair. "Hey, sorry. I must have fallen asleep."

Kyle kisses his temple and then sits at the table, putting a bag with a cheeseburger and fries in it in front of him. "No worries. Eat. Everything okay?"

"Turn Back protested outside of the clinic today," he says. His fingers make slow work of unraveling the cheeseburger wrapper. "God, thank you. I was starving." He chews. "The media was there. It was awful."

"Have we been authorized to dig up dirt on that organization and take it apart yet?" Kyle asks.

"It's not a priority." Brian wipes his mouth on a napkin. "But I did do some checking. They've been operating almost as long as we have. Publicly, I mean. Which is interesting. Of course, it's impossible to figure out who funds them or pulls their organizational strings. It's all anonymous donations and pseudonyms on the official record. No one wants to be associated with a conservative hate group unless they can use religious conviction as a means of justification. They have a little of that, too, but it's not solely a 'vampires are immoral, unnatural creatures' platform. A third of their members are actually vampires."

"What? I didn't know that. The chapter they have on campus seems all human, from what I can tell."

"That's one of their secret weapons. They recruit vampires who hate what they are—who are willing to fight against the movement. It's an ace in their pocket, for sure. Makes it look like vampires have a reason to be suspicious of their own. They've been light-handed about it in the press, though. When they're questioned, they just say things like 'our membership is diverse but shares the opinion that vampires are not what our government would like us to believe they are,' et cetera, et cetera."

When he stops talking and the food is gone, he looks up at Kyle for a long moment. His boyfriend looks tired but calm, the tension that has recently been so present on his face hardly visible.

"Working hard, babe?" he asks, pitching his voice lower.

"Yeah," Kyle says. "Hungry, too. I haven't seen a client or been to the center in days."

Brian's chest aches. He wants to be close to Kyle very badly. "Do you have plans?" The answer has been "yes" more often than not lately.

"No. Could we—could we take a bath? Together?"

"I'd love to. Do you want to eat?" Heat pounds in Brian's cheeks. It's been a while since they've done something that leisurely at home together.

"If you feel up to it."

That's an understatement.

"Of course I do."

Brian fetches the kit that contains their first aid apparatus as well as the supplements he takes to help him recover from blood loss. He turns off his laptop and throws away the food wrappers. Standing at the kitchen sink, he listens to Kyle run their bath. Affectionate warmth rushes through him in waves when he smells the bath oil they both like wafting under the bathroom door on a wave of humid air.

Being around Kyle still makes Brian's body and mind ping at the same frequency, as if he is exactly where he should be.

He shrugs off his T-shirt and walks into the bathroom, which, with a tub and a detached shower and room to move around, is much nicer than the bathroom in their old apartment.

Naked beside the tub, Kyle's body is tight and pale. His reddish-brown hair and blue eyes are vibrant against the off-white color scheme of the bathroom. His sharp jaw and the tips of his ears make Brian weak with longing to touch them. Something about Kyle's body has always driven Brian completely insane, and that feeling hasn't diminished in the slightest.

"Shower first? Don't want the bath water to get bloody."

Brian nods as he steps out of his underwear, takes Kyle's hand and tugs him into the shower. They stand beyond the spray of water against the far wall. All Brian sees are those beautiful eyes before Kyle kisses him, cups his face and then pushes fingers into his hair. By the time Kyle's lips trail down his neck, he's breathing heavily and squirming to get their bodies closer together.

"Feels so good," he says. He clings to Kyle's broad shoulders.

Brian isn't sure what the limits of their shared telepathy are. He only knows that sometimes when they're close, he can tell exactly what kind of mood Kyle is in. Tonight, Kyle feels as if he's happy to be wrapped around Brian. The sensation of being wanted goes through Brian like sunlight through shallow water. He breathes it in, feels it pound beneath his skin, and when Kyle's mouth closes over the apex of his neck and shoulder, it comes tumbling back out of him in the form of pleas that echo from the ceiling tiles.

Mine, he hears, and he's not sure which of them is thinking it. *Mine mine mine mine.*

"Yeah." He gasps, clawing at Kyle's back. "Please."

Kyle doesn't give him warning. He bites down, hard and fast and deep, and when Brian's knees buckle, Kyle takes him by the back of his thighs and hauls his legs around Kyle's waist.

"Hold on," he rasps, blood-thick and growling.

"*Oh.*"

Brian wraps his legs around Kyle's hips as the pain lashes his body. When he begins to grow dizzy, he feels Kyle become sluggishly aware of the change. Kyle pulls off with a wet smack and surprises Brian by kissing him immediately. In the shower, the mess isn't a concern. Brian suckles at Kyle's bloody mouth, not minding the sharp, metallic taste of his own blood as it smears across his chin and drips down onto his chest.

"Turn around," Kyle says, his tone chest-deep.

Brian whimpers and turns, not ready for it when Kyle licks a stripe down his spine to the crack of his ass. The vulnerability he feels is off of the charts—it makes him shake and twitch. "Shit, *shit*—"

Kyle nuzzles his ass. "Spread your legs for me, honey."

Brian almost slips, but Kyle steadies his calves and, when he's still again, leans in and begins nibbling kisses around his rim, and then licks, broad and firm, over his hole, again and again.

"Oh, my god, oh, my *god*," Brian moans. He clutches the shower wall as Kyle's chin digs in and sets itself, as his mouth begins to move in time with his tongue, hungrily eating Brian open. Brian buries his face against his wet forearm and tries to breathe through the waves of sensation.

"Move," Kyle says. "I know you want to."

"Kyle," Brian gasps. He lets go, allows his ass and hips to churn back against Kyle's face. His cheeks and neck and shoulders flush. It feels incredible, especially when Kyle's tongue slides in and he has something to clench around.

"That's it. Make yourself feel good, come on."

He doesn't hear Kyle reach for the lubricant bottle, but suddenly slick fingers paw his cheeks apart and Kyle's tongue isn't enough. He whines, canting his pelvis back.

"Fuck me," he pants. "Fuck me."

Kyle stands and breathes rapidly over the back of Brian's neck. "Too fast. Let me—"

"No, do it. Just do it. Want you closer."

Kyle's fingernails dig into Brian's hip bones and angle his ass up so that when he thrusts down and in, the head of his cock catches on the rim. Another sloppy spill of lubricant and hasty fingers holding him open and then blunt, burning pressure, all the way in, making his muscles seize and his throat close up. It's a shock, being stretched and stuffed that quickly, no matter how many times they do it. Brian huffs frantically through the first few push-pulls, until Kyle applies more lubricant and the glide back in is smooth and slick. He calms at that, his belly pushing out against the tile, but with extra lubricant, the friction dies off and the angle is awkward.

"Fuck me on the floor," he says.

"I can hold you up."

"Want to move. Be on my hands and knees."

Kyle kisses his shoulder. "Okay."

They collapse together, grunting and shifting until Brian is comfortably wedged against the wet bathmat and can set his knees and hands safely. The first, long thrust back onto Kyle's cock in this position makes him cry out. Free to do what he likes, he's pleased when Kyle allows him to do most of the work.

"Shit, *fuck*, oh, god, keep doing that," Kyle says, wrapping his hands around Brian's cheeks and holding them apart. "Look so good around me."

He lets Kyle fuck him for longer than usual, ignoring the erection bobbing below his belly and the sway of his balls between his legs and allowing the fullness of a cock inside of him to suffuse his entire body. The drone of the shower water draws him into a lull and the light-speckled darkness behind his eyelids deepens. Kyle's soft, satisfied noises dust his skin like confectioners' sugar, airy and sweet.

"Do you want…?" Kyle asks, dragging his fist up Brian's cock.

Brian whimpers. "Stay inside. Want to come with you inside."

"Mmm, okay." The pace of Kyle's hand is steady but slow. He knows what Brian likes.

Brian's lungs race to keep up. Clawing up his spine and between his legs, his impending orgasm is making him weak. "Close, I'm so close, *oh*."

Kyle's lips touch the skin between his shoulders blades, and something about the gesture shatters his resolve. He comes pulsing in Kyle's fist, his body shaking and his hips stuttering. For a few seconds, he can't draw breath. Kyle kisses down the top half of his spine, milking his cock until the head stops giving up its release and then edges his pelvis back. Brian tightens up on him as he pulls all the way out and pushes all the way back in. His ass clings to the thick shaft.

"Fuck," Brian says.

He puts his forehead on the floor of the shower, lifts his ass and takes Kyle's cock, deep and slow, then deep and fast, and then somewhere in between, past the point where it begins to twinge, past the point where his body begins to scream in protest from being on his hands and knees on the unforgiving shower floor for this long. He doesn't care—he wants to be used, completely and for as long as Kyle lasts. And he knows that Kyle can last.

"Ah," Kyle blurts, suddenly, and goes still. "*Ah*, ah."

Brian rocks back onto his cock. "Mmm, yeah. Yeah." That's all it takes. When Kyle comes, he feels the corresponding twitch all along Kyle's thighs, across Kyle's chest and belly where they're plastered against his back. They laugh in the aftermath, breathless and sated, Kyle still on his knees, stroking Brian's back and shoulders.

"Shit," Kyle says, "your neck."

Now that Brian isn't focused on being fucked, he feels the pain. He retrieves one of the antiseptic, adhesive, waterproof bandages from the first aid kit, cleans the blood off of his skin and then applies the bandage carefully. He pops a pain reliever, an iron pill and a blood booster in one swallow. He's sustained worse feeding injuries—there's nothing extreme about this one.

"Ow," he says. He lets Kyle help him get to his feet beside the shower.

The bath water is ice-cold, so Kyle refills the tub. Brian enjoys the view of him sex-loose and flushed, his cock sticky and shrunken between his legs, his mouth tinged red-brown-black with dried blood.

"Sorry, I should have stopped before we—sorry."

They climb into the tub together, Brian in front. Brian cuddles back against his chest, dizzy and satisfied. "Don't worry about it." He turns sideways so he can put his cheek on Kyle's sternum and one arm around his torso. "I love you." He feels Kyle smile against his hair.

"I love you, too."

"How's the studying going?"

"Great, actually. The performance piece is in final rehearsals. Everything else I have blocked out for study sessions. And I was able to turn in a Theater History essay way early, which means I don't have to take the final."

"That's awesome." He smiles. "How's poly sci with Lee?"

Kyle laughs. "She has never let me live it down that I didn't notice her in class. Every time she comes into the room, she reintroduces herself to me, with exaggerated direction to where she sits."

"I'd like to meet these new friends. They sound cool. They're the first specific people you've mentioned."

"It took me a while to figure out how to make friends, I guess."

"Nothing wrong with waiting for the right people."

Kyle kisses Brian's hair, and then trails his fingers through the bath water to gather soap and the loofah from the tub's edge. He begins washing Brian's back with slow, even strokes.

"Elisa's not going to drag you off again before the holiday, is she?"

Kyle shakes his head. "Nothing until July."

As they wash, the stresses of the day fade away. It's lovely to simply be with Kyle and talk about mundane things.

"I had an elderly patient today," he says. "She was seventy-something when she turned. A really fun person. She had a great attitude, especially considering that she's showing signs of pancreatic cancer."

"Another one like the others?"

"Yep."

"Clara must be all over that."

"I don't think she sleeps." Brian turns his face into Kyle's neck and closes his eyes. "What I'm seeing so far is treatable. Thankfully, I haven't had to give out any hopeless prognoses."

Kyle's fingers card through his hair. "But it's hard for you."

"For vampires, disease and degradation, like aging, is essentially in stasis. It's one of the perks. Strength. Agility. Longevity. Not having to worry about what ailed you when you were human, at least not for a long time. I mean, sure, if you're on death's door, being turned isn't going to save you. But if you're turned before disease or injury develops or becomes critical, you have a good chance of living as long as several human lifetimes without experiencing a single symptom. So to have to tell them they're losing their immunity and not be able to explain why…" He shudders. "Yeah. It's hard."

Kyle tips his face up and kisses the tip of his nose. "You're the best doctor they could have."

"Thank you." He smiles. "So, since I have you in such a good mood, would now be a good time to talk about the menu for Thanksgiving?" Brian bats his eyelashes.

Kyle smirks. "Man, a human feeds you a few times and they think you want to help arrange one of *their* meals."

Laughing, he splashes Kyle.

* * *

"'Hunter green' and 'dark sage' are two entirely different colors!" Michael says. His voice carries, as it is wont to do, and Brian laughs behind his hand at the panicked look on Jenn's face.

"Oh, look, drinks!" she says, in a pitch identical to Michael's, and grabs Brian's arm, booking it for the fountain drink and pretzel kiosk they just walked past. "Why," she whispers, so that only Brian can hear. "Why napkins? Why do napkins matter so much? I can't even speak English anymore. *Help.*"

Brian is sure that she's one centerpiece question away from tearing the shiny, shoulder-length brown hair she's currently sporting right off her scalp.

"You did say yes when he asked you to marry him."

"In small doses, do you think animal tranquilizer would be safe to use on a male vampire of approximately Michael's size?" Her hazel eyes narrow thoughtfully.

"Your patients may have four legs and mine two, but you're still a doctor of medicine. For shame, Jenn Chapelle. For shame."

"Damn our ethical code," she hisses, deadpan.

Michael catches up with them and slides an arm around her waist.

Brian is amused. Who would have thought his older brother would turn out to be such a terror regarding his own wedding?

"Are you sure about Halloween?" Michael asks him.

Michael and Jenn are hosting the Halloween party for Jenn's veterinary hospital this year, but Brian made plans to celebrate Halloween with Kyle's friends and coworkers at *Mi Corazón Sangrante* months ago.

"RSVPed already, sorry."

"That's okay," Jenn says, smiling. "You're cooking for us on Thanksgiving, anyway."

"For you, maybe," Michael says. "I do sometimes miss meat. Sigh."

"Oh, please," Brian says. "You can afford the best black market blood there is."

"I have no idea what you're talking about. I am offended at the implication."

Brian laughs. "Uh-huh."

"I need to pick up my scrubs," Jenn says. "Do you want to meet somewhere else after I'm done?"

"No," Michael says, kissing the tip of her nose. "We'll be here."

For the moment Michael takes to gaze into Jenn's eyes, Brian sees their mother's fairer features shine through—Michael's slate-gray eyes and light brown hair are nothing like the chocolate-brown coloring Brian inherited from his father's side of the family.

When they're alone, Brian asks, "We will be?"

Michael's change of expression tells him they're out of joking territory. "Look, I haven't wanted to ask, but have you talked to Dad?"

The question surprises Brian. They don't often talk about their semi-estranged father.

Their family maintained a tenuous harmony at best—their father an attorney and their mother the CEO of her own dot-com company, and both of them always busy. They expected a lot of independence and drive from their sons, but never had much one-on-one time for them.

"If I had, you'd know," he says.

"One of my partners forwarded me some interesting media regarding dear old Dad. It's all pretty vaguely worded, but what it boils down to is that he's definitely moved up in the world."

"How 'up' are we talking?"

"Department of Justice up."

Brian sits back. "Whoa."

"I don't like what I'm hearing. I just wanted you to know he may be even worse than he was when we saw him last. And I'm not sure how he's going to react to Kyle."

Neither of their parents were openly homophobic, but Brian is sure they would have preferred both of their sons to be straight. They never engaged him on the topic, but were polite, if cool, to his high school boyfriends. Work ethic and money-making and business expansion were the entire axis upon which their affluent family spun. Anything unrelated to career paths took not a second but third or fourth place in their household. Brian wasn't abused or outright neglected, but he can't recall any genuine warmth, either.

"If he can't handle me having a partner, I don't know what to do about that," he says. "I'm not going to censor my life to gain his approval."

"Brian," Michael says, leaning across the table. "I'm not talking about you having a boyfriend. I'm talking about the fact that your boyfriend is a vampire."

"What?"

"I know you haven't wanted to be in the loop, but you have to know by now that Dad's politics are rabidly anti-vampire. That's what I'm trying to tell you."

Brian always knew his dad disliked vampires—before his mother's death when Brian was seventeen, and even more fervently after the attempt to turn her into a vampire to save her from cancer failed—but he had no idea the personal bias became a professional one as well.

"Shit." Brian tears a piece of pretzel in half. "Shit. Well. Okay. I'll warn Kyle—and we'll limit the amount of time he spends with Dad."

"I feel awful about this," Michael says. "I invited him. I just… I don't think Mom would have wanted us to exclude him. She would have said family matters, even when they disappoint you."

Brian exhales. "Honestly? I don't see it that way. You know how much family means to me, but let's be honest, our upbring-ing was as cold as ice, and there are so many disappointing things about our parents that we didn't learn about until we were older." He shrugs. "You got to see a slightly more positive side of Dad for a while because you were following in his footsteps and he approved. Mom defended my performance dreams, so I got a view of her that was more flattering. But still, even with that, in the end, we weren't enough for them. That failure—*their* failure—matters. And then my career in vampire medicine and your law practice's public defense of vampires, and Dad just—dismissed us and moved across the country to start a new family. As if it wasn't his choice to abandon us. As if *we* were somehow responsible. We shouldn't forget that. I think it would be a good idea to forgive and move on, for our own sakes, but forgetting or pretending it didn't happen…"

"I hear you," Michael says. "I'll be honest: I almost crossed Dad off the guest list a hundred times."

"Hey, it's your wedding. Maybe seeing him will help us put the past behind us. Or seeing us will affect him positively. Either way, he's going to be there—unless he sends his regrets at the last minute."

"Ha. Wouldn't that make it easy?"

"You know what else would make it easy?"

Michael groans. "Brian—"

"Stop driving your fiancée nuts. She's going to start sleeping at the hospital to escape you, I swear."

"Color schemes matter! The music matters! We only get to do this once." Michael stops suddenly and smiles. "I love arguing with you. Is that stupid? It's nice."

Brian has to agree. During his medical school days, he and Michael were not close at all. They weren't very close as kids, either, due to the ten-year age gap, and their mother's death and family's fracturing had not helped them grow any closer as adults, but in the last couple of years, they've made time for each other and become true brothers.

He throws a bite of pretzel at Michael. "Stop it before you make me cry, you big idiot."

"How's that best man speech coming?"

"Oh, no. No, no, no. We are not talking about this now."

"Does it lack emotional depth? Do you need a copyedit? A thesaurus?" Michael's face goes dramatically soft. "The removal of a thesaurus?"

Brian stands. "What I need is a refill."

"How many paragraphs are dedicated to praising my smoldering good looks?"

Brian cracks up in front of the drink fountain, feeling lighter than he has in days, despite the worrying talk about his father.

* * *

MI CORAZÓN SANGRANTE DECKED OUT in Halloween décor is a sight to behold. Kyle can't believe how cheesy they've gone—fake cobwebs, decals of stereotypical witches, vampires, werewolves and ghouls, bowls full of "eyeballs" (peeled grapes), skeletons dangling in doorways, machines playing "spooky" noises. Every Halloween item that can be purchased from a party store is present and accounted for.

Standing in the kitchen where Clara is stirring a bowl of "blood"— spiked fruit punch for the human guests—Kyle laughs until he almost cries.

"Please tell me you aren't taking this seriously," he says.

Clara is dressed up like Morticia Addams; Elisa is her matching Gomez.

"What other holiday can we go completely overboard with, huh?" she asks. "Besides, we don't celebrate any differently than they do, although our food and drink of choice is quite different."

The Halloween party is hours away, but Kyle has been helping them set up all afternoon. The guest list is long—all of
their clients have been invited, as well as friends and family of
employees—and if everyone who agreed to attend shows up,
they're definitely going to have a full house.

Kyle is nervous about introducing Brian to his friends.
He's also regretting his costume choice. He thought it would
be funny to dress as a "sexy doctor"—a scrub-green tank top
and shorts with a stethoscope around his neck and a name tag
pinned to his chest—what with Brian being *his* sexy doctor,
but now he realizes he has no idea what Brian is wearing. What
if they clash? Should they have coordinated beforehand? He
should have asked.

Kyle arranges a bowl of spicy cinnamon candies labeled
"blood drops" and asks, "Do I look stupid?"

"You look like a twink," Elisa says, breezing into the kitchen
in her suit and slicked back hair. "Good job! That is, if Halloween were about dressing up as what you *are*." She pauses
dramatically and looks at Clara as if seeing her for the first time.
"*Cara mia!*"

"*Mon cher*," Clara says, laughing as Elisa kisses up her
arm, tugs her in by her wrist, and kisses her on the lips, long
and hard.

Kyle clears his throat.

Elisa lets a dewy-eyed and flustered Clara go. "I can see your
religion in those shorts."

"I'm a sexy doctor!"

"Oh, my God, did you seriously—"

"Hey, hey," Clara says. She slides her arms around Elisa's
waist. "He looks nice. Shush."

Elisa winks at him, and he smiles.

"You both look awesome," he says.

"What's Brian going as?" Clara asks.

"Not sure. It'll be a surprise, I guess." Kyle pops one of the candies into his mouth to cover the awkward silence. He blinks. "Are these made with real blood?"

"Sort of." Clara waves her hand. "What? I labeled them. Of course, sometimes the label matches what's in the bowl and sometimes it doesn't. It's fun!"

They set up a trick-or-treat trail in the rooms throughout the building's upper floors, carnival fun-house style. Kyle doesn't have to cover his room until later, so until then, he's hoping to party with his friends in the basement common room where the bar and music are set up.

He's still not sure how he feels about the basement. It's to this room—to that very chair at its center—that he led the vampire who followed him all the way to Chicago from his hometown. Using a trap Clara planted on the chair, he successfully captured his pursuer and ended the chase.

The guy, Jeffrey Simmons, was one of Kyle's peers in high school. Jeffrey was a confused social outcast, both like and unlike Kyle, who had been under the impression that Kyle would want to be with him if he were a vampire, too. He kidnapped Kyle after their high school graduation, tied him up and took his blood. Kyle managed to break free and fight him, then fled the scene fully convinced that he'd killed Jeffrey in the process when, in reality, Jeffrey was successful in taking enough of his blood to effect the change and survive.

Kyle recalls the way that it felt to watch Jeffrey unable to move in that chair, to feel the rage and sickness in his mind—as Jeffrey's maker, Kyle could not block all of his thoughts—to see the boys Jeffrey had fed from and killed on his way to finding Kyle, to hear the thoughts he'd had as he killed them and… other things.

Shuddering, Kyle tucks himself against the bar. The room is filling—mostly with employees—but he doesn't expect the hand on his arm and he jumps.

"Whoa, hey." Max comes up behind him. "Sorry. You somewhere else?"

"You could say that." Kyle's cheeks heat up at the sight of Max in a T-shirt, jeans and a leather jacket. His hair is artfully rumpled, and the fit of his costume shows off the lines of his lanky frame very well. "James Dean?"

"Yes, sir."

He looks good. God, he looks good.

"We, um, we opened up the surplus for the party," Kyle says. "Can I get you a drink?"

"O-pos, if you've got it. Thanks."

"I remember." Kyle smiles. He tries not to blush. He tries not to be flirtatious. He's pretty sure he's failing on both counts. "Where's Lee?"

"She and Ms. Baxter decided to do last-minute matching costumes and went to get accessories."

They stand off to the side of the bar, sipping shot glasses of blood. "Can I be the one to tease her first?" Lee swore up, down, and sideways that her dating luck wasn't going to change, but she and Caroline have been inseparable for weeks now.

"If you're a good boy, maybe," Max says.

Kyle's neck goes hot. For the twelfth time in the last three minutes. He clears his throat. "Your costume is nice."

"It was an easy one, and a classic." Max smiles, licks blood off of his upper lip and says, over the rim of his glass, "You, now. You look—wow."

"It's stupid. I thought it would be edgy, but I just feel naked."

Max laughs. He stops and starts talking once and then again before he says, "Uh, well, I mean, there's a certain naked element to—to it, yes, but I wouldn't say it's stupid." His smile curls at its edges, digging dimples into his cheeks. "You look hot."

Kyle is saved by Lee and Caroline arriving dressed as Thelma and Louise.

"Oh, hey, you guys," he says, as Caroline orders herself and Lee blood. "You look great."

"The words 'I told you so' are not to pass your pretty pink lips, Hayes." Lee loops an arm around Caroline's waist.

"That's okay," he says. "Max can do the honors for me."

"So I get to take all the heat?" Max puts a hand on Kyle's shoulder. Kyle leans into the touch.

During a lull in the conversation, he checks his phone and is disappointed when he reads a text from Brian saying that he's staying late with a patient and might be a couple of hours.

Suddenly in possession of time to kill, he decides to dance. The basement is darker than usual with the overhead lighting turned off, and the center of the room that's been cleared for dancing is ringed in dim orange lights. He's comfortable disappearing into the crowd, but remembers his manners and asks Caroline to dance. He can tell she's unsure of her place in their group, and knows all too well how that feels. She's majoring in biology. Kyle asks about her finals. She seems perfectly nice, from her sharp, upturned, pale nose to her dirty blonde, short-cropped hair. She might be good for Lee, who obviously doesn't want to relinquish her new girlfriend for long—she claims Caroline after only two songs, and Kyle lets her go with a polite, friendly smile. He turns toward the bar and isn't surprised when Max crosses his path.

"There you are." Max slides his fingers over Kyle's forearms. "Want to dance?"

"Sure."

From the start, it's too much. Max's palms against the dip of his lower back. Max's body, all denim and leather and the smell of an uncharacteristic overabundance of hair product.

Kyle closes his eyes. He feels guilty. He shouldn't want to be close to Max, but he does.

He turns his face into the underside of Max's jaw—their height difference allows this to happen perfectly—and pushes up with his nose, inhaling sharply when Max's fingers skim the soft cotton waistband of his shorts. A pre-arousal tremble starts low in his belly.

Max inches them, step by step, into a secluded corner. Kyle swallows a noise when Max's face tucks into his neck. They don't stop dancing, but Kyle feels an unstable shift in Max's body's movement—just before their pelvises line up, and *oh, god, shit,* they're both getting hard.

"Max," he says. Max's fingers skim the upward curve of his ass, neatly skirting the border between groping and petting.

"Just dancing." Max's lips ghost down Kyle's neck.

It's not just dancing. Kyle's body is humming and he's getting harder and all he wants to do is rub his dick against the bulge in Max's jeans. It's such a basic, animal urge that he is forced to take it for exactly what it is—he is being a tease and a cheater and he can't believe how easy it is to tumble down that path. It's like his brain shuts off the second he starts to get turned on by Max.

"I need air," he says, when he realizes that if he doesn't stop swiveling his hips against Max's, he's going to have a problem in these loose shorts that he can't conceal.

"Okay." Max lets him go, though he's breathing heavily himself and it seems to pain him to unwind his arms from around Kyle. "Okay, okay."

Kyle pushes through the crowd, all the way to the double entry doors and into the hallway, which is equally crowded. The party is in full swing. He checks his phone. He has another text from Brian, about twenty minutes old that reads "omw," which means Brian should be here already. Breathing out a sigh of relief, he climbs two flights of stairs and heads for the kitchen. A little window on its far side opens up onto an alleyway, and he sticks his head out into the freezing air and breathes.

He is embarrassed to have to reach down and adjust himself, but he does.

"Fuck," he says, to no one at all.

He's alone for maybe five minutes when Elisa strolls in, empty bowls in her hands.

"Shit! Fuck, you scared me," she says. "Creep a little louder, huh?" She takes one look at him and he knows that she knows something is wrong. "Oh, boy. Oh boy. What's up?" When he hesitates, she adds, "Don't lie to me, *gato*, I can smell the fucking sex musk from over here."

There is no escaping this woman. Kyle really kind of loves her a lot.

"It's Max," he says.

"Oh, shit."

"Yeah."

She sits down at the table where they have shared countless meals and conversations.

He remembers the first time he was lucid after he collapsed on their doorstep and she and Clara took him in, fed him and offered him a job biting humans for pay. It took so long for him to learn to trust them, and even longer to realize there was more to *Mi Corazón Sangrante* than met the eye: that it was a front for the vampire research facility they had created. Now, he probably trusts her and Clara more than anyone else in his life besides Brian.

"You can't say anything," he says. "I mean it. I am so—I am trying not to make a mistake."

For once, there isn't a trace of inappropriate humor or sarcasm in her tone. "I wouldn't do that to you."

He joins her at the table. "I feel this pull toward him, and I can't figure out whether it's because he makes me horny or because there's more to it. Whenever he's around, I just—react. It's unconscious. And I don't feel that way about guys all the time."

"Look, don't take this the wrong way, but your experience with dudes isn't exactly extensive. It's new to you, to feel that way. To trust. To want. You never did before *el doctor*, but now that you know what it can be like…"

Kyle empties his lungs. "I guess?"

"Have you talked to Brian about this?"

"Oh, god, no. How could I?"

"You're dating, not dead." She smirks. "And please, no 'undead' jokes. Especially not tonight."

"How could I expect him to react calmly to something like that?"

"He loves you." Kyle swallows around the lump in his throat. "Do you think he'd put you out on your ass for being turned on by another guy?"

"No," Kyle says. "It would be worse. He'd tell me he understood. He'd thank me for being honest. And all the while, he'd be dying inside and trying to hide it from me. But I would be able to feel everything—and I would hate myself more than he ever could."

"Look at you, all grown up and shit," Elisa says, her voice unusually soft. "This is one of the reasons why loving humans is so fucking hard for us. We feel the things they try to bury."

Kyle's eyes feel as if they're burning. "What do I do?"

"Just be with him. Be with him and keep trying and see how you feel. It all comes down to forgiveness, when things go off the rails. And true forgiveness is rare." Elisa stares past his shoulder and out of the open window. The kitchen is getting cold with it open, so she stands and crosses the room to close it. "If you can forgive each other, you can do anything together." She touches his shoulder and walks to the kitchen door. "He's downstairs, but your room shift is about to start. Go on up."

He doesn't know what to say to that, so he simply does as he's told.

It's warm inside the client room. There's a bowl of candy and some items that count as tricks—exploding or noise making party favors with Halloween themes, mostly—and he tries to allow serving the partygoers to take his mind off Max.

Soon enough, though, every partygoer has had a chance to receive either a trick or a treat, and the door to his room remains shut. It's quiet for too long.

He sits on the bed and eats some of the blood candy, but it must be more glucose-derivative than blood because it makes his stomach hurt. He sits back against the pillows and wedges his body halfway between them and the wall to get comfortable. In no time at all, he's sleepy and thinking about Max and Brian, and he starts rubbing himself through his shorts. He doesn't conjure up a particular scenario—he just touches himself until he gets hard, and then slides one hand down the front of his shorts and starts jerking off.

The fact that the door is unlocked excites him. Would it send his clients running if they were to walk in on him like this? Would some of them like it? When they have his teeth in their flesh and his mouth on their skin, do they ever think about him like this, hard and warm and aching to come?

The first time he fed off of a willing human was here at the club during his training. Further experience taught him how to make taking his clients' blood clinical in some ways but intimate in others; both are necessary to ensure the exchange is satisfying for them. But he has to admit that there are times even now when he takes clients who simply turn him on. It's this generic attraction he thinks about as he touches himself.

When he comes into a tissue, though, the orgasm feels like nothing. He's sticky and hot, and as light and hollow as brittle bone on the bed. His body twinges with missing the intimacy of being close to someone after sex. He dozes off briefly and is woken up a short time later by a knock on the door.

He can smell that it's Brian.

"Come in."

Brian enters, smiling. "Trick or treat?"

It takes Kyle a second to realize who he's dressed as. He's wearing skinny jeans and a *Star Wars* T-shirt and big glasses with no lenses; his thick, dark hair is styled into a flyaway mess.

"Oh, my God," Kyle says, laughing. "You're Tray!" Brian dressed as his favorite character from *Dusk Until Dawn*. He looks amazing.

"Phew," Brian says, and sits down next to him. "I thought the resemblance wouldn't be obvious enough." Kyle's throat closes up. Brian dressed up *for him.*

Brian switches on the bedside lamp and looks at him. "And you are… oh." He chews his lip, and then kisses Kyle. "If the other med students looked like you, I never would have graduated."

Kyle makes a noise and clasps Brian's arms. "Come here." Dragging Brian down on top of him, he wraps his arms around Brian's shoulders and kisses him, perhaps too intensely given the situation. Brian makes a contented noise and presses Kyle down into the squeaky mattress.

"You really like this character, don't you?"

Kyle laughs. He takes the glasses off of Brian's face because they're getting in the way. "I like you. I love you." He's so needy that he flips them over, not holding back his strength, and pins Brian's arms above his head.

Brian breathes out harshly, his chest pushing against Kyle's. "Oh. Okay."

"I want to dance with you," Kyle says. He kisses down Brian's neck. "Are you too tired?"

"No, I'm okay." Brian relaxes beneath him. "I want to meet everyone. Not sure how long I'll be able to stay up, but…"

Kyle has an afternoon class tomorrow but the morning off, and he knows Brian's morning is also free. They can go home whenever Brian likes and then spend the morning lounging in bed.

Sounds like heaven.

"Agreed," Brian says.

Kyle tenses. He didn't realize how hard he was mentally projecting. He reins in his thoughts. "Sorry."

Brian smiles and kisses along Kyle's jaw. "No problem. Although—you could have waited for me. I would have helped." He cups Kyle through his shorts. "I can feel it in your mind, sometimes, when you've had an orgasm."

"It's okay. I—I was worked up. Too much blood at this party." He only hopes his mental walls are strong enough to prevent Brian from sensing the lie. He's already feeling guilty that Brian naturally assumed he jerked off; Brian doesn't even suspect Kyle of being capable of cheating on him. He pushes the thought to the back of his mind and sits up. "Let's go dance."

Lee greets them near the door, half of her costume off and Caroline clinging to her waist from behind. "Well, here he is, finally!"

"I'm already a celebrity." Brian swaps hugs and cheek kisses with the pair. "Lee, I assume?"

She nods, and shouts over the music, "This is Caroline, my date."

"Nice to meet you!"

"And this idiot is Max. He's an engineer," she says, with a wink.

Brian laughs but then smiles, firmly shaking Max's hand. "Max. The engineer."

"I introduced myself to her that way and she's never let me live it down." Max pumps Brian's hand with equal force. "The man himself. Kyle never stops talking about you."

Brian leans into Kyle's side. "Good to meet you."

The tension between them is palpable. Kyle isn't surprised. He has a life with Brian, but he's drawn to Max, and Brian can sense Kyle's feelings. Even if Kyle is blocking the details of his thoughts, Brian knows something is happening here that he can't quite put his finger on.

Kyle wants to reassure him—and to stop giving him a reason to worry. He takes Brian's hand. "We're going to dance."

"How much blood have you had?" Brian asks as they cut a path through the crowded dance floor.

Kyle wraps his arms around Brian, slots their bodies together, and begins to sway to the beat of the music. "A bit."

"You're really warm and sensitive. Every time I touch you, you shiver." Brian presses close and buries his face against Kyle's neck, near his ear. "So. This *is* a sexy doctor costume, right?"

Kyle laughs. "Yes."

"You dressed up like a sexy doctor for me." Brian nuzzles kisses against Kyle's earlobe.

The way it felt to dance with Max—dangerous and sexy—is different from the way it feels to dance with Brian. With Brian it's not only hot, but comfortable and familiar. Brian knows his body and what to say to turn him on. When Brian's fingers grasp his waist and lead him into a dark corner, he doesn't feel guilty. When Brian's hands squeeze his ass and pull him close, when Brian's thigh slots in between his, he feels free and sexy.

Kyle attempted to style his hair into thick waves for the costume but only partially succeeded. Brian's fingers quickly undo whatever progress he'd made.

"So if I'm the vampire," Brian says, raspy and low, "and you're the doctor…" Brian's mouth opens over Kyle's neck. Kyle can feel the blunt press of teeth that are longer than usual.

"Are you wearing fangs?" he asks, his voice breaking. How had he not noticed *that* before?

Brian pulls back to let him see. He's wearing false fangs that are convincing enough to pass for real ones in this light. "You mold them to fit your teeth."

"Oh." Kyle can't explain it, but there's something ridiculously hot about Brian trying to look like a vampire. When he goes back to kissing Kyle's neck, Kyle's heart begins to race again. "That's interesting."

Brian mimes biting him, pressing the curved plastic teeth into his neck, a little rough and fast. Kyle gasps. His back bends beneath Brian's hand, and his pelvis jolts against Brian's.

Brian laughs into their next kiss. "You *have* had a lot of blood."

"Or you're just inspiring."

They back up into the wall behind them, kissing until their mouths are humming from the friction, Kyle's fingers in the back pockets of Brian's jeans and Brian's in his product-sticky hair.

"We're supposed to be dancing," Brian says.

Kyle licks over the plastic fangs. "This is dancing. Kind of."

When they exhaust the limits of decency, they wander back into the light to mingle with Kyle's friends. Max keeps his distance, but Lee and Caroline are excited to talk to Brian, and when Kyle sees them getting along, he swells with pride and happiness. He gets them another round of drinks and stands opposite them, his hand in Brian's, and the rift that has grown between them ever since he made new friends and never introduced them to his boyfriend closes.

While Caroline and Brian debate about a detail of cellular mitosis, Kyle gives Lee a squeeze and whispers in her ear, "I like this one."

"She is so out of my league. What do I do when she figures that out?"

"Oh, stop. She is not. You're a catch."

Lee kisses his cheek. "So keeping you for the ego boosts." She nudges him. "Your boyfriend is sexy as well as sociable. 'Grats." She tilts her head. "Where have you been hiding him?"

"Our schedules are insane. We almost never get to go out together anymore."

She laughs. "What exactly do you do after school that keeps you so busy, huh? I know it's not the club because I've seen the shift sheets and you barely work there anymore."

Kyle hesitates. The truth is that the people closest to him who know what he does also *do* what he does, so he doesn't have an excuse handy.

"It's mostly Brian's schedule." He doesn't like lying to her, but what other option is there? "Have I mentioned he's a very important doctor?"

"*No*, really?"

She drops the topic, for which he is grateful.

He takes the opportunity to look for Max. He's feeling sensitive about what happened earlier and doesn't want to leave the party without them talking about it.

He finds Max sitting at the far end of the bar.

"Hey," Kyle says.

"Hey."

He puts his elbows down onto the sticky counter. "I'm sorry."

"You don't have to apologize."

"No, I do. I haven't exactly been pushing you away." His face burns. He's never had to reject someone, at least not like this. "I'm attracted to you, I mean, that's been obvious since we met… but it's fucked-up, and I keep letting things happen, and I'm sorry."

He can't read Max's face, and it's freaking him out. "He's your first boyfriend. That's all I'm gonna say."

"What?"

"I just think you're narrowing the playing field too soon, that's all."

Kyle shrugs. His stomach tightens with irritation and embarrassment. "That's my choice. It's really none of your business."

"We're friends, though, aren't we? I care about you."

"If you were my friend, you wouldn't try to make me feel bad about not wanting to break my boyfriend's trust."

Max flinches. "Okay. Fine. True. Look, *I'm* sorry. I've had a lot of blood, and you drive me crazy. But that's on me, not you. I'm gonna head out. I want to—I want us to talk again, when I'm not like this. Have lunch with me at the center, tomorrow before class?"

Kyle exhales and nods. "Okay. I'll text you."

He's rattled after Max leaves, but not truly upset. He can handle this—he just needs to tread lightly and be mature.

The party is a lot of fun. Brian meets many of Kyle's clients, which proves to be hilarious instead of mortifying. Elisa and Clara ply Brian with alcohol, but by the time the party begins to wind down, they're nowhere to be found.

Kyle asks Brian if he's seen them. Brian laughs and coughs, his cheeks bright red. "I, uh, well. I kind of walked in on them in one of the client rooms."

"Oh, god. You didn't."

"Elisa was very busy. Clara looked as if she had no complaints. I didn't interrupt them."

"Oh, my god, *stop*."

Brian laughs. "Sorry, I know for you, that's like talking about your parents getting it on."

Kyle makes a face. "Images. Blargh."

"I'll give you some new ones." Brian is drunk-touchy as he kisses Kyle. He lowers his voice and thumbs Kyle's bottom lip. "I have wanted this mouth all night. Wet and swollen and wrapped tight around my cock. If I take you home, will you do that for me?"

Kyle stifles a whimper. Heat rushes through his body. It has been a crazy night, and the thought of going home and taking care of his boyfriend makes it all seem worthwhile.

5

"Please tell me you're here for reasons other than grilling me about my security checks." Erica throws an empty—and thankfully sanitized—blood bottle at Brian's chest. He catches it.

"I'm here for reasons other than grilling you about your security checks," he says in a monotone, and then smiles. "I also wanted to ask if you've done something with your hair. It looks *great*."

She laughs and puts down the box that she's holding. "You're such a jerk, Preston."

"You're the last center on my list, Szeto. I saved the best for last."

She takes a stack of papers from a safe that's hidden behind her desk and hands it to him. "This is our activity for the last twelve months. We don't allow remote access, as you know, so it's all internal."

He sits on the edge of her desk. "Thanks, hon."

"I'm not in the loop on this one, but can I ask how it's going?"

He sighs. "Clara wrote formulas for detecting data patterns. We have techs running them day and night. I'm doing most of the back-end analysis."

"Sucks being the newbie, doesn't it?"

"I know it well," he says, with a laugh. "Hey. How are you? How's John? Does Mom miss me?"

Erica, her boyfriend John, and her family were Brian's closest friends, almost like a second family, before he strengthened ties with Michael and met Kyle. He's sad to say that his and Erica's lives have taken separate paths since—Erica is need-to-know only at the facility, whereas Brian has been drawn in much deeper.

Erica smiles. "I swear, it's like she has no one to feed anymore."

"Let me know if you have time," Brian says, "I'd love to take you all out for dinner. I owe your mom a few."

She surprises him by hugging him. "I'm not looking for inside secrets, you know. I just miss you, dummy."

Guilt floods his chest. He hugs her back for longer than usual. "I'm sorry. Things have been insane."

"I get it." Pulling away, she looks around the room. "We had good times here, didn't we? I wasn't the worst boss ever."

"We had *great* times here." In fact, despite frequent inter-actions with violent vampires, he remembers his stint at this distribution center fondly.

"I'm glad that you're where you always wanted to be," she says. "I really am."

Some days it's that simple, and some days it's not. Still, this is neither the time nor the place for that conversation.

After he finishes at the center, he bundles up and leaves with a coffee shop in mind. He loves the cold, loves this part of town, especially now that he's able to enjoy the protection that the smell of a vampire on him brings. Humans and vampires alike are less likely to harass a human who reeks of contact with a vampire as strongly as Brian does, from constant exposure to his patients and Kyle.

As he orders his coffee and a bran muffin, he thinks about the latter.

That Kyle's mind has been concealing things has become glaringly obvious in the past few weeks. The silence surrounding his hidden thoughts has deepened, and Brian worries that Kyle is keeping something vital from him. He isn't sure whether it's personal or related to something Kyle is doing for the facility and has been asked to keep confidential. The second scenario is a definite possibility; they don't have a full disclosure policy with each other regarding work. It's just not doable.

But the way Kyle has begun to put walls up in his mind reminds Brian of the same strange silence he projected when he was trying to hide his past after they first met. Kyle didn't want Brian to know he had killed someone—even in self-defense, even though he was wrong about how much harm he'd done—and as they grew closer, physically and otherwise, he kept those thoughts carefully shielded. Brian didn't realize then what mental shielding in shared telepathy felt like—but he learned the ins and outs later, when Clara explained how vampires and their lovers or donors often develop mental connections with repetitive bites, to facilitate communication during the act, which often makes reliable or coherent speech impossible.

Kyle is still his—still wonderfully, amazingly his—but Kyle's mind is no longer an open book, no longer his to peruse, and he isn't sure when that change occurred.

Is this something they can talk about? Is this something Brian is *ready* to talk about? These questions plague him all the way home.

At the door, he shrugs out of his damp outerwear. It's warm in the apartment—Kyle knows that he loves to step out of the cold and into skin-tingling heat during the winter months. He doesn't hear any movement in the apartment, and Kyle's mind is a blank hum, so he ducks into the bathroom, washes his face and hands out of habit and then wanders into the bedroom on light feet.

Kyle is asleep on a textbook in bed, his feet near the pillows, wearing a T-shirt and a pair of ratty jeans he only wears at home. The hem of his shirt has ridden up to reveal a slice of skin between it and the waistband of his jeans. Brian tilts his head and smiles.

Kyle has changed so much, right in front of his eyes, in the short time they've been together. He was a gorgeous, smart, witty, yet conflicted young man when he stumbled into Brian's blood center one night with nothing but the clothes on his back, fear in his eyes and an empty belly.

He revealed himself by layers—his sarcastic sense of humor, his naivety, his underdeveloped sense of his own likes and dislikes due to years of neglect and abuse at school and at home, the open wounds he carried from the assault that was his turning, all blazing brightly into something new when he was allowed to live and love freely. He started reading books, watching movies he'd never seen and, when he started college, his life became three-dimensional practically overnight. Simple dreams of performing on stage became a reality, at least in tutelage, and this year, after his exposure to the social work department, he seems to finally be finding his place.

For some, the patience required to be with a younger man who is going through these changes might prove to be a burden, but Brian has enjoyed every second of it. It's the revelation of the man he loves in measured time, allowing him to appreciate every facet of Kyle. But for the first time he wonders if he and Kyle are on the same page. He wouldn't be surprised if they weren't—he isn't naive, and is perfectly aware that they are not at the same stage of life—but he isn't sure how to approach this issue.

He sits on the end of the bed, combs his fingers through Kyle's hair and smiles, flushing warm when Kyle's cheek pushes up into the curve of his palm.

"Mmm, hey," Kyle says. When he sits up on his elbows, his T-shirt and jeans stretch tight across his back and ass, and Brian allows himself to appreciate the view. He loves Kyle when he's domestic-grungy.

"Hey, sleepyhead." Brian tugs the drool-stained book out from under Kyle's cheek. "How far did you get?"

"Far enough. I don't think I can read anymore."

"Have you eaten? We could just go to bed."

"What time is it?"

"Nine thirty-ish."

"It's early."

Brian frowns. "You look exhausted."

Kyle stares at him for a moment and then smiles. "Yeah. Can I be the little spoon?"

"Any day of the week."

He changes while Kyle shrugs out of his jeans and into a clean pair of underwear. After the lights are off and the television fills the room with a blue glow, Brian turns down the bed and takes Kyle into his arms. He savors the alignment of their bodies— Kyle's shoulders against his chest, Kyle's ass snug against his crotch, Kyle's calves tangled with his. He feels like a phone with a low battery plugged into its charger at the end of a long day.

When it's quiet and their breathing is even and slow, he kisses Kyle behind his ear and says, "You know you can tell me anything, right?"

The only response he receives is the desperately hard—almost painful—clench of Kyle's right hand around his left.

Something is wrong. It's only a matter of when, not if, Kyle will clue him in.

* * *

Elisa stares at a pair of turkey-shaped salt and pepper shakers. "Home goods give me hives."

Kyle laughs. "You'll survive. We haven't even approached the battlefield that is the produce section—I need you by my side."

"I have no idea how I let you talk me into these little excursions."

"It's Thanksgiving, the club is a ghost town, you and Clara aren't celebrating so you have nowhere to be and nothing to do, and Brian is having a mental breakdown over everything we forgot to buy, so I figured I would dive into the crazy and save the day."

"You become more of a lesbian every day, *gato*," she says. "I'm so proud."

He chucks a bulb of garlic at her. "We need parsley."

They split up in search of the items Kyle and Brian missed on their pre-Thanksgiving Day grocery run. The store is a madhouse, but Kyle could have easily managed it by himself. The truth is, he feels awkward about not inviting Clara and Elisa to their dinner, but Brian wanted it to be just them and Michael and Jenn, and Clara and Elisa didn't seem to mind.

"Thanksgiving and Christmas were always nightmares for us," Clara explained. "We're more than happy to have a quiet evening alone instead."

Kyle wants to say that holidays weren't any nicer for him growing up, but he holds his tongue. This time of year doesn't hold a spiritual significance for him—neither he nor Brian harbor those beliefs—but becoming a part of Brian's family has changed the way he views celebrations. It's nice to have people around on those days. It's nice to feel as though he has a place and a purpose. Enjoying a holiday still feels like a shoe that hasn't quite been broken in, but he's getting there.

"Sometimes I think about how weird the holidays will be as the years go by," he says.

They use little blurs of vampiric speed to get around human shoppers, and Kyle suppresses a smile when a child they pass gasps in delight at the display with an excited, "Mom, did you *see* that?"

"Yeah?" Elisa asks him.

"It didn't hit me until recently," he says. "I was thinking about the four of us: me, Brian, Michael and Jenn. About how Brian's and Jenn's faces will change every year while mine and Michael's won't. About what a weird foursome we'll be fifty years from now."

They stop in front of a crooked pyramid of onions. Kyle rummages for a big one. They bought yellow onions for cooking, but Brian wants white for the salad.

Elisa is unusually quiet, and then she says, "Rude question."

"Shoot." He prepares himself, because if she's looking for permission to ask a rude question, it must be *really* rude.

"Do you think you'll make it that long?"

Kyle frowns. He was right; that's harsh, even for her. "What?"

She takes the onion from his hand and puts it into a plastic bag. "Twenty years from now Brian will be pushing fifty and you'll still look like a high school student. Do you think he'll be comfortable with that?"

"Physical looks don't correlate with age anymore," he says. "Since the Outing that has become a pretty mainstream concept."

"That isn't what I asked."

Kyle never thought about it before. He doesn't care what Brian looks like. He thinks that Brian is gorgeous, and knows age will change him—but just as vampires view many human conditions differently than humans themselves, he hasn't found the idea of Brian visibly aging problematic. Then again, he was never one of those teenagers who got hung up on looks, either, so perhaps it has more to do with who he is as an individual than a vampire. He has to admit, though, he's never considered how Brian might feel about it. Will it be too strange for him? Has he thought about them together that far into the future?

"I don't know," he says. "We've never talked about it."

"Don't get me wrong, I don't think you should obsess over it. We live long lives. We usually have many partners, whether we pair up with humans or vampires." She shrugs. "The human experiences just last for shorter periods of time."

He exhales. "It hurts to think about it like that."

"You need to prepare yourself for the possibility that your forever and his might not turn out to be the same thing," she says. "That's why enjoying every minute is so important." She thrusts the bag of groceries she's carrying into his arms. "So go baste a fucking turkey, give your man a blow job and live it up, kid."

Not bad advice, he thinks, with a twisted smile.

***

MICHAEL AND JENN ARRIVED AT the apartment early and have thrown themselves into the meal preparation. Music is playing, Michael is chopping vegetables at breakneck vampire speed, and Jenn is laughing with Brian at the kitchen table. Kyle stops in the doorway to watch them, so grateful for their presences gathered together that he could cry. The somewhat melancholy conversation he had with Elisa at the store seems far away. Or, more accurately, it seems inapplicable to this scene.

Brian is wearing a pair of designer jeans and a dark purple sweater that hugs his torso like a second skin. He becomes visibly giddy when he sees Kyle, and the giggle that bubbles up in his throat makes the corners of his eyes and mouth wrinkle. Kyle's chest contracts with emotion. He almost destroys the grocery bags in his arms clutching them too tightly.

"There you are," Brian says. He shuffles tipsily across the tile floor.

Kyle puts the bags down on the counter and puts his hands on Brian's jaw on either side, accepting the sweet kiss that Brian offers longer than he usually would with Michael present. Brian's face is warm and his breath smells like fermented grapes. When they part, Kyle tips his face against Brian's cheek and breathes out, then breathes in the scent of him, pungently human, a unique combination of fresh bread and salt-tang that Kyle has never smelled anywhere else. Lust—both carnal and hunger-based—swells for a moment, sharp and sudden, and he nuzzles his way to Brian's ear.

"You look great," he says.

Brian laughs. "I'm a little drunk. Jenn is finishing the—all the delicate—sorry."

"Awww, do I get a drink, too?" Kyle runs a fingertip down the side of Brian's neck.

Brian nips at Kyle's jaw. "At the first available opportunity."

"All right, all right, give it a rest," Michael says. "We've been slaving over this food for hours for you human types—"

"We've been here for twenty minutes," Jenn says.

"I've been up since six, you ingrate," Brian says. He jabs at Michael's arm, but allows himself to be pulled away from Kyle and into a brotherly embrace.

"I'll set the table, then, Julia Child," Michael says.

Jenn carries an armful of first course bits and bobs into the dining room while Michael collects plates, cutlery and napkins. The tablecloth and centerpiece and glassware are already set out.

When they're alone in the kitchen, Kyle puts his hands on Brian's hips and kisses him again, softer, slower.

"Sorry I took so long," he says. "I stopped by the club after I dropped Elisa off."

"No problem. We were at it all morning. I could tell you needed some air."

"This domestic stuff is still kind of new to me." Kyle inspects the food on the stove. "Holidays with my family were like court-ordered interactions. Food I was made to feel guilty for eating. Presents I was made to feel guilty for receiving. And after I was turned, I sat there at the table with my blood packet like an unwanted freak…"

He doesn't realize how shaky his voice is until Brian's hands land on his shoulders. "Hey. Last year was kind of a blur. And I know I was a little insistent on the arrangements this year. Too much?"

Kyle exhales. The food smells like so many overly sharp, unappealing things—sweet, salt and something too intense, almost like ripe garbage. He doesn't miss human food, and it doesn't always smell offensive to him, but being unable to enjoy it is sometimes depressing—especially on days like today, when human food is symbolic of bonding and family.

"No." Kyle puts his hands on top of Brian's and tugs them farther around his neck. "These are the kinds of things I want to get used to. I want—I want a life with you, a full life. Sometimes I just feel disconnected. Like I can't experience things the way you do."

"You don't have to. You don't have to experience things the way I do to appreciate them. In fact, I'm glad we're different. Our life would be pretty boring if we saw everything the same way, don't you think?"

Kyle's eyes fill with tears. He puts down the wooden spoon he's been holding and turns into Brian's arms. He isn't sure where these emotions are coming from—all he's done today is shop, chat with his employers and get blood at the clinic—but he feels raw and exposed.

"I do. But hearing that and feeling it are two different things," he says. "I'm trying."

Brian rubs Kyle's back. "I want you to be happy. Just come have some blood and amuse my stupid brother and be happy."

Kyle laughs. "I think I can amuse your stupid brother, at least."

Dinner is lovely. The food, a mish-mash of recipes that they cobbled together from vague childhood memories and preferences, seems to impress. Brian bought one of the newer, nicer blood-serving pitchers for Kyle's sake. Made of two layers of crystal with a warming and anti-coagulation mechanism, it keeps blood thin and at a chosen temperature while also facilitating neat pouring. It comes with matching glasses they're now calling "blood glasses," which are a hybrid of the wineglass bowl shape and the taper of a champagne flute. Kyle has never felt so upper-class. It takes the edge off of the bitterness he feels at being unable to share food with Brian and Jenn.

"We had these awful suits," Michael is saying, "and we dreaded them all summer long. Starched shirts and collars and ties so tight we could barely swallow our food. There were so many overdone rituals. The food was catered. The family we invited was so tense around my parents that they hardly relaxed the entire time."

"I remember overpowering perfume and cologne and sharp, poky jewelry," Brian says, sitting back in his chair with one arm around Kyle's. "Being nervous until the adults went off to talk and drink because I knew I was going to say something that would get me a sharp look from Mom or Dad."

"We still managed to have some fun together."

"We were too far apart in age to really tolerate each other for long periods of time, though."

"Especially when I was a teenager," Michael says.

Brian laughs. "You were always trying to find ways to sneak out and visit your girlfriend, and I didn't get what the big deal was."

"It was just me and my mom," Jenn says. "Small but nice."

"No comment," Kyle says, and then laughs. "Yeah. Mine was never—I dunno. I never felt that I had much to be thankful for."

"Well," Jenn says. She lifts her wineglass. "I think we can agree that now, at least, we're all where we want and choose to be. I call that progress. I'm thankful for that."

"Hear, hear," Michael says.

Brian leans over and kisses Kyle's cheek. "I'm thankful for us."

Kyle's face burns. He's been drinking donation blood all evening, not keeping track of how many times Brian has refilled his glass, and he's humming with it. Even though it's a holiday, it still feels indulgent. Drinking more blood than a vampire is used to over a short period of time is much like intoxication in that it overwhelms and makes him feel almost too wild for human company. Kyle, who frequently interacts with human clients while blood-glutted, is used to suppressing this reaction for their benefit, but in current company, he doesn't have to worry.

Stressful topics of conversation are avoided—the wedding, finals and Brian's trials and tribulations at the clinic—for which Kyle is grateful. After a while he spaces out, commenting here and there but mostly just floating deeper into the circle of Brian's arm until he's cuddled there with his head tucked up beneath Brian's chin. Under the table, his fingers trace the inseam of Brian's jeans. He is very relaxed.

"Since you did the shopping and cooking," Michael says, "we'll clean up. Go pass out on the couch or something."

"Or something," Jenn says with a sly smile as she and Michael disappear into the kitchen.

Kyle and Brian relocate to the couch with grateful sighs.

"Like they aren't going to indulge the second they're alone," Brian whispers, laughing.

Kyle doesn't often think of Jenn and Michael doing the things that he and Brian do, but of course they must. "In our kitchen?"

Brian rolls them over so that Kyle is the little spoon, and kisses the back of his neck. "Maybe it's just a donor thing, but I can pick up that vibe between vampire and human couples pretty clearly now. When the pull gets really strong."

"Oh." Kyle goes hot down the back of his neck.

Brian's voice drops. "Case in point." He drags his fingernails over the inch of visible skin between Kyle's ridden-up sweater and the waistband of his pants.

Predatory awareness flickers within Kyle, a shudder shot through with vibrant color and sound, and when Brian winds his forearm around Kyle's chest, Kyle's eyes tick unconsciously to the vein throbbing down its center.

Kyle kisses the pulsing blue line. "Do you—do you need me to?"

"God, yes, please." Brian shifts their bodies together. "Are you too full?"

Kyle licks at Brian's salty flesh. "Can you be quiet?"

"Maybe?"

"Can you stop your dick from getting harder than it already is?" he asks, playfully cruel.

"Oh, my god, you're such a tease."

Smiling, Kyle hums into Brian's forearm, and then pulls back a hair's breadth to allow his fangs to drop. The quiet noise that this makes draws a whimper from Brian. "I love you like this. Can't help it." He brushes the smooth front of his fangs back and forth over Brian's skin. "What if they hear us?"

"I don't care." Brian trembles where his muscles are straining.

"You need to be quiet." Kyle sucks kisses into Brian's arm.

"I will."

Kyle holds Brian's arm at the wrist and pins it with his shoulder at the joint. The excitement of being allowed to bite down, to take, is as strong as the sexual arousal that results from moving against Brian's body. The two desires twine and undulate, playing with each other as they wind tighter and tighter. Kyle lets the thrill ring in his ears for a moment before he bites.

The sparkling rush of Brian's blood is like ice cold water compared to the tepid dribble of donor blood. It's alive, full of thoughts and desires and familiarity and love. He drowns in waves of *Brian*, pulling at the wound until he can't feel or taste anything else.

He hears Brian sob against his shoulder, and then Brian's teeth when he bites down to muffle the noises he's making. The pain is brief but pleasurable; a spark in the darkness. When Kyle stops, dabbing the wound with his tongue, Brian rubs against him.

"We're not alone." He's breathless, his throat thick with blood. Brian's fingers close around fistfuls of his shirt. "So close."

"Don't. Wait a little longer for me?"

"O-okay. Okay."

They rearrange themselves. Brian puts a bandage over the wound and pulls his sleeve down to cover it. Kyle turns the television on and, after ten or so minutes of background noise, Michael and Jenn begin walking back and forth between the dining room and the kitchen, carrying dirty plates. Kyle can smell Michael's excitement and Jenn's blood easily—Brian wasn't wrong about that.

After the cleaning is done, they gather around the television as if nothing unusual occurred, and Kyle realizes this is yet another way that the four of them can relate. Michael and Jenn understand human-vampire relations; it's not embarrassing for them that they needed the alone time. He likes that.

Brian's blood is thick with alcohol, though, and Kyle is woozy for the remainder of the evening. They walk Michael and Jenn downstairs to their car with leftovers, take their time saying goodbye and thank you and love you, and Kyle is content. It was a lovely evening.

But the second that they're back upstairs and the door is shut and locked, he has Brian against its panels, and Brian is tearing the sweater off of his shoulders.

"Do you remember the first time I fed off of you?" he asks. "It was just like this."

"I came in my pants humping your leg and then passed out." Brian jerks Kyle's jeans open.

"Shit," Kyle says when Brian drops to his knees.

"Is this not," Brian says, "sorry, I'm—blood loss, and—I have no idea what's with me today. I'm so horny I can't think straight. Did you want to do something else?"

His boyfriend is on his knees, his plump, pink mouth hovering inches away from Kyle's tented underwear and he doesn't think that this is something Kyle might want? Kyle considers the advice Elisa gave him this morning and laughs.

"A certain employer of mine told me to be the giver and not the receiver today."

Brian laughs against his hip. "Meddling lesbians."

Kyle cards his fingers through Brian's hair. He can't remember ever feeling so thankful.

* * *

FINDING A COFFEE PLACE THAT'S vampire-friendly, satisfies the humans in their lives and has enough room for everyone to spread out with books and laptops over the course of several hours to study is a never-ending struggle this December. There are a few new options near campus, and they try them all before settling on a cafe called Equal Ground, which touts itself as a vampire-human mixing place. Kyle thinks it's all right.

Today it's just him and Max and he's okay with that. They haven't seen each other in a while and have a lot of catching up to do.

They get blood at the center first, and then walk at a leisurely pace to the coffee shop; snowfall dusts their dark outerwear. Kyle's feet don't quite feel the slippery sidewalk. The blood is bubbling in his veins. He keeps waiting for it to slow down—feeding usually only affects him for an hour or so—but today, it isn't slowing.

After they've caught up on the basics and settled at a table, their laptops plugged in and their books open, Max asks him about his Christmas plans.

"We were originally going to do more family stuff, but Brian wants to show me some sights. The Museum of Science and Industry has a Christmas exhibit that's a big deal, apparently. The Christkindlmarket in Daley Plaza. Ice skating at Millennium Park. And there's this string of boutiques—Prada, Wolford, that kind of thing—we usually avoid because I know he's going to drop serious cash on me, but it's *Christmas* so, I dunno, why not?"

Max smirks. "First-world problems."

"Oh, shut up. We're doing well and I'm completely aware of how lucky I am."

"In that case, buy a poor engineering student a mug of tea to warm himself over?"

He does so, and when he comes back with the tea, he asks, "Why did Lee say no again?"

Max shrugs. "She has a cold. Didn't want to come out in the snow."

"Ah." Kyle shuffles his note cards. The truth is that he had no reason to come out today, either; he's more or less finished studying. He only agreed to come because he felt guilty about having not seen Max since the Halloween party. They didn't get together for the lunch they talked about having that night and neither of them has brought up this fact yet; Kyle suspects that they both want to sweep the incident under the rug.

Behind them, on the television playing in the corner, a newscaster's voice is overtaken by shouting and then a clearer voice saying, "... *Entitled to express our concerns for our brothers and sisters, both vampire and human alike, about exactly what kind of medical treatment is being dispensed...*" The newscaster's voice reasserts itself, "... *The sentiment we've heard expressed many times today outside of Chicago's first federally-funded vampire health clinic, after a weekend of similar demonstrations on campus at…"*

"Hey," Max says to the employee fiddling with the remote, "you mind changing that?"

"That's what I was doing," the employee replies. "Sorry."

"I am so tired of Turn Back and their fucking fronting," Kyle says. At some point between tea refills, they migrated toward the same side of the booth they've been occupying all afternoon, and when he leans closer to Max as he speaks, their elbows brush. The unintentional contact sends warmth surging up his arm. "They just want public assistance taken away so that vampires get desperate enough to act out and prove all their crackpot 'naturally violent and a threat to humanity' theories."

Max nudges their elbows together. "I'm going to take that as 'studying done, can't no more with the learning.'"

Kyle smiles. This is true. His brain feels like mush. "You go ahead and do that."

There is a pause, and then Max says, "I missed you."

Kyle bites his lip to stop himself from immediately replying that he missed Max, too. There's just something so *easy* about Max. He never has to put much thought into their interactions. Max is—receptive, as if no matter what Kyle chooses to be or how he presents himself, Max will find him fun and amusing and attractive. Kyle so rarely gets that from people that he feels uncharacteristically clingy with Max.

In the end he risks a casual, "Same."

Hours pass. He forgets that he should probably get home. He forgets that they originally planned to leave early and take something hot over to Lee's place.

He sprawls out in the booth, his nose twitching at the overpowering combined scent of tea and coffee and baked goods, and the strong vibe that Max, as a vampire, gives off. He takes up so much more mental space than Brian, because of that and also because he isn't as neatly integrated into Kyle's mind. Sometimes Kyle enjoys this because Max is so mentally present when he's *physically* present.

Someone changes the television channel again, and this time it's a *Dusk Until Dawn* rerun.

"Is this the one where they go on a double date and the vamps try to switch all night because their humans are not doing it for them?" Max asks.

"Ugh, I hate that one."

"Oh, my god, why? It's so good."

"Come on, who could resist those humans? Tanya is a *darling*, and Andy has the cutest little neck. And the actors who play the vamps in this arc have like, no chemistry."

"Bullshit." Max laughs. "They are smoking."

"You being the foremost authority on females."

"They can't take their eyes off each other! Besides, they are about ten times more interesting than the humans they're dating."

"Awww, I dunno."

"What, you don't think two vamps can have as much fun together as a vamp and a human can? I wonder what your lovely employers would have to say about that."

Kyle laughs and turns into Max's side. Max's arm slips from the lip of the booth to fall around his shoulders. Kyle's face goes hot and his muscles tense up.

"It's not that—I mean, trust me, I've seen and heard more than I've wanted to, there. I know that those are some happy ladies in the sex department," he says, "I just—with Brian, it's such an inescapable hunger. It's a *need*. And he feels it, too, and I can't imagine what it would be like without that."

"Oh, man," Max says. His fingertips trail down the back of Kyle's bicep. "You really think it's that simple? Human equals food, vampire needs food, yin and yang? It's so much more complicated than that."

"I didn't say that. It just feels right when I'm with him, that's all."

Max's thigh lines up with his beneath the table. His breath is warm on Kyle's earlobe. "Have you been with a vampire? Since you turned?"

"Not—no." Kyle's whole right side where they're touching is tingling wildly.

"Oh, honey," Max drawls, and suddenly his hand is a warm weight on Kyle's leg. "There's nothing like it." Kyle shivers, sucks in a breath. "Imagine yourself on your craziest day—blood in your veins, power like static crackling under your skin. You can smell every human, vamp and creature with a heartbeat for miles." Max's lips brush the sensitive spot below his ear, and he bites his lips shut. "You feel aggressive, powerful and sexy—you would fuck anyone who so much as looked at you sideways, so hard and for so long they'd feel you for weeks."

Kyle's pelvis wants to move, to shift his cock, which is throbbing against the zipper of his jeans. He wishes that it would not pay attention right now. The betrayal taking place in his thoughts is more than enough.

"And then imagine," Max says, stroking Kyle's thigh, up and down, down and up, dipping toward the inseam with every stroke, "that there's someone else who feels exactly the same way. And you can let go with this person completely without worrying about hurting them. They know what you're feeling and they can give you what you need. It's like tidal waves colliding. You could destroy buildings together getting it out of your systems, and come out smiling."

"But what about the blood?" Kyle shakes. He's filling the front of his jeans—he can't help it.

"You've never had another vampire's blood?" Max's fingers squeeze his kneecap and then glide back up, splaying wide across his thigh.

"No." His heart pounds.

God, touch me. Touch me touch me touch me.

"It won't satisfy your hunger, but it's still delicious. Smoky. Spicy. Thick. It's like tasting a vampire's mouth with a kiss, or—" Max's lips curve against his neck. "Other places you might want to taste. It's intimate. You need to trust another vamp if you're going to let them at your veins."

Kyle can't breathe. The walls are closing in. He sits up. "Can we get out of here?"

Max nods. They pack their bags, Kyle pays their tab, and then they're outside in the snow-frenzied air before Kyle has a chance to think twice. He *can't* think. Everything is fuzzy and the cold is doing nothing to change that.

Max doesn't let up. He slides an arm around Kyle's waist, guides him two blocks south, and then blurs them between two buildings with a sudden twist of his body.

This isn't over.

Kyle gasps. "Max."

"Take my blood." Max presses him into the icy brick facade of the building behind him.

"What?"

"Do it. I'm safe. I'm clean. We trust each other. Bite me. I want to show you what you're missing out on." There's warm breath against his neck and Max looming tall and hard against him, bringing to life every wicked fantasy of the two of them that he's ever had.

Biting is... okay. Isn't it? It's just blood.

Doesn't matter want it just want to be closer fuck fuck touch me.

It's strange, reaching up to push his fingers into Max's hair, bending his body to bring them closer together. Max's arms cradle his head against the brick and away from the cold.

Everything is fracturing around him.

His teeth come down with a soft *snick*. Max's fingers flinch, go as hard as steel, and he feels the lash of that snap through his body, and—it hurts, just for a second, when Max shoves him into the wall and pulls on the hair at the nape of his neck. It hurts in a way that makes his cock twitch.

"Do it," Max growls, lifting him right up and off of the snow.

He puts his legs around Max's hips and his arms around Max's shoulders because he doesn't know what else to do now but give in. Effortlessly held up, he bends his back and then drives his teeth into Max's neck in one quick lunge. Max's blood tastes and feels, for lack of a better comparison, *condensed*—it's syrupy and pungent and strange, like a sauce from a dish that he's never tasted before, a combination of spices and textures he has no experience with. It makes his mouth and throat and belly tingle and his cock harden so fast that it almost shocks him. Deep down at the center of this black hole of sensation, he simply flails, aroused and lost and overwhelmed.

Max's fingernails rake the back of his neck. He feels the marks they leave behind. "That's it." He clutches Kyle's legs around him. "Suck it. It's okay. Feels good, and you're so hard, baby, I know. It's okay."

He tears his mouth away a breath later, and feels as if his heart is ripped out at the same time. He wants and needs more, but this is—this is not right. This isn't him. This isn't something that he does.

And it isn't just about blood. *Why did I think it could ever be just about blood?*

"Stop, stop," he says, panting. Max's blood is dripping down his chin. It tastes so good; he wants to lick it back into his mouth, he wants to latch back on to Max's throat, he wants to thrust against Max's belly until he comes. "I'm—I can't take anymore."

Max puts a tissue to his neck with one hand, but continues stroking Kyle's bloody jaw and cheek with the other. "Okay. Shhh, it's okay."

"Too much." He clings to the wall behind him, digging his fingernails in between the gritty, cold bricks until it hurts, which provides some clarity.

"Just breathe. And move. Moving helps burn some of it off. Come on." Max takes him by the waist and walks him out onto the sidewalk. "I'll take you home, come on."

"Oh, my god, I can't even walk straight."

"Nothing straight about you, darlin'."

Kyle laughs and chokes on a breath at the same time. "No. Bad. Bad joke, no cookie."

"Can we blur a little? We're farther from your place than I thought."

"Yeah."

"Hold on to me."

The rest of the trip is blocks zipping by, pedestrians and cars neatly avoided, and Kyle is okay but queasy by the end of it. It feels as though there's too much blood inside his body, as if his skin is going to split, and the taste is lingering on his tongue, coating the walls of his throat, reaching tendril-like fingers of sensation deep inside of him, giving him thoughts and feelings he doesn't want and would not normally entertain.

"Are you good to be alone?" Max asks when they arrive at Kyle and Brian's apartment.

"As long as I can be horizontal, I'll be fine, yeah."

"I'm going to text or call before I go to bed, just to make sure you're okay."

"Okay."

He needs to be alone. He *has* to be alone, or he's going to do something he'll regret. And there is as much paranoia in him right now as there is lust.

Brian isn't home. He washes his mouth out, strips down to his underwear, and crawls into bed, breathing a sigh of relief. But he doesn't rest for long. It's only an hour later, barely that, when Brian arrives, smelling like salt and sweat and wool and snow, so *human*—so much like food, like the kind that Kyle needs—it makes his mouth water and his cock stiffen. He's been at half-mast since Max left him, but Brian's presence takes him the rest of the way in a matter of moments.

It's not only lust, though. He feels strange—disconnected and too connected at the same time. He doesn't realize that he's moving until he's standing in the bedroom doorway.

"Baby?" Brian asks. Brian's worried tone doesn't surprise him. He probably looks like hell, and he doesn't want to know what his thoughts must feel like to Brian right now.

Feels good, and you're so hard, baby, I know. It's okay.

He almost groans as he tamps down the memory. Did that happen? Did he let that happen? But it didn't, at least not all of the way, and he's here with Brian, not Max, and that's better than the worst possible scenario.

He takes Brian by his shirtfront and draws him in, trying to hold back his strength but failing. The material pulls too hard, too fast under his hands. He kisses Brian, shaking, and when Brian's hands cup his ass and pull him closer, he whimpers.

"Need you." He feels the hunger, the animal need, course through his body. It refuses to be denied.

"God." Brian exhales, grips Kyle's ass harder, spreads him open beneath his underwear and shoves him back against the dining room table. "Right now?"

"Fuck me."

He doesn't breathe evenly until Brian comes back with a tube of lubricant and bends him face-first over the table, until Brian's hands tip his ass up and peel his underwear down. His skin is crawling—too warm—and his heart is beating—too quickly— and he can't seem to get oxygen to his lungs.

"Fuck, honey, you're burning up."

He squirms, tilting his hips up, shamelessly desperate. Brian pulls his cheeks apart and places a cool dollop of lubricant right over his hole.

"Oh, my god, yeah," he gasps. "Fuck me." It's thrilling, there on his belly, gripping the edge of the table and listening to Brian jerk himself to get hard, and then feeling the silk-over-steel pressure of the head of his cock. Kyle pushes back, breathes, relaxes and then impales himself, inch by glorious inch.

"Oh god, oh god, oh my god," Brian moans.

"Fuck yes," Kyle hisses, rocking back and forth. "Hard. Fuck me, hard. Make it hurt."

It's not enough, but it's close—the table shakes, creaks and jars forward a half of an inch, an inch, with every thrust. It's all blind pressure and blunt stabbing and Brian's fingernails marking his back. He smells his own blood, briefly, and hears every slap of skin against skin.

Brian cries out when he comes without warning or delay, gripping his waist.

When Brian doesn't try to get him off in return, he turns over, separating their bodies. He isn't prepared for the hurt look on Brian's face.

"Were you—were you with someone else before I came home?" he asks, his voice breaking.

"What?"

"You smell like someone else. Your thoughts aren't—on me."

Shit. Shit, fuck, shit.

His first instinct is to confess. "I drank vampire blood. I—I didn't know it would do this."

Brian does up his pants with shaking hands. "Are you serious? Why would you—from someone you know?"

"Yeah, a friend, someone who goes to the same center; he's clean, he's fine."

"Why in the world—what does that even do for you?" He spares Kyle the jab of reminding him they both know perfectly well that vampire blood does nothing, nutritionally speaking, for other vampires. Kyle is equally aware that he doesn't deserve the kindness.

"I'd never done it and I was curious and he offered. It wasn't a big deal. We were just out on the street and it happened. It—it was intense, and I wasn't prepared. He walked me home. Made sure I was okay. That's all."

Brian sits on the back of the living room couch. His belt is hanging undone around his waist even though his fly is zipped, and Kyle knows that he's truly upset because he hasn't noticed.

"I know that signs are pointing to the likelihood that vampires can't contract or pass on human diseases and infections after they've been turned, and that vampires most likely can't pass things on to other vampires through blood, either, but—we don't know for sure yet. Why would you risk exposing us both to something?"

It would be simple if that was the source of his hurt, but it's not. Kyle feels the pain in his mind, feels how devastated he is that Kyle sought intimacy elsewhere, even this kind, and it devastates him. *What have I done?*

"I'm sorry," he says. "I wouldn't have—he's someone I know, I mean, I—"

"Max?"

The silence is thick. He nods.

Brian's lips thin into a line. He wraps his arms around himself and turns away.

Kyle's body freezes with the shock of realizing that Brian thinks he's confessing to cheating on him. He surges forward, a little blur, and puts his hands on Brian's stiff shoulders. "It's not like that."

At least it's not as bad as you think.

"He's hot." Brian sounds both amused and broken. "I get it."

"He is, and I'm not going to lie and say there isn't a physical attraction, okay? But we haven't—done anything."

Brian turns to face him. "Do you think I don't find other men attractive sometimes, too? We're in a relationship, not dead below the waist. I'm not mad at you for that." He cups Kyle's face in his hands. "But he's in your head, you smell like him, and he—his blood made you like this. I'm jealous, okay? You just *used* me to get off on the way he made you feel. Don't you realize how upsetting that is for me?"

Kyle's eyes glaze over. His jaw ticks. He looks away, overcome with guilt and self-loathing, and then presses himself down into Brian's arms. "I'm sorry." His throat closes up around the words. Tears streak down his face. "I am so, so sorry."

Brian's body is tense with resistance at first, but after a moment he begins to give in, and his arms slide around Kyle's naked shoulders. His fingers push into Kyle's hair. Kyle trembles with relief—his body is still humming from sex, though he didn't come and has lost his erection. His back is healing, but the scratches Brian left behind sting.

Max's blood is finally leaving his system, and he feels more like himself. The gentle collapse into Brian's embrace and loving, though injured, thoughts, is like sinking into a warm bath. It feels like home, and again Kyle is assaulted by the question of why this seems so distant when he's with Max.

"I love you," he says, into the curve of Brian's neck. "I love you so much."

"Loving each other doesn't mean we can be everything to each other," Brian whispers. He strokes Kyle's hair. "We don't—we can't be. Thinking that we can or should is asking for trouble."

Kyle feels young and stupid. He grips Brian hard enough to bruise him. "I hear what you're saying. But that—that doesn't change anything for me." He cups the back of Brian's head and presses in against his ear and jaw. "I'm still yours, and you're still mine."

They sit on the carpet, fingers laced and bodies shaking. When that becomes uncomfortable, Kyle sits with Brian in the kitchen while he eats dinner.

Brian takes a shower, and Kyle uses the time alone to check his phone. He has multiple messages and a voice mail from Max, but instead of looking at any of it, Kyle texts him, before deleting his number, "We can't be alone together anymore. I can't do this."

He turns off his phone without waiting for a response and goes to sleep beside the human he can't seem to stop hurting.

6

LEE AND KYLE GO OUT to celebrate the weekend after finals and before the holiday break. They dress up to patronize one of the more upscale vampire nightclubs. Kyle gets to hear the latest about her relationship troubles, a topic they haven't delved into lately because exams have taken priority over everything else these last few weeks. Things with Caroline didn't work out, but then there was Kevin and Janeel, both fun if short-lived dating sprees. Romance has given Lee a run for her money, but in a good way. She seems happy. She also plans to go home to her brothers and sisters for Christmas, which has her lit up extra brightly.

"So, elephant in the room—why did you ask me not to invite Max?" she asks.

"Who says I didn't just want to hang out with you?"

"My dear, my brain is a barren landscape of essay books, multiple choice questions and extensive knowledge of how to fuck around with word processing settings to make papers look like the right length when they are not at all the right length. I am a cranky woman. Don't make me dig."

Kyle shrugs, making the shiny, fitted button-up that he's wearing shimmer in the dim club lighting. "Things got complicated. And I was stupid."

She shoves his arm. "Shit. Don't tell me you slept with him."

"No, but I might as well have. We flirted, got way too cozy and then—ugh. I drank his blood and we almost fucked in an alley."

"First time drinking vamp blood?" Lee's face is screwed up into a very easily read, "You're a dumbass, my friend," expression.

"How was I supposed to know it did *that*?"

She laughs. "It enhances whatever you want at the time. So if you almost got it on, it's because you wanted to get it on."

He groans and pushes his fingers through his hair. "I know, I mean, I'm not trying to excuse what I did, at all. Anyway. So, he took me home, and I thought I had plenty of time to come down—and then Brian came home early."

"Oh, no."

Kyle sinks lower into his chair, his face growing hot. "I practically begged him for it, and he sensed Max on me as soon as we got close."

Her mouth drops open. "Did you tell him?"

"I told him what happened. I told him that I found Max attractive, but we didn't have sex." He exhales. "Feeling his pain… I can't even describe it. It was this giant, red, throbbing ache, like a wound, only in our heads. *Suffocating*, and I—I texted Max that we couldn't be alone again, ever, and then I deleted his number."

"Man, self-control: I know you have it. So what's the deal?"

"That's just it," Kyle says, "I have no idea. I've never had trouble telling myself, 'No, you have a boyfriend' before. It's Max. We spend time together and it's like my brain shuts off."

She rolls her eyes. "Which brain?"

"I know it sounds like an excuse, but I'm telling you, with him, it's different. I can't explain it."

She works her bottom lip against the top, and watches him for a moment. "Well, look. At least you're learning. If you need to cut him off completely, I get it." She takes a sip from her shot glass, licks blood from the corner of her mouth, and then touches his arm. "I think it might be for the best, actually."

"Agreed. I need to stay far, far away."

"No," she says, "I mean, Max—how can I put this?"

"Let me guess: He swoops in, fucks whoever he wants to fuck, and then disappears after the damage is done?"

"Nah. I haven't seen him fuck around much at all. I just get this feeling you're better off leaving that one behind you, at least in the intimacy and trust department."

He tilts his head. "Why?"

"Call it a gut instinct. He's a nice guy and all, but I haven't known him forever, and since you came into the picture, he's given me a weird vibe."

"Interesting. Okay."

He's surprised. This is the first time that Lee has said an unkind word about Max—the three of them have been close all semester, spending time together at the vamp shelter and blood center, studying and enjoying the city's nightlife—and he isn't sure what to make of the odd, shuttered look on her face or the fact that her mental walls have suddenly gone high and smooth. But her intentions seem genuine and he feels at ease. He's willing to take her advice—vampire instincts are rarely far off of the mark.

He smiles and reaches over to affectionately tweak the bow on the wrap that she's wearing around her high hair. "Thanks. Your logic is good logic."

She leads him out onto the dance floor by way of response, a matching smile on her face. "Just stay out of trouble while I'm away. That's all I ask."

"I hope you have a good time. I know how much you miss your family."

"I'm doing well enough now to bring home gifts and stay a while," she says. "It'll be nice to see the looks on their faces."

He hugs her. "Text me pictures?"

"Duh."

A drink server goes by, and she touches the woman's arm, checks her tag as she turns. "Hi. A-pos?" She glances at Kyle, who shakes his head. "Just the one, then." Kyle holds her waist loosely as she tips the server and then knocks back the shot. Her pupils dilate and she shivers, putting her hands back on his biceps. "Okay, no more drama. Let's dance. Finals are over!"

Kyle touches their server's arm before she walks away. "Change of plans; I *have* to drink to that."

* * *

THE FRIDAY BEFORE CHRISTMAS WEEKEND, Brian has to work late. The doctor scheduled to relieve him is running behind and there are patients still waiting. By the time he's free to go, he's exhausted, a predictable state that's been exacerbated by too many shifts and too much lab time clocked at the facility.

He and Clara hoped to have an explanation for their security issue and its possible connection to the strange medical and behavioral patterns that they've observed in the Chicago vampire community by Christmas, but they aren't there yet. The arranged data is taking ages to categorize, and when Clara fell asleep on her laptop the night before, Brian insisted they stop for at least a few evenings. They both deserve some time off.

Kyle and Brian have a weekend of holiday-themed recreation and shopping planned, and Brian hoped for an evening of relaxation before that, but it looks as though that hope isn't going to amount to much.

He changes out of his coat in the back room, shrugs on his winter coat and gloves and scarf, all with enervated deliberation. He has no messages from Kyle, which brings him down even farther. He's late, they had plans and the silence hurts. Will he have to get used to this feeling?

He steps out into the night and, as he takes his first cleansing breath of cold, snowy air, notices Kyle standing near the curb, wearing a sleek knee-length coat, a bouquet of pink, red and white striped amaryllis in his hand.

"Merry Christmas, Doctor Preston," he says, closing the distance between them.

Brian's eyes burn. He expected—he was *so*—and here Kyle is, reminding him of how easy it is to lose faith in something when it doesn't always meet your expectations.

He buries his nose in the flowers and takes Kyle's free hand. "Oh, honey. Thank you. Were you waiting long?"

"Since I got your text," he says. "It's okay."

Brian slots their fingers together as they walk. "Are you done at school?"

"Just handed in one last assignment, made sure my major switch went through, and yep. I'm all yours." He kisses Brian's temple. "Should we stop at the center? You're tired. I don't want to make you weaker tonight."

Brian scoots closer to Kyle; snowflakes dot his eyelashes when he tips his face up. "No. No, I took a booster at lunch, and I—no. I'm good." He wants Kyle tonight, in more ways than one, and he isn't going to change those plans just because he's tired.

The last few months have been a roller coaster of challenges and domestic instability, and for the first time in a long time, Brian feels something settled between them. It's nice not to feel left out in the cold by Kyle's mental walls, to sense genuine affection, to feel the romance between them play out as sweetly as it did when they first started dating. It isn't the same, of course, but it's grown in its own way, up and around the expectations they've had to adjust and the ways they've changed as individuals.

At home, he watches Kyle unravel his scarf, tug off his gloves and take off his coat. He watches melted snow glisten along his hairline where his hair is more red than brown. He watches the sweep of those beautiful, thick eyelashes over his high, pale cheeks.

He feels far too much. This graceful, silly, still-maturing young man is his.

"Get a fire going?" he asks Kyle.

The apartment is decked out in fresh pine garlands and cinnamon-scented candles. Brian inhales the delicious blend of aromas as he fetches the medical kit from the kitchen and places it discreetly beside the couch, on the end near the chaise where he intends to settle. As a last-minute indulgence, he pours himself a glass of wine. By the time he's finished, Kyle has rolled up his sleeves, and a healthy fire crackles in the fireplace.

He sits on the chaise, stretches his legs out and says, "Tell me a good Christmas memory."

Kyle bites his lip, smiles and leans against the fireplace mantel. "There was a Christmas market in Mansford that was put up every year the day after Thanksgiving. I was too small to realize how dingy it was. I remember at least one or two trips, before my parents died. They would make a big show out of letting me pick out wreaths for the house. They would always buy me a pastry or a decoration or a toy. I remember being so excited—as if that market was a magical world put there just for me to explore. I went back later as a teenager and realized that it was a gross parking lot full of small-minded people and cheap things. But when I was a kid, when I had my parents with me, it was magical. They made it magical."

Brian sits up, folds his legs in front of him, and puts his elbows on them. "Mine was a vinyl record my mom had. It was a two-sided record with twelve Christmas songs on it. Oldies stuff, you know, Nat King Cole, that kind of thing. She would play it once—only once, and Michael and I knew to be there when she was ready. She would sing the songs with us while we helped her unpack the Christmas decorations. We never put them up ourselves—they had people to do that for us—but the unpacking and the singing always went hand in hand. She never told us why she chose that record or that particular activity. She just did it for us. With us. I would think about how happy it made me when we were sitting through formal dinners and company Christmas parties and lining up to be kissed on the cheek by distant relations who barely spared us a glance once the gifts were handed out."

Kyle sits on the end of the chaise sideways, facing him. The firelight glows behind him, casting his profile and styled hair into sharp relief. "What's your Christmas fantasy?"

Brian's mouth twitches. "We're getting there."

"I'm serious."

"I'm serious, too." He drags a knuckle across Kyle's collarbone, right above the neckline of his scoop-neck sweater. "I think about being warm and sleepy and safe, knowing I've done my job for the year, knowing I'm about to taste your lips and tell you I love you and hear you say it back. That's my Christmas fantasy." He smiles. "Helped along by half a glass of wine, but no less true."

Kyle laughs and shifts onto his hands and knees, inching forward until Brian is reclining beneath him. "Are we going to make with the kissing now?"

Brian grazes Kyle's lips with his. "And the 'I love you.'"

Kyle kisses him, parts his lips and licks inside. "Can I throw in an 'I want you'?"

Brian puts his wineglass down on the coffee table unsteadily. "Oh, you sure can."

They lie down side by side, slotting their legs together from the knee down. Brian lets Kyle take control of the kisses, until all he feels is heat from the fireplace and heat beneath his skin and Kyle's body squirming against his. Their shared mental connection sizzles—a unified, undeniable mass of intimacy.

Kyle kisses down Brian's neck a dozen times before he stops over the bite mark, teasing it with slow, sucking passes of his lips and tongue before taking it into his mouth and *pulling*. Even with that whip of sensation cracked, Brian's hips come forward slowly—everything is wonderfully unhurried.

Kyle moves forward until his weight is on Brian's side, and then takes Brian's shirt off. Brian returns the favor, and they reach for their belts at the same time, laughing and helping each other, with the clink of buckles and creak of leather and snap of the wood in the fireplace all around them. Brian licks his lips and brushes the ridge in Kyle's jeans with the side of his hand. Kyle rolls over on top of him and spreads him out on the chaise, pressing his hands into the cushions on either side of his head. He wraps his calves around the back of Kyle's knees.

Kyle's fingers tuck into the waistband of his slacks. "Lift up?" He's naked in short order, breathing faster when Kyle reaches for the towel and lubricant bottle sitting beside the medical kit. Kyle kisses him, and strokes his thighs until he starts to quiver.

He turns his face so that Kyle's mouth can slide down the column of his throat. "Can we," he asks, "can you—fingers first?"

Kyle already has one hand on the inside of his thigh, and when he asks this, the fingers on that hand cup and lift his balls. "Yeah?"

"Please."

Kyle kisses his knee, sits up in between his legs, and tips his pelvis back. He wraps his legs around Kyle's torso, flushing hot when he feels the cool slide of lubricant and Kyle's long fingers dipping between his hairy cheeks. It's been a while since they've gone slow enough to start with fingers, but Kyle hasn't forgotten that he likes to begin with two. They burn all the way in and Brian holds his breath, waiting for the sensation to even out.

The crackle-snap of the fireplace seems to set the rhythm— Kyle works him open carefully, adding a third finger only when he begins to move and whimper. Brian feels the sympathetic arousal pound through his boyfriend's body and mind, sexual lust as present as blood lust as present as love as Kyle lets cautious little blurs of vampiric speed rush his fingers.

Brian cries out, spreading his legs. "Oh, god, yeah." He will never get used to these displays of power, woven so neatly into their sex play.

"How open do you want to be?" Kyle asks, sweet as sugar, as his fingers fly. "So open that I could just slip inside? Or less, so you'll feel it?"

"More," Brian gasps. He tugs Kyle down on top of him, barely leaving enough room for Kyle's arm between their bodies, between his legs, but he needs to be closer. Kyle latches onto his mouth with a throaty noise.

"Love you," Kyle whispers. "Love you. Love you." He kisses down Brian's jaw, all the way to the bite mark, which is throbbing in anticipation of another application.

"D-don't. Not until you're in me. Want you in me first."

Kyle huffs a breath over his collarbone, kisses across his nipples and the sharp rise of his sternum, then presses against the back of his thighs until he yields, letting them press into his shoulders, exposing his ass to the air and Kyle's roaming hands. Nothing excites him quite like hooking his knees over Kyle's shoulders, knowing that he's only moments away from being full of the man he loves.

Kyle kneels higher on the chaise, below the curve of Brian's ass. He shakes his jeans and boxer-briefs from around his knees to the floor. Brian touches the smooth, milky flesh of his belly, then squeezes the jut of his erection and groans at the feel of it.

Kyle bends over him, kisses him and steadies his legs.

"Let me in," Kyle says. The muscles in Brian's arms quake as he reaches between them to guide his cock. "Let me in, oh, f-fuck."

Brian whines, sinks his fingers into Kyle's hair and pulls him close. He doesn't want to talk, doesn't want to think—he just wants to feel their minds and bodies come together.

"Brian." Kyle moans and presses his forehead against Brian's shoulder.

"Bite." Brian scrabbles his fingers down Kyle's back. "Bite, *bite.*"

The tension cinches and snaps in the span of two heartbeats. Kyle doesn't hold back—he comes down hard and digs in deep, clutching Brian hard enough to bruise him. The pain is blinding. He cries out as Kyle's teeth slip free of his flesh—he actually hears the blood gush as Kyle closes his mouth around the wound, careful not to spill any. The mental backlash is stronger, clearer; Kyle's thoughts blow up with color and sound and shape as the blood floods his throat.

So good so good good good so good love you mine mine KyleKyleKyleKyleKyle fuck me

The couch creaks as Kyle honors his request, long sucking pulls at his neck alternating with powerful thrusts that drive his ass up onto Kyle's thighs and his legs almost vertical against Kyle's shoulders. When Kyle stops drinking, he feels how much blood Kyle took, feels the bruise around the wound, feels the pain spread, checked only in part by the numbing agent in Kyle's saliva. He doesn't care. The sensation is just right, makes everything too much, too perfect.

Fuckmefuckmefuckme

Even with that urgency beating furiously alongside his racing heart, Kyle slows down and kisses the bow of his upper lip, which is damp with fresh sweat.

"Hey," he croons, while Brian's eyelids flutter. The bite mark aches. "Stay with me. Feel so good. God, you feel so *good*." He inhales audibly when Kyle licks at the punctures, soothing them, tasting them, feeling the bumps and ridges of injured skin. He receives no warning at all when Kyle blurs them around, placing Brian on top of him.

"Oh," he whispers.

Kyle guides Brian's ass down around his cock again. "Sit. Just like that." He begins thrusting up, slow-paced and shallow, encouraging Brian to bring his weight down fully.

Brian makes a noise and rolls his ass back. "Oh, *god*."

"Go slow." Kyle strokes Brian's chest and belly. His fingers glance off of Brian's jaw, and Brian turns his head to take Kyle's fingers into his mouth. "Oh—oh." Brian sucks at them; his eyelashes flutter over blown pupils as he rises and falls on Kyle's cock.

The room is warm and smells so good, above and beyond the sharp tang of sweat between them. Brian closes his eyes and moves, and allows his body to be moved. Kyle does most of the work, but Brian loses himself in the way their bodies connect.

He makes a soft noise when Kyle's fingers wrap around his cock, and lets the glide of Kyle's fist take him higher. Everything comes together—the plunge of Kyle's cock, the tacky thrust of his cock through Kyle's hand, the heat of the fire on his back and ass, and the pain from being bitten. He feels blood on his skin, sticky and drying, as far down as his collarbone. He tilts his head back; a drop of sweat trickles down his temple and hangs onto his jaw.

All of the sudden he's *right there.*

"I'm gonna come," he says, the words uneven, and Kyle milks the head of his cock just the way he likes. His vision goes blank as the orgasm crests, his body convulsing with every jolt, spilling ropes of white all over Kyle's chest. Kyle hums, jerking him through it from root to tip, and then pushes back inside of him. The sensation is jarring but he clenches up appropriately. Kyle rolls them over again.

"You're going all limp on me," Kyle says.

This time he spreads out, folds his legs up on either side of his body and lets Kyle kiss him and slide deeper. He sucks kisses down Kyle's impossibly long neck. The grooves above Kyle's ass cheeks are perfect hooks for his heels, and he puts them there as Kyle fucks him into the couch, faster and choppier.

"Come," he says.

Kyle hammers into him and he holds on, dragging his fingernails across Kyle's shoulder blades, their bodies and the couch shaking. Kyle comes silently, his face buried against Brian's shoulder. He makes a noise after, when the muscles in his back and thighs loosen.

"Oh. God, that was incredible."

Brian hums affirmatively. He can't remember the last time it felt that good. "You have become very, very good at that."

"I had a good teacher."

"You still think of it that way?" He hasn't considered their disparate levels of sexual experience for a long time.

"It doesn't turn you on, remembering how you taught me to suck you?" Kyle kisses up the sweaty rise of his shoulder. "To eat your ass? To fuck you? To love taking your cock?"

"You know I'm not young enough to go again yet. Tease."

Kyle laughs, pleasure-loose and sprawled on top of him. "I'm just asking."

"My fantasies evolve as we do, I guess. The way we are now—it's more than enough to get me off."

"Have I ever told you that you have the best lines?" Kyle wraps a few of Brian's wayward, sweaty strands of hair around his fingers.

"That's because they aren't lines."

Kyle kisses his chest and plays with the hair there. "Exactly."

They use the towels and medical kit, cleaning themselves enough to slide on underwear and separate. Kyle stokes the fire while Brian gets a blanket from the other end of the couch for them to cuddle under. He finishes his wine, savoring the lightheaded sensation that a combination of blood loss and alcohol bring.

"Did you want to turn the television on?"

Kyle puts his head on Brian's chest. Together, they watch the flames in the fireplace dance. "No. No, this is nice."

Brian is asleep within minutes.

* * *

SATURDAY IS A WHIRLWIND OF shopping for gifts for each other bought by means of sneaky, brief escapes—Kyle purchases a slew of things to redecorate the areas of Brian's clinic that he's allowed to alter—gifts for family and friends mutually debated and decided upon, and finally they check in with the carpenter who is assisting Brian in executing his combined Christmas and wedding gift for Michael and Jenn.

"All they've done since they moved into the new house is complain about Jenn having to take her veterinary work home," Brian explained months ago, "so, with Michael's input, I'm having the garage they're using as a kennel expanded inside and out, and cat walks and animal door flaps installed around the house."

They also plan to donate a lump sum of money to Jenn's veterinary hospital and the vampire nonprofit organization that Michael often works for. Kyle has a bead on Jenn's personal taste, and he wants to pick out some clothes for her to wear on her honeymoon. As far as Michael's gift goes, the facility was kind enough to toss some vampire paraphernalia prototypes Kyle's way, mostly convenience items they were sure Michael would get a kick out of: grooming tools and blood holders with superior anti-coagulant and temperature-control technology.

Brian and Kyle don't make it to the exhibit at the museum, but the German Christmas market in Daley Plaza is a wonder. Brian eats sausages and stollen and sugared almonds as they stroll through the timber lodges. They buy glass and wooden ornaments for their tree and huddle together in the cold. Kyle wishes that he could feel more connected to the sheer humanity of it all—and then they manage to find a corner of vampire-friendly stalls, and he drinks blood that tastes like salt and pepper. Brian laughs. He dabs the corner of Kyle's mouth with a napkin.

"You're all squinty."

"It tastes funny!"

By the time they hit the ice rink at Millennium Park the next day, Kyle is worn out from shopping but overwhelmingly happy. Ice skating is one of the things he became fairly good at as a child. Brian is mediocre at best, and Kyle takes great pleasure in letting Brian hold onto him while using his powers to whip them around the rink at alarmingly high speeds.

There's a vampire-only rink, a human-only rink, and a "mix if you dare" rink that requires its patrons to sign a waiver.

"Segregation makes me nervous," Brian says, as they slide onto the ice of the mixed rink.

"It's only because of the physical risks. We *are* flying around with razors on our feet."

"It still feels weird, to be split up like that unless you're willing to sign a piece of paper."

"I know, babe." Kyle kisses Brian's cold-flushed nose tip. "But there are a lot of humans here, a lot of kids. You never know. All it takes is one stupid showoff or blood-pumped vamp."

All around them, groups of humans and vampires skate and mingle freely—friends of all colors and ages and genders, couples who only have eyes for each other, and even families in which no one could tell at a glance who is human and who is a vampire. These open, happy displays are quite different from the way things were just a few years ago, and deep down Kyle feels good about that, even if the other rinks make him wary.

He kisses Brian. "Come on, newbie. Show me a spin."

"I picked the fencing lessons; don't judge me."

Kyle grins. "Trust-fund baby. I'm gonna laugh when you fall on your ass."

"Will you kiss it better?"

"Oh, smooth. Maybe."

The bright light bouncing off the ice makes Brian's brown eyes shimmer, almost clear around their edges when Kyle glances at them sideways. His thick, dark hair is standing high, mussed by the cap he was wearing earlier. His tanned skin is pinched pink and red from the cold.

Kyle's chest seizes with adoration—he is so in love with this man.

* * *

MICHAEL AND JENN DECIDED TO forgo the traditional rehearsal dinner, so instead of panicking over the venue and the introduction of family members to the rest of the wedding party, all Kyle and Brian have to do the day before the wedding is pick up their tuxedos from the tailor and panic about a million *other* details instead. Brian took the week off whereas Kyle still has classes to attend, but between the two of them, they manage to check in with the caterer, event organizer and florist to make sure that everything is in order.

The wedding ceremony is a civil one because neither Michael nor Jenn are religious. It's officiated by one of their closest friends in a hall at the Langham—even Jenn was won over by its romantic, European charm—with the reception to take place in the hotel's Devonshire ballroom, which boasts a newly reinforced structure and décor that are vampire- and human-friendly.

Kyle isn't sure how he feels about weddings in general, but who could resist being dressed in a designer suit so expensive that Brian actually refused to let him see the receipt? It was a sweet but pointless gesture—Kyle took one look at the suit and knew the designer and that it came from this year's line, and even though he isn't into labels as a rule, he knows enough about men's fashion to know how much it cost.

"How is this going to survive cats and dogs?" he asks Brian, who is standing behind him, his reflection showing in the three mirrors Kyle has in front of him.

The reception will also play host to the staff of Jenn's veterinary hospital, who are bringing their pets and foster pets, and all of the wedding guests were invited to do the same. Kyle thinks this is the coolest part of the whole event by far, but what about all of those beautiful tables and dresses and suits?

Brian's lips part. His cheeks are delicately flushed. "*I* have to survive it first."

Kyle blinks, and then smiles slyly. "Oh. Really?" He does a turn, letting his hips lead, and smiles wider when Brian swallows visibly, his fingers twitching at his sides. "You've seen me in a tux before." They'd attended at least two funerals in the last year.

"Not one that was tailored to fit every curve of your body," Brian says, his voice rough. He trails the pads of his fingers down Kyle's lapels. "You look incredible."

"You, too." Kyle bites his bottom lip. He has a better poker face than Brian, but that doesn't mean he's unaffected by the smooth lines of those slacks over Brian's ass and thighs, and the way the jacket cuts in to frame Brian's tiny waist.

"I think we're good," he says, pronouncing them properly attired. It's been a long day.

Brian kisses his cheek. "I'll get Marco to come take these suits off of us."

After everything has been finalized, Kyle breathes easier. "I think you deserve a nice meal," he says. "Don't worry about me. Let's go out."

He knows Brian loves the Korean place around the corner, and he's feeling that urge he often has when Brian is hungry—to watch Brian eat and experience the smell and taste of the food vicariously. It's almost a sensual pleasure, when the mood is right, observing humans doing things that he as a vampire can no longer do.

"Are you sure? We could stop off at home or the club first—feed you," Brian says.

"I'm sure." His skin tingles at the suggestion, but he's learned how to hold back.

At the restaurant, Brian eats and Kyle people-watches. They've reached that point in their relationship where constant conversation is neither required nor expected. But after the edge is taken off of his hunger, Brian stops and starts speaking a few times, and Kyle knows there's something on his mind.

"Are we having third and fourth thoughts about the suits?"

Brian dabs his mouth with a napkin. "Oh, god, no, that's like, the tenth time we've been refitted. I just—it's funny, Michael and Jenn got engaged around the same time we got together. I feel like their wedding has been almost a state of being for us for a long time. We've been running around doing prep for months." He shrugs. "But we've never really talked about it."

"Talked about it? Do you think they shouldn't get married, or…?"

"About how we feel about that kind of traditional—I mean, having that kind of ceremony, making that kind of commitment."

His belly twists with nerves as the awkward silence that follows Brian's statement deepens. Is it time to have this talk?

Brian puts down his drink. "Okay, I'm getting the 'Do not want' vibe. I'm sorry if I freaked you out bringing it up. I'm not asking you to marry me, babe." He smiles. "But I'd like to know how you feel about the concept."

Kyle takes a deep breath. "Fair enough. Could you go first? I need a second."

"Sure. I'm conflicted," Brian says. "My parents had a pretty superficial marriage, and seeing that from a young age colored my views pretty heavily. But when I see couples like Michael and Jenn or John and Erica, I see a healthier side of it. I'm not religious, so it's not a belief thing. But I also don't know if—I mean, the heteronormative stuff sometimes gives me pause. Is that us? And now the *humanness* of it, I mean, couples where one half will live for hundreds, maybe thousands of years and the other won't… that changes the meaning of commitment in a pretty drastic way. I think marriage needs to be examined under a new lens, but I'm not sure how. I like the idea of it, though, in any case."

Kyle picks at the placemat beneath his empty plate. "I'm a little conflicted, too. It's hard to explain, but when you're—when you have a lifespan like that, you think about things differently, even when you're young, you know? It's something we never forget. I only started thinking about it recently, for obvious reasons. Before you—well, I mean, I guess I never really knew my aunt and uncle well enough to judge their relationship. I know that my parents were happy together." He smiles, but it's weak, and when he shrugs his emotions knot inside of his chest. "I have to be honest; I'm not sure how I feel."

"That's totally fine." Brian reaches out to touch his hand.

"I love you and I'm happy. Is that enough for now?"

"It will always be enough. I promise."

Two errands—and one frantic phone call from Michael later—they're home in bed with their phone alarms set to a frighteningly early hour.

"So give me pointers on how not to make an ass out of myself in front of your dad," Kyle says, already half-asleep.

Both Michael and Brian have dropped some pretty heavy hints about their father, and even though Kyle hasn't wanted to psych himself out about it, he supposes that they should talk about it now. Brian is quiet for an unusually long time.

"I can't remember the last time we had an actual conversation, much less saw each other in person," Brian says. "But, he's—he's not a warm person. He's always been disappointed about me being gay." Another pause. Brian's fingers sweep up and down his side. "He's not vampire-friendly, either."

"I got that. Why is he even coming?"

"Michael is his first-born. That alone would demand his attendance. That kind of thing matters—or, mattered—in my family. I don't know how he really feels, but I'd go out on a limb and say he's feeling guilty and curious, too. Michael's name is better known in certain circles than his now, so maybe it's a competition thing, as well? I don't know. It's complicated."

"I'm used to jerks." Kyle shifts around just to feel Brian's hand move against his waist. "Look, don't get me wrong—it drives me nuts that I won't be able to make a good impression. But if that doesn't matter to you, I'll try to not let it matter to me. I just want to focus on Michael and Jenn's day, and on us having a good time after all the work we've done to make it special." He smiles. "Also I'd like to not get pooped, if at all possible."

Brian laughs, burying his face in Kyle's chest. "I think that last part's doable, at least."

7

"RUNNING WATER IN THE TEMPORARY kennel became an issue," Brian says as he rushes to Kyle's side. The polo and jeans he's wearing until he changes for the ceremony are askew, and he's red to his jaw line. "Sorry I kind of—ran off."

"Is everything okay?" Kyle asks.

They walk to the lobby—Kyle has never seen such beautiful glass and stunning furniture and high ceilings. The cunning uses of space and the modern architecture take his breath away, and he wants to stop every few feet and stare. Brian's hand cups his elbow.

"Jenn's mother is having last-minute panic attacks over her shoes and whether she's going to trip walking Jenn down the aisle," Brian says. "The hospital's dog mascot Monkey ate a wedding favor and they had to induce vomiting, Michael has almost caused two hotel employees to quit, one of his colleagues is concerned about the view of the river from the ballroom because his wife has a fear of bodies of water, and my father has yet to check in, so all things considered—well. I'm considering alcoholism. Your thoughts?"

Kyle steers Brian to the window. "Look at that view. And breathe."

"It is gorgeous." From where they're standing, they can see the Chicago skyline on all three sides.

"Is Monkey going to be able to carry the ring, still?" Kyle asks.

"He seems fine now. We'll just have one of the vet techs walk beside him to be safe. I know Jenn thought it was awesome that they were able to train him to walk down the aisle on his own, but…"

Kyle slides his arms around Brian's waist. "Is there anything I can do?"

Brian breathes in and out. "You're already doing it."

Kyle presses his lips to Brian's ear. "I think you'd be a terrible alcoholic."

"I think I would be, too."

"I want to stare at these floors forever," Kyle whispers with a glance downward. "Have you *seen* these floors? Oh, my god."

Brian laughs. "This place is amazing." He pauses. "Oh, and I had one of the boys go to the dummy location we advertised in the paper, and sure enough, Turn Back has been protesting outside the building all morning."

"Not surprised. It was a really good idea to place that ad."

"I have no idea how long it'll take them to figure out the wedding is taking place here, but if we're lucky, it'll be long enough to seat the guests, at least."

Kyle is worried about that possibility, but there's nothing they can do about it unless Turn Back breaks a peaceful assembly law.

"The organizer kicked me out of the kennel with strict orders to decompress and make myself beautiful, so shall we go upstairs?" Brian asks. He looks much more relaxed.

"You're sure you don't want to wait for your father and his wife?" Brian had said he wanted to intercept his dad before Michael had the chance to run into him first.

"Honestly? I need a break. He'll probably hide in his room until the ceremony, anyway."

Their suite is a deep, rich blue against a backdrop of pristine white, with a view of the river and a king-sized bed that Kyle has been acquainting himself with on and off all day. The bathroom is cleverly segregated marble and granite and limestone, with not only a soaking tub but also a rain shower and dual sinks. It's ten times more luxurious than their apartment's bathroom, and Kyle is a little in love with it. He's been imagining Brian's tanned, tight body under that spray or a film of bath bubbles for almost as long as they've been checked in. That particular indulgence may have to wait, however.

He's resolved not to feed on Brian today—Brian needs to keep up his strength—but the desire to undo him in some way is present, even nagging, as they enter the suite. Brian pops the two buttons on his polo. Kyle follows the motion with his eyes. Brian chugs a bottle of water and eats a packet of M&Ms from the mini-bar, and then flops across the width of the bed with a sigh.

"God, that's better."

Kyle kneels on the mattress, savors its firm spring, and then straddles Brian's hips and undoes the button on his jeans. "It could be even better."

Brian, his arms splayed wide, lifts his head. "Really."

Tooth by tooth, Kyle lowers Brian's zipper. "Really." He bends to put his mouth on Brian's collarbone and then his earlobe. "Silence your phone?"

Eyelashes rising and falling slowly, Brian asks, "Why?"

"I'm going to need your undivided attention for at least ten minutes." The corner of Kyle's mouth turns up. "Or five, if you're feeling quick about it."

"Hon," Brian says, laughing but sprawling eagerly at the same time, as Kyle kisses down to his belly and pushes his shirt up, "I am useless right now."

"Allow me to increase your uselessness." Kyle brushes his mouth along Brian's still-soft cock.

It only takes about seven minutes, all told. After, when Brian is gasping and swatting him away due to oversensitivity, he shows off a little, works his arms beneath Brian's body, and uses his strength to effortlessly carry Brian fireman-style into the bathroom.

"Oh, my god," Brian says and then laughs. "Your blow jobs aren't that great. I can still walk."

Kyle swats those plump buttocks in retaliation for the teasing. "Jerk. This rain shower is calling my name. Come on. Let me wash your back and then we'll get out of each other's hair to get ready."

"Aw, I didn't mean it. Your blow jobs are *always* great. Let me return the favor?" Brian asks.

"You need to focus on being the best best man you can be. Don't worry about me." After a few moments of warm, wet silence, Kyle tips his cheek against Brian's shoulder. "However—I wouldn't complain about you considering renovating our bathroom to have one of these."

Brian's shoulders shake with laughter. "We might have to move to a slightly better neighborhood to find *that* kind of renovation potential. Food for thought, though."

With the knowledge that time is not precisely on their side, they separate and wash. Kyle steps out of the shower before Brian and goes to unpack their garment bags. Everything after that is a whirlwind of dress clothes layered on piece by piece, makeup and sewing kits, a frantic last-minute triple check on the box that contains the rings, and fussing around each other until the room gets too warm. Kyle takes a walk to the ice machine and back to relax the mood.

"Are you nervous?" he asks when he returns. Brian is doing turns in front of the body-length mirrors on the closet doors.

"A little. More about drama than my duties, though."

"Understandable." Kyle looks at his watch. "We should touch base with the wedding party. Check the hall and kennel."

Brian stops dead in the middle of rubbing a cloth over his shoes; a smile tugs at his lips. His eyes go hazy and then refocus. Kyle puts a hand to his jacket and then his rigidly coiffed hair.

"What? Lint?"

Brian's eyes sparkle. "You look stunning."

"You've seen me in a tux before." Repeating this conversation has become a running joke.

"Not all done up like this." He closes the distance between them and puts his fingertips on Kyle's lapels as if he's afraid to dirty them. "You're so beautiful." His cheeks darken. "I'm spoiled, having you every day. Sometimes I forget."

Kyle's faces warms at the praise. Words are one thing, but the way Brian is looking at him, as if he hangs the moon, is something that can't be articulated. It just is. It's just *them*. And sometimes he forgets, too.

"You're also indescribably gorgeous right now." The intensity of Brian's gaze makes him useless, verbally and otherwise. He presses their lips together. "And if we have any energy at all left tomorrow, I intend to put this room to good use."

Brian's mouth moves against his, and he feels it in his bones when Brian whispers, "I booked it through the weekend."

"Oh," Kyle says, on an exhale.

"I want you on every surface of this room," Brian says. The words fall hot and heavy along the seam of Kyle's mouth. "I want you against those windows. I want you in that bathtub. I want you on this bed."

"Oh, god, stop, I'm going to—"

Brian cups the ridge of his cock through his pants, a wicked smile curling his lips. "Save this for me?"

Kyle lets out a noise like a balloon being stepped on. Forget the wedding; he'll be lucky to survive the walk down to the lobby.

IT HAPPENS THE MOMENT HE stops looking over his shoulder, in the room that they're using as a temporary kennel.

The noise of yowling cats and barking dogs forms a cacophony around them as Brian tries to talk to two vet techs at once. Kyle is busy fixing ribbons onto the animals' collars. In such a posh environment, this barely controlled chaos feels a little ridiculous, but, as always, money can normalize any situation. The hotel has treated them like royalty since the first deposit check. No part of him, however, wanted his reunion with his father to take place in a room that reeks of dander, which is, of course, exactly why the universe has conspired to make it happen.

One of the employees standing behind him says, "Sir, this room is open only to certain members of the wedding party."

"I'm the father of the groom, son," Edwin Preston says, in that understated, raspy, authoritative tone that regularly made a teenaged Brian quake in his Oxfords.

For a moment, Brian doesn't know what to do. It's been years since he's seen his father, and in the last few years, their communication dwindled to cards on holidays and birthdays. Neither he nor Michael were invited to the wedding when their father remarried. He's been thinking about how to handle this meeting since the day that Jenn said yes to Michael's proposal and now, standing here, surrounded by well-dressed hotel staff, his adorable boyfriend blurring around the room gently securing animals, and a party of people expecting him to take charge, he has no idea what approach to take. The performer in him tells him to simply go with it. He looks good, he feels good and he's successful. He's a grown man. He's in his element. He can do this.

The fact that his father has to trip over a wayward hamster to enter the room, however, *does* take the edge off of his confidence.

Kyle streaks past him in a blur of black and white, shouting, "No, Tippy! Bad hamster!"

Brian sighs.

Edwin takes in the room in one grand sweep that ends with his eyes on Brian. He's a short man—even shorter than Brian, who isn't tall—but that does nothing to diminish his presence. His bright white, perfectly coiffed hair, lofty expression and expensive watch and suit announce him as a person of status.

"Brian," he says, reaching out his hand. Brian shakes it, or it shakes him—he can't tell. "Quite the spectacle for this sort of venue." Every single thing about him screams, "I am judging you."

Brian steadies himself. "Dad. I hope you're checked in and comfortable?"

"Yes, yes. Anita is upstairs now."

"Good. Great. I, uh, I'm looking forward to meeting her. Finally."

Edwin's mouth squirms in an attempt at a polite smile. "So this is—the bride's side of things, I take it?"

"She's the administrator of one of the city's largest animal hospitals, yes. She wanted something a little more personal, something fun to offset Michael's more traditional wedding."

Kyle secures the hamster with a yip of triumph and hands it to a vet tech. "I've still got at least six cats to put ribbons on, so here. Thanks!"

Brian tries to gauge the timing, but in the end, he just reaches out to snag Kyle by the sleeve. "Please have someone else do that. You'll get cat hair all over your jacket, sweetheart."

"It's no big deal—they've got industrial-strength hair-removing things, they're kind of scary, actually, like duct tape on steroids," he explains, breathless, pink-cheeked and happy, and when he leans to kiss Brian he notices Edwin for the first time. He freezes, clearly waiting for Brian to make the introduction.

Brian wishes that this happened differently, but it's too late now. He smiles, squares his shoulders, puts his hand on Kyle's lower back and says, "Dad, I'd like you to meet my boyfriend, Kyle Hayes. Kyle, Edwin Preston, my father."

Kyle's face goes blank.

"Really," Edwin says, pumping Kyle's hand. "For a moment I thought he was one of the veterinarians in training. But age *is* difficult to judge with your kind, I suppose."

Kyle's face goes pink. He plasters on a careful smile. "It's a pleasure to meet you, sir."

Embarrassed, Brian curls his hand around Kyle's waist and holds on. He thinks, loudly and intently, *I'm sorry*, and hears Kyle's sympathetic response in the back of his mind.

"Well," Edwin says, looking bored and unimpressed, "plenty of time to catch up at the reception. I'll let you two get back to your—ahem—animal husbandry."

Brian could say any one of a thousand scathing things, but all he does is watch his father disappear and then breathe a shuddering sigh of relief.

Kyle turns into his side. "You were not kidding."

"I am so, so sorry."

"Don't apologize for him again."

It's not that simple, unfortunately. Brian feels gutted, vulnerable in the way that only his father's disapproval can make him. It's an awful feeling. It makes him doubt himself. It makes him want to hide. It makes him feel as if he has to justify everything he's done or said since they last spoke. He hates it, but more than anything he hates *believing* it, even for a moment before he remembers he's done nothing wrong and there's nothing wrong with him.

"Hey," Kyle says, when he doesn't respond. Kyle leads him out into the hall where the air is clearer and rubs his arms. "Hey, hey."

Brian is horrified to feel tears burn behind his eyes. He buries himself in Kyle's arms. Kyle is the only thing in the world that he can count on right now, and if his tears do fall, Kyle's shoulder will catch them.

"Just think about Michael and Jenn, okay? Let's make sure everything is ready. It's almost time."

That, and a hastily procured vodka tonic, gives Brian the strength he needs to move his feet.

Aside from a few overactive animals and a handful of last-minute guest cancellations, the ceremony goes off without a hitch. The hall is a beautiful blend of sage and gold, seating approximately three hundred of Michael and Jenn's closest relatives, friends and colleagues. Brian is impressed by how sweetly relaxed the whole affair is, considering Michael's high-profile life and Jenn's notable career, but the officiant is well-spoken and the vows simple—in places, even humorous—and when Monkey the ring-bearer dog trots down the aisle dressed in a frilly green collar looking very pleased with himself, noises of surprised pleasure ripple through the crowd.

Brian holds himself together through vows, the exchange of rings and the final "I do" moment, but when it's over to grand applause and his brother is clasping his wife in his arms, he can't stop the tears that have been on hold since he saw his father. Hazy-eyed, he finds his father and his father's new wife in the crowd. He's surprised and even pleased to find that in defiance of the second wife trophy stereotype, she's a short, round woman. They're applauding politely, but Brian can't read their faces.

Kyle's head comes down on his shoulder. "That was really sweet."

"Cocktail hour time," Brian says, and follows Michael and Jenn through the throng. He wants to congratulate them, but mostly he needs to move, to do something, to feel useful.

Kyle reaches for his hand. "Are you okay?"

No. But I need you to think that I am.

"I'll be fine."

Kyle's mouth tries to smile. He draws Brian close—Brian thrills at the strength in that tug—and kisses the bow of his mouth. "I'm so proud of you." Brian's heart turns a circle in his chest. He smiles, touches Kyle's cheek in thanks, and then breaks away while he still has the will to do so.

Michael and Jenn and their entourage have slipped out of a side door and into the hallway. Brian isn't surprised to see his father and Michael in a huddle with Jenn and his father's wife. For a moment, he isn't sure that he can do this, but he has to. He straightens his posture and walks up to them, though his pulse is spiking and his palms are sweaty.

He's just opened his mouth to speak when Jenn's mother grabs his arm. "I'm going to check the reception hall, dear."

"Thanks, Ann," Brian says, his eyes still on Michael and his father. As he resumes his approach, Michael breaks away from the group, takes his arm and steers him in the opposite direction. He should protest—insist on sharing the burden of socializing with their father—but he doesn't have it in him.

"Have the wackos found us yet?" Michael asks.

He even planned to crack a height joke to break the tension—Michael inherited that gene from their mother's side of the family, and is one of the only Prestons to break the six-foot mark—but Michael seems too irritated for humor, so Brian abandons the idea.

"No, the street is clear on both sides. I don't know what magic we worked, but they either haven't figured it out or don't care," he says.

"Good." Michael's jaw is tight.

"Hey." Brian stops them and puts his hands on Michael's biceps. "Congratulations."

Tension drains from Michael's face. Smiling, he bends down to hug Brian. "Thank you for being my best man."

"Don't thank me yet. I still have a speech to mess up."

Michael laughs and jabs him in the ribs. "True." They walk toward the reception hall. "So. You've spoken to him, I assume?"

"Yeah. Just him, though. He caught us in the damned kennel."

"Of course he did."

"How was he with you?"

Michael shrugs. "Probably the same way he was with you. Cool. Smarmy. Superior."

The way he is with us may be the same, but what it does to me isn't what it does to you.

"Jenn wants to see if she can warm things up," Michael says, as they stop in front of the doors to the reception hall. "She was pretty insistent."

"Maybe she'll bring some new magic to the family mix."

"Maybe I can convince her to drink enough wine to get *me* drunk later."

Brian laughs. "I have a feeling that Kyle may ask the same of me."

"How was Kyle, meeting him?"

"Stone-faced polite. He didn't have much of a choice. The phrase 'your kind' was used."

"For fuck's sake," Michael says. He braces himself in an obvious attempt to not lapse back into the foul mood his father put him in. "All right. Getting over it. I have dancing and posing to do and frown lines are so unattractive."

The cocktail hour is a never-ending chain of greeting guests and Brian doing his best not to succumb to the temptation of drinking until he feels less anxious. The food is excellent, and the floating blood donors who are serving the vampires are as professional and discreet as money can buy. More than once, Brian spots Kyle chatting with one of them, and he's so grateful for the ways in which he and Kyle are different in social situations, and how that allows them to engage the crowd in different but complementary ways. When they find each other again, it's time to move into the dining room. They make their way to the family table hand in hand.

"How are you doing?" he asks.

"This is kind of exhausting," Kyle says. "Elisa and Clara helped a little."

"I haven't even *talked* to them tonight." He has been favoring the guests he's more unacquainted with in an attempt to be polite.

"They're keeping a low profile. There are some well-known vampire rights types here tonight they don't get along with."

Brian is glad he hasn't been drawn into a debate or business conversation by any of said types. He wants this evening to be about Michael and Jenn and not work.

He glances down the table and takes a deep breath. The wait staff has poured the drinks and disappeared into the shadows. The dogs and cats have been secured by handlers. It's time. He stands and raps his champagne flute with a fork to draw the attention of the room.

"I promised my brother and sister-in-law that I wouldn't open with a party animal joke," he says, and then waits for the corresponding laughter to die out before continuing. "Which means that I had to rewrite a few paragraphs—but what can you do?" More laughter, another pause. Brian looks at Michael and Jenn and smiles. "It's kind of wonderful, how family can change. Just a few years ago, I'm pretty sure I wouldn't have been Michael's choice for his best man, and it wouldn't have surprised me or concerned him much. But life and circumstance sometimes brings you together with the people you maybe should have been with already. I can't say that I'm solely responsible for my brother and me coming back into each other's lives…" He spares Kyle a glance and a smile. "But I can say that I'm grateful for and humbled by how close we've grown. And I'm just as lucky to have Jenn in my life. She's the sister I never had, and seeing how happy she and Michael are together makes me believe in the good in this world, and in how easy it can be to make difficult things work when they really matter." He raises his glass. "I believe that they'll continue to amaze us all for many years to come. To the bride and groom." The phrase is parroted back amidst clapping and whistling, and Brian sits down when Jenn's maid of honor stands to deliver her speech.

Kyle's hand folds tightly around his under the table. Michael and Jenn blow Brian kisses. He laughs and reaches up to wipe his eyes.

This, at least, feels good. This is home. Brian is finally able to relax.

The food for humans and blood donors for vampires circulate. Kyle declines a donor and puts his hand on Brian's thigh under the table—code for "later."

Animal handlers pass around the dogs and cats and hamsters and lizards and snakes that have been brought from the hospital for petting and attention. Most of them are available for adoption. Brian hopes that as many as possible leave the wedding to go to forever homes.

Brian enjoys the first few songs the live band plays. The music for the evening is a mixture of jazz, classical and remixed seventies and eighties songs that make the crowd laugh with delight. It's a solid representational blend of Michael and Jenn's tastes—and, coincidentally, a choice that puts a constipated look on their father's face, which only makes them enjoy it that much more.

Brian is well on his way to being partied out, but he can't refuse when Kyle leads him out onto the floor to slow dance to a romantic song. They tangle their bodies, Kyle's arms around his waist and his around Kyle's neck, his face tipped against Kyle's jaw. The room is kissed by dim lighting around the edges of the floor and walls, on the tables and around the windows; the strings are woven sparsely so there's enough light to socialize by but not enough to illuminate. It's like floating in space, with the windows making huge rectangles of the evening outside and the city shining beyond the only clear view.

He's here, and even though the wedding has brought difficulties, he's glad to be: glad to see how content Michael and

Jenn are, glad to see the thoroughly mixed crowd of humans and vampires and, most of all, glad to have this beautiful man in his arms.

He drags his palm along the hair at the back of Kyle's head. "I love you."

Kyle smiles against his temple. "I love you, too."

"Do you have a donor thimble?"

"Yeah, just in case we ran out."

"Can we," Brian says, turning a flushed cheek against Kyle's shoulder, "can we be alone for a minute?" He wants to feel something familiar that might also excite his body's chemistry.

"Right now?" Kyle holds him tighter, almost unconsciously. The strength and unknowing possessiveness in the touch makes Brian's heart beat faster. "Here?"

"Plenty of dark corners." Kyle is particularly skilled at finding those.

When they are successfully tucked away, Kyle fishes the thimble from his pocket and slides it over his thumb, adjusting the collection bubble on the bottom so that it's facing the right away. He deliberates over Brian's arm for a moment, and carefully unbuttons the cuff of his jacket's sleeve, and then his dress shirt's cuff beneath that, folding the cloth over twice so that it's nowhere near the inside of his forearm.

Brian lifts his arm, meeting Kyle's mouth halfway. He bites his bottom lip inward as Kyle kisses and suckles his skin to numb it. Anticipation slinks through his body, finding homes in his pelvis and face and neck. Kyle cups his arm below the elbow, then holds it hard and down and brushes the point of the thimble's tip across his skin.

He inhales sharply at the tease of pain. "Yeah. Yeah, please."

Kyle presses down.

The painful sting sends rushes of adrenaline and arousal through his body. He holds on, breathing unevenly as his blood trickles down to fill the bubble. He watches as best as he can in the almost-darkness as the deep red of the blood spurts against the glass. Kyle removes the bubble when it's full, bends to lick the wound until the coagulant in his saliva kicks in, and then places a cotton ball and an adhesive bandage over the wound in two smooth motions.

Brian reels, lightheaded and turned on. Kyle courteously rearranges his shirt and sleeves, and then twists the thimble's bulb and tips the blood back into his mouth. It's barely a mouthful, but Brian feels the tug of its consumption in his chest and between his legs. Kyle's hunger being even minutely satisfied makes his own body ache with sympathetic contentment. As soon as Kyle has swallowed and licked his lips clean, he drags Kyle into a kiss. He knows that this is neither the time nor the place, but he feels like himself for the first time in hours, and when he tastes the coppery tang of his own blood in Kyle's mouth, he goes a little wild, flattening his hands on Kyle's chest and driving their hips together.

"*Ah.*" Kyle's grip on his arms tightens.

"Sorry. Shit. Sorry."

"It's okay, there are just—a lot of people."

After he shakes it off, they walk back out onto the dance floor. They're just passing the bar when a woman who Brian belatedly recognizes as his father's wife touches his arm.

"Brian?" she asks. "Your father would like a word."

The moment he realizes his father has been at the open bar for some time is the moment he almost turns around, politeness be damned, and walks away, but he's frozen in place. Anita is a stranger, and his manners reassert themselves.

"Brian," Edwin says, "my wife, Anita. Anita, my younger son, Brian." His tone is half a beat behind his inflection. He's at least a little intoxicated.

Brian forces a smile. "It's so nice to meet you, ma'am."

"Charmed," she says. Brian can't tell if she's being kind or sarcastic or both—she's difficult to read, despite the fact that she's smiling. "I'll let you two catch up." And then they're as alone as they can be, given the situation.

"You and your brother seem… settled." This is high praise, coming from Edwin Preston.

"Thank you, sir. We've had a good year."

The other shoe drops the second Brian stops waiting for it. "I still don't understand why he had to turn his career into a fiasco with that turning nonsense, but then he always was one for grand gestures. I suppose it's earned him some measure of success. If you call *this* success." Edwin sips his drink, his lip curled. He's obviously amused by his own jab and doesn't care if Brian shares in that. "He managed to find himself a decent human woman to marry, at least. Though I don't see how that kind of union can possibly last, myself."

Brian's blood runs cold. He's seven years old again, repelled by his father's words without understanding why, wanting to run and hide because they make him feel fear as well as shame. But he wants to try, so he says, "Times have changed. I hope you'll come to change your mind, too."

Edwin stares at him, red points stark on his cheeks. "Don't trot out that liberal nonsense around me, son." Brian's stomach withers. "You've got a pair on you, strutting around this upscale gathering with that vampire child on your arm. It was bad enough when your brother involved himself in this nonsense. I thought you were coming around in medical school—finally honoring your heritage and all of the sacrifices your mother and I made for you. But now I see that you've fallen in love with the vampire sickness as badly as your brother. Not only recreating but living with one of them, and working at a clinic that caters to them—what kind of life is that? Where will that career path lead? And what will you do when that *creature* has finished using you?"

Brian can't draw breath. The world goes fuzzy-dark around the edges of his vision. He didn't expect an open attack. How many times has his father seen the bottom of that glass? How long has his father been waiting to unleash this tirade? Could the floor open up and swallow him whole this very instant?

"Please don't do this," he says, his voice shaking, his throat closing up.

"Obviously someone has to," his father says with a sneer. "There isn't a single person in this room with your best interests at heart. That much is clear. And you wonder why I've kept Anita and my daughter well clear of this insanity."

"You have—I have a sister?"

"*I* have a daughter, yes. She's no sister of yours."

Brian's knees wobble. He becomes keenly aware that he is only a few labored breaths away from passing out. "Excuse me." He turns and walks out of the room as quickly as his feet can carry him.

He doesn't see Kyle fleeing in the opposite direction.

KYLE STOPS IN THE LOBBY, because it's beautiful enough to take the edge off of the pain in his chest. Brian's father's words cut through him, like so many shards of broken glass.

It's not as if they haven't encountered hostility or judgment before. But this is personal. This is Brian losing his family because of who they are and how they love. This is a little girl somewhere who is being denied the love of two brothers because of a father who will inevitably not accept her for who she is. It's the ugly side of family, similar to the neglect he suffered living with his aunt and uncle, and yet somehow worse because it's *present* today—most notably in Brian's heart, which was torn to shreds by only a few sentences.

Then there's the other side: Kyle's side. There's a place deep down inside of him that's screaming, "Why didn't you stand up for me, for us? Why didn't you say something?"

Brian has faced down medical professionals twice his age, stood up in front of doubtful peers and blown them away, danced verbal circles around federal employees and even took on Elisa on her best day, all without hesitating or faltering. But this…

Kyle sits on a white leather ottoman near the windows and stares out at the city.

Behind him, Clara clears her throat.

"Oh," he says. "Hey."

"I figured I wouldn't be missed." She sits on the armchair behind him. She's wearing Vera Wang in a deep shade of green and her strawberry-blonde hair is whipped up into loose curls around her face. She looks stunning. "I see you finally met the folks, huh?"

He laughs, and it comes out half-sob and half-giggle. "You could say that."

"I could offer ladylike advice, but screw that," she says, in her trademark raspy purr. "Edwin Preston is a conservative fuckwit and you shouldn't give a single shit what he thinks."

Kyle breathes out with difficulty. "I don't. But Brian does. Not consciously. But that man is his father. And I think deep down he's always tried to—to impress him, or prove to him that his accomplishments matter. And now he sees that he can't, but maybe he'll think that if he makes changes it might still be possible, and I'm—"

"Important to him." Clara puts her hand on Kyle's knee.

Kyle pushes his fingers through his hair, even though he knows that he's ruining the style by doing so. "Do you ever just wonder if it's—if it's just us versus them, even when you don't want it to be?" He stares down at his expensive dress shoes. "I feel like I can see past the pettiness, the immediate future, like noticing background details in a painting at the same time as the foreground ones and being able to—see the whole picture, at a glance, just like that. But Brian can't do that. And sometimes I want to *shake* him. I want him to see the way I see—but I don't want him to change—fuck!"

"Imagine how much you'll be able to see decades from now." Her voice is soft but her words are hard. "Kyle. It's always going to be that way, when your partner is human. You either accept your disparate natures or you walk. It's a choice you'll be forced to make over and over again." She tips his face up. "But I don't know if *this* has anything to do with your natures. I just think that, for the first time, maybe you're seeing the cracks in what seemed like perfection."

"It hurts." He clutches her wrist, hard enough to harm a human but not her. "It hurts so bad."

"I know," she says. "I know."

Kyle watches her fingers stroke up and down his forearm. "Normally, I would go to him, but I can't—I can't do that right now. I just need to be away."

"Come with me?"

"Where?"

"There are dozens of donors here tonight. Let me find one who won't sexually excite you—a woman—because I don't think you need that complication right now, and let's take her together, if she would like that. Blood sometimes makes things very simple."

Kyle takes a breath. He wants to go with her. "Okay. That—okay."

He's curiously excited. He's never fed from a woman. He's never felt Clara quite so intensely; her bloodlust comes before her like a wave. She's much stronger than he is. He needs that kind of companionship right now.

She speaks to several donors hovering around the edges of the room. He lets her choose—or be chosen, he isn't sure—without comment, and, when she beckons, obediently follows her and the donor upstairs to the room that she and Elisa share.

The donor's name is Siobhan. She has shoulder-length brown hair and hazel eyes. When Clara kisses her cheek and pushes her hair behind her ear she turns a delightful shade of pink. She sits on the end of the bed, and then pushes down the collar of her shirt, which is designed to stretch so that she can do just that for her clients without removing her clothing. Clara sits beside her, and motions for Kyle to sit on her opposite side, which he does. He's shaking. He isn't sure why he's so nervous.

"Are you comfortable?" Clara asks her. "We can have someone stand watch if you would like."

"Ma'am," she says, "I know who you are. I'm comfortable."

Clara smiles. She drags her thumb over Siobhan's jaw, which is shivering. She's already breathing faster. "I'm glad."

Kyle can't drag his eyes away from the pulsing vein that runs down the side of her neck all the way to her upper arm. He wants her blood in a primal way that makes his body sing—but he waits, because Clara is his superior in more ways than one. He watches her kiss down the woman's throat to where her neck and shoulder meet. He watches her open her mouth and suck until the skin there is shining and flushed.

His heart slams against his chest.

Clara's fangs come down with a soft *snick*. Siobhan only has the time to whimper once before they pierce her flesh. Kyle's body flashes hot at the smell and sight of blood and her pleasure and pain. He wants her. He wants her wants her wants her blood *now*.

When he hesitates, she wraps her fingers around the back of his neck and pulls him closer.

"You can bite," she whispers. Clara's throat bobs with hungry swallows. Out of the corner of his eye, he watches her eyelids flutter.

Kyle cups the front of her throat, lets his teeth descend, and buries himself against her before he thinks twice. He inhales inside of the humid space between her skin and his mouth, and lets her feel him once before biting down. Her soft cry and the way that her body bends into the pain makes him moan. He draws his teeth back, closes his lips over the wound and drinks.

Her blood is like fire—heat and light and life. Everything and anything that matters.

When he's finished taking the amount of blood he safely can, he opens his eyes to watch Clara writhe against Siobhan, who puts one hand on Clara's and presses it to her breast. Kyle's thoughts stutter. It's strange to be privy to this.

"Please." Siobhan moans.

Kyle wonders if Clara is reading her mind—he isn't—because the next thing she says is, "It's not necessary, my dear." Her mouth is bloody. She licks it clean, her throat heaving with breath.

"Please, *please*, I want you to."

Clara raises an eyebrow. Kyle stares, enthralled, when she slides her hand down the front of Siobhan's skirt and between her legs.

"Oh," Kyle says.

"You don't have to stay," Clara says to him.

He can't bring himself to move, though—and doesn't particularly want to. Siobhan is clutching his arm and has one leg thrown over his lap and—he doesn't want to do anything to or with her body, but he would like to watch her enjoy herself. The bite marks flanking her neck satisfy the predator in him, and her pleasure is beautiful to his human and vampire sides alike.

Clara's fingers move beneath her skirt, taking her higher and higher still. He lets her hold onto him the whole time, and towards the end she begins to shake and give off the most delicious musky smell that Kyle has ever breathed in. She is violent in passion, with her face screwed up and her skin red and her hips churning. When she comes, the shallow, temporary bond they formed during the feeding allows him to feel it clearly. Surprised, he grips her thigh hard enough to leave bruises and savors the responding whimper.

Clara withdraws her hand politely, wipes her fingers clean with an impish smile, and then puts Siobhan's clothing back into place.

Siobhan laughs. "Oh, my god."

"How do you feel?" Clara asks.

"Dizzy. Incredible. Thank you."

"Let's see to these bites, hmmm?"

Kyle jumps up to retrieve the first aid kit and recovery supplements. This is familiar territory. Taking care of a donor is second nature to him by now. It settles his frayed nerves. By the time she leaves, smiling from ear to ear after receiving several polite kisses to her nose and cheeks from Clara and a hug from him, he feels like himself again.

Clara rinses out her mouth and then sits on the bed with him. "Better?"

His face is red. "Ummm."

She laughs. "You've never…?"

"No. Never."

"I haven't traumatized you, have I?"

"You're beautiful. She was beautiful." He laughs. "I'm gay, not repulsed by the female form." He sits back on his hands. He feels content. "Is Elisa okay with you…?"

"I don't make a habit of it, but she and I both sometimes pleasure our donors. We see it as a courtesy. It has no bearing on our relationship." She shrugs. "I don't linger with them. I don't really have any desire to. Elisa is my partner."

Kyle bites his lip in thought, and then nods. "Thank you. I feel like I can breathe again."

"Being true to your nature affords you that kind of peace." What she says rings true, and the gratitude that he feels for her wisdom is beyond what he can articulate.

"I should go find Brian," he says.

"I would go back to your room if I were you. Elisa went after him. She won't let him slip away." She pats his arm. "Give him time."

Normally, he wouldn't be okay with that, but tonight he's too exhausted to argue.

Elisa finds Brian on the street, two blocks down from the hotel. She blurs the distance in the span of three heartbeats, but he isn't paying attention and doesn't stop until she's right in front of him.

"For god's sake!" he says. "Warn a guy."

"Come on. About face."

"You have no idea—"

"Actually, I do."

Brian sighs. "Of course you do. What was I thinking?"

They turn around. Elisa puts her arm around his waist. "Your brother and I had a long chat about inviting abusive fathers to important life events. I think it went well. I refrained from rearranging his face. Go team me, am I right?"

"It was his choice. His wedding."

"*Mira*," she says, walking him into the lobby of the hotel. The heat feels wonderful. He can't believe he ran outside without a jacket on. "I know what it's like to have the kind of parent who can make you feel like you've been stabbed with one word or look."

He collapses into a chair and puts his elbows on his knees. "Elisa…"

"No, shut up." She arranges her slacks along her legs as she sits. "I get the anger. I get the despair. It's fucking good to feel those things. You know you're alive when you feel those things. But there are people in this world who are like fortresses—you aren't going to break down their walls and they aren't going to invite you inside. They'll throw boulders and boiling oil at you before they give you an inch. Sometimes it's a relative, sometimes it's a friend, sometimes it's a lover. But when it's a parent—that's a special kind of pain. They know where your weak spots are because, half the fucking time, they put them there."

Brian shudders. "I went to therapy for years after high school. Trust me. I've heard it all."

"And now Kyle is here to share that pain with you."

He looks up. "What—what do you mean?"

"He heard everything. Clara is with him now."

Brian stands. "Oh, my god. Oh, shit."

Elisa grabs his hand. "Give it some time."

"I don't *have* time. I'm supposed to be there for the rest of the party, but…" The cake cutting, the bouquet and garter toss and the last dance mean nothing if Kyle needs him.

"And you will be, because fuck Edwin Preston. But let Kyle calm down. Let yourself calm down."

"I thought I was ready," he says, sitting down again, "but he sunk his claws in so fast."

"Let me guess: booze makes him mean?"

"Loose-lipped, more like. But yeah."

She tosses her long, thick, dark hair back over her shoulders. "Fuck me. We should have stayed outside. I could use a smoke." She sighs. "Look, so what can you do? And I don't mean that rhetorically, doctor. I mean like what in the actual fuck can you do right now? You aren't going to win against him. So you're going to go back in there, shake that bubble butt, and give your brother and his wife a proper honeymoon send off."

Brian's mouth curls into a wobbly smile. "You make it sound so easy."

"Because, my dear, sometimes, it can be."

IT'S JUST PAST TWO IN the morning when Kyle hears the keycard in the door. The mechanical whirr of the lock opening wakes him from a dead sleep. The bed is beyond comfortable—at least there's that.

The room is dark, but Brian doesn't turn any lights on. He puts a plate on the table beside the bed and says, "I brought cake, and then in the elevator I—well, I remembered that you can't eat it."

Kyle sits up, drawing his naked legs beneath his body. "Went okay?"

"Yep." Brian sits sideways on the edge of the bed. "With Clara and Elisa running interference." He reaches across the mattress. "I owe you an apology."

"No. No, you don't. Look. You were never going to win that fight. And neither of us was prepared for it to begin with. I—I don't want to talk about it tonight."

Brian wets his lips. "Okay."

Kyle can't explain how finished he is with this whole event— he listened to every word Clara said and he appreciated the advice she tried to give him. But he's tired. He's still half-asleep and they're together and he missed most of the reception and he just wants to not talk anymore. He sprawls out on his side, closes his eyes, and bites back a moan of relief when Brian's hand traces his side from his ribs to the curve of his hip.

"Just sleep with me," he whispers. "Okay?"

Brian slides wordlessly beneath the covers.

8

THE WEEKEND DOESN'T TURN OUT to be the sexual escapade
that either of them envisioned, but it does have its moments—in
the absence of conversation, they hold hands, sleep spooned
together, share the bathroom and take advantage of the hotel's
luxurious amenities alongside wedding guests who are also
staying the weekend. Kyle goes shopping by himself one afternoon. Brian has a lunch date with a colleague. They recover, in
their own ways, and then manage to come back together again.

By the end of the weekend, Kyle is blood-starved, but he can't
imagine asking Brian to provide right now, and the thought of
using the hotel's donor services makes him uncomfortable, so
he goes to a blood center for a morning and an evening ration,
spending the hours in between exploring the area. He's tempted
to call Lee to find out if she'd be interested in joining him, but
the thought of divulging the details of his latest drama to her—
an inevitability if they were to spend any significant length of
time together—is too much for him to handle. Besides, it's nice
roaming around by himself. It reminds him of the way he lived
after he and Brian first got together—exploring the city at night

when Brian was at work, with hopes for a brighter future taking root inside of him.

When it gets dark, he texts Brian that he's going to be out late, and avails himself of not one but three vampire-human nightclubs set along a dense strip of Chicago nightlife. Going alone to places like this always attracts immediate attention, and he isn't surprised when he has to pry both humans and vampires off of himself. But he doesn't mind—the blood from the center is humming in his veins, and that buzz takes on a new dimension every time that he swallows a thimbleful of blood from a donor, which he does at least a dozen times over the course of the evening. When he's more relaxed, he allows bodies against his own, dancing with strangers until strobe lights become normal and everything outside is too dim and still.

The blood changes the world around him. Every color, every sound and every source of light takes on a life of its own.

He loses track of how many donors he pays. All he knows is he's spent all of the pocket money that Brian gave him for the weekend.

He feels like a bloated tick. He's been away too long. *Brian.* He has to get back to Brian.

He picks the quickest, safest option and calls a taxi. Ten minutes later, he's being escorted up to their hotel room by a discreet hotel employee, who makes sure that Brian is there to greet him when he crosses the threshold. Brian fusses over him and tips the porter.

"Are you okay?" Brian asks, when they're alone. "It's late."

"I'm sorry," Kyle says. Brian smells good: deliciously human but also like home. "I needed to be alone." He nuzzles into Brian's neck. He's not sure if he deserves affection, but that doesn't stop him from wanting it.

Brian isn't stupid. "How much blood have you had?"

He hesitates. "A lot."

"If you needed to gorge a little, I could have come with you. It's no different than a human getting drunk to let go once in a while. Don't be ashamed and sneak off to do it by yourself."

Kyle sinks down to sit, and realizes only once he has that he's sitting on the floor. "It's not like being drunk, though. You don't forget things. You can't escape. Everything just becomes—more." Brian's mouth crumples into a frown. He sits opposite Kyle on the rug. "When I heard your dad saying those things about me, I wanted to rip his head off." Kyle's pupils dilate seconds before his fangs drop—he can't control them right now. "When you didn't—when you ran away, it felt like you were running away from me instead of him."

"Oh. Oh, god, no."

"I know that you were overwhelmed." Kyle twists the carpet between his fingers. It tears, but he can't stop himself from holding on to it. "But I had no control over what I felt. And I thought, 'This is it. This is always going to be something that holds us back. His dad will never approve of us. He'll never know his sister because of us.'" Kyle paws at Brian's arm, then grapples for his hand and holds it too tightly.

Brian squeezes Kyle's hand. "Only my father is to blame for that, but I understand why it hurt you."

"Every time I think I'm ready for the life we've chosen, something happens to remind me I'm not." Kyle leans in close, letting their foreheads touch. Brian's fingers frame his mouth. "But I *want* to be."

Brian surges forward and kisses him, and Kyle's fangs nick the tender flesh of Brian's bottom lip. Kyle moans, opens his mouth and kisses back, this time putting his lips ahead of his fangs.

"We can do this," Brian says, fervent and hot against Kyle's jaw, where he drops kiss after kiss. "We can do anything together." Kyle grasps the front of Brian's T-shirt and hauls him up, all but carrying him onto the bed.

He doesn't know if he believes what Brian is saying, but it's a beautiful dream.

GOING BACK TO WORK AFTER Michael and Jenn leave for their honeymoon in Greece is, in many ways, a relief for Brian. He knows it hasn't been that long a break, but the emotional wringer that the wedding put him through on top of the stress of his best man duties was, without a doubt, more draining than the first few grueling months he spent training for his role as part-time underground vampire scientist and part-time vampire doctor.

He and Clara dive back into research on their security issue first thing, going so far as to give other projects to junior members so that they can make it their primary focus. They run multiple lanes of testing at the same time—everything from tissue sample analysis to database dives to pattern-matching software.

In the end, it's Clara who makes the discovery.

It's eleven o'clock—they've been at it all evening—and Brian is on his fourth cup of coffee. Since the wedding, he and Kyle have given each other space, but this time in a healthier, more mutual way. Kyle's course load is heavy, his change of major having forced him to double up on prerequisites, and between that and Brian's case load, they are both more often than not at school and work. It's interesting, the difference deciding to do something together can make—it's as if they're working toward something now instead of going in opposite directions.

Clara sticks her head into the kitchen. "Hey. I have something."

Brian chugs the rest of his coffee and rushes to her workstation.

"Okay, I narrowed it down to the fifteenth data field on the delivery manifest." She points to the screen. "I don't think I've ever looked at it twice; it doesn't exactly contain vital information. The twelve-digit number here is the batch number. It indicates warehouse of origin, ship date, delivery date and a six-digit personnel security code."

"Okay."

"Now. Every month we change the security codes, using an algorithm so that they're entirely random. The codes are viewed only by the employees who give final authorization on blood shipments and who receive those shipments at their final destination. I'm not sure if they've gotten lazy about checking, or if it's a system error, or what, but for the last eight months, there are instances of zeros being replaced by Os. Sixes and nines being swapped, you know, that sort of thing. It could be—and probably has been—written off as data entry or scanning error."

"How do we find out if it is or isn't?"

"That would be almost impossible to do if it wasn't for what I found next. Get this. The error occurred only on blood shipments with the destination of our original, downtown center in Chicago. Not cross-country, not in the Midwest, not even just in the state. That's why it took so long to find it: needle in a haystack."

Brian collapses into the chair beside her. "Erica's center? It's just the *one center*?"

"Someone is fucking with that center's blood delivery."

"Which means someone is messing with the blood."

"Which means someone is doing something intentional to our local vampire population."

"I need to run this against my patient list. That's—that'll be the final call."

Brian transfers the data by flash drive to be safe—he doesn't want it on the network—and sits beside her on his laptop to run the formulas.

"Just give me the most recent cases." Judging by her hovering, she's as nervous as he is. "Or the most extreme."

"Yep, got it." It takes a few minutes to run even a small slice of that data. When the columns populate, Brian sits back in his chair; a wave of nausea sweeps through him. "They're all registered at Erica's clinic. All of them. How did we miss this?"

"It was so basic we didn't even think to check."

"Oh, my god. There's something in the blood. There has to be." He pauses. "But we ran the blood. We didn't find anything abnormal. So it has to be something we can't see, or something new, something we have no frame of reference for."

"What's the end game, though?" She sits down, looking flummoxed. "Half of them have the flu or chicken pox or—I mean, if someone could tamper at that level, why wouldn't they just insert something fatal?"

"You're thinking like a predator," Brian says. "You're assuming that killing vampires—efficiently or otherwise—is their only goal. Maybe it's not. Maybe they want vampires to suffer. Maybe they're using vampires as lab rats. An extermination attempt would be big news—social outcry, media coverage, interest groups circling like vultures. But when people die of 'natural' illness in small numbers, no one asks questions."

Her mouth curves. "And they ask me why I hire humans."

He nods, tight and fast. "What do we do?"

"We have to stop the bad blood distribution. It may take a few days, but it's doable. I'll need to send people I trust to remove boxes with incorrect delivery codes. Only every third or fourth box has been tampered with, so even though we'll be tight on supply, we'll still be able to serve. It's the only way I can think of to do this without letting them know we know."

Brian is thrilled that they've had a breakthrough, but the long term ramifications of an infection (if that's what this is) elude him. As for putting a stop to it entirely—what if they can't? What if there is no solution?

"We need to talk to Erica," Clara says. "Everyone in the know should be on notice to go to other centers for blood."

Brian barely hears her. His mind is racing. "I want to start testing, but I have no idea where."

"Start by collating samples. Get the newbies on it. In the meantime, you hit the samples from the cases you're already treating for symptoms. Chances are they are the ones who've been drinking the tampered blood for a while. If we're lucky, prolonged exposure makes whatever this is easier to see." She stands, clearly ready to get to work. "Call Kyle and Erica. I'll call Elisa. We might as well bring everyone up to speed all at once."

It's the loudest, most disorganized meeting they've ever had. Erica is flabbergasted and also feels personally responsible, even though she isn't the one who does the manifest checks. Elisa prowls the conference room with her fangs out, so angry that for once she's speechless. Kyle, in a hastily thrown-on university sweatshirt and house jeans, hugs his elbows looking lost.

"All those sick vampires," he says. "And—well, we've all got it, don't we? We've all had blood from the center."

Brian tries not to react visibly. Of course that was his first thought—his patients the second—but if he lets panic take hold right out of the gate, he's going to lose his grasp on the situation before he establishes it.

"Not necessarily," he says. "It's not every box. It's not even every shipment. And you, Elisa and Clara have shown no symptoms."

Erica's hands curl into fists. "I can't believe what I'm hearing. How high up does this go?"

"We have no idea," Clara says. "I can only poke and prod so much without risking notice."

"We have to play this very carefully," Elisa says, "even though I'd like to eat someone right now."

Clara smiles. "She's right. So we stop the distribution of the tampered blood. We try to figure out how to tell if a vampire has had it. We see whether the affect it has is something that can be reversed—or if not, treated. To be safe, inside staff should avoid centers altogether if they have access to other sources of blood. But we can't alert the public or anyone in our lives who has no knowledge of the facility. I know that's going to be challenging, but we have no choice. We have to control the flow of information as tightly as possible. Wide-scale panic that would result in whoever is responsible for this finding out what we know is not going to help us." She looks around. "Do you all get that?"

Brian knows that Kyle is thinking of his friends at school. He himself is hard-pressed not to think of every vampire he has recently come into contact with. It will kill him to remain silent, but Clara is right. They have to be careful.

"Erica, you can't distribute the synthetic stuff," Elisa says. "We can't have vamps talking about changes at the center, and you know if you mess with their food supply, they will talk."

Erica sighs. "I hear you."

She stays behind to talk strategy with Clara and Elisa while Kyle follows Brian to the facility kitchen. They sit at the table together after Kyle fixes Brian another cup of coffee.

"Are you okay?" Brian asks.

"I want to believe that if I haven't shown any symptoms, I'm okay, but Max and I hit the clinic twice a day last semester. How is it even possible?"

"Have you felt different in any way?"

Kyle forces a smile. "Are you going to ask me to show you where it hurts, doc?"

"Babe, come on."

"No. I haven't."

"Then don't worry about it. For now, let's just focus on figuring out what's going on."

Kyle puts his hand on top of Brian's. "You're right."

Despite that, he's displaying that contained, nervous sparkle Brian knows all too well—he's scared. Brian only hopes he doesn't have reason to be.

* * *

THE THING IS, BLOOD IS always an issue, and now it's an even bigger one. Kyle avoids the centers—he doesn't trust any of them now—and that makes his social life awkward because suddenly he's saying *no* and *goodbye* and *maybe later* every time that he's asked along.

Not having the center blood to rely on means relying on Brian instead, at least most of the time, or the on-campus donors, with whom Kyle has never developed a relationship and whom he feels strange around even now. Turn Back is constantly distributing fliers outside of their office, which doesn't make going there any easier. The visits are nigh-on impossible, anyway, considering their limited hours and his crazy schedule. He can only buy blood from donors at bars so often before it becomes too costly—the thimble-sized servings are pricey and not meant to satisfy hunger, in any case—and he has no experience navigating the blood-for-money trade that goes on in back rooms and alleys and dilapidated buildings in bad neighborhoods that are nowhere near as safe as Elisa and Clara's club. He almost stopped taking customers at the club because of the time demands of school. Now, when he tries to pick that back up to compensate for the blood he isn't getting from the centers, Elisa tells him she only has so many human clients and they're bursting at the seams with employees looking to feed. There's only so much blood to go around.

So the hunger lurks, and lurks and lurks, and by the time Brian comes home, Kyle is dancing around the apartment like a forest cat in search of the faintest stirrings in the underbrush. He hates *needing*, hates relying on Brian as one of his only blood sources, but then Brian is there, smelling like food, and Kyle is incapable of resisting when he rolls up a sleeve or tugs aside a collar or takes off his shirt. He ups his blood booster dose and tells Kyle he's okay.

Brian's heartbeat is a constant torment. Whenever Kyle is near or whenever it pounds faster, he feels it like a second pulse in his own body, pressing up against his flesh like something that wants out. He becomes distracted by Brian-as-food in ways he never has before.

"I think I'm psyching myself out," Kyle tells Erica, whom he has volunteered to help at the center. "Like getting paranoid because one of my food sources has been cut off, you know? Fixating on another."

Erica smiles, hefts a box, checks the packing slip on the side, and says, "If he's okay with it, I don't see the problem, I guess."

"I feel so selfish. Half the time he's working—like 'about to pass out on his laptop' working, trying to find a marker or whatever it's called in the cell samples so that we can tell who is infected and who isn't, and there I am circling his ankles like a starving animal who also happens to be in heat."

Erica laughs, nearly dropping the packet in her hand. "Oh, my god."

"It's true!"

"All right, kitty. Quit stalling. We have boxes to move. I *was* promised the services of your preternatural strength."

He smiles, and flexes, just to make her laugh again.

* * *

FINDING A CLUB THEY CAN agree on is challenging. They both prefer a mixed-age crowd that leans toward the more mature, they both like classics and pop music, they both like to see vampires and humans, and neither of them wants to watch couples having sex on the dance floor, but Kyle would rather go to clubs that are popular with the people he goes to school with, whereas Brian would rather go to clubs that boast a more diverse sampling of the city's population. For obvious reasons, food and alcohol quality is a sticking point for Brian but not for Kyle.

But lately, none of these preferences seem to matter much when Kyle has Brian wrapped around him on the dance floor.

He isn't sure where his friends have gone—the guys and girls from his urban youth outreach group fell in love with Brian immediately, so it's not a question of social cohesion—but his brain is sizzling in his skull, Brian is wearing a pair of slacks—black with a shimmering thread woven down the sides—and a button-up—pink—so well-fitted that nothing is left to the imagination. Every individual in this establishment with an interest in male bodies has had their head turned by him. Kyle's hackles are up, in the best way possible. Brian is his. Brian is *his*, and if anyone—blood sucker or otherwise—tries to put a hand on him…

Kyle growls, low and sudden, and reasserts his grip on Brian's ass. It's so thick that he can't get his hands around it completely. Brian makes a noise into his neck and twists closer. Kyle thinks that maybe he was too rough. He can almost feel the bruises form, feel the shape of the pain in Brian's mind, as well as excitement and—the faintest hint of embarrassment?

Brian is not a possessive person, and neither of them has ever found anything attractive about jealousy, but Kyle is getting pleasure feedback from Brian's mind in response to his aggressiveness that he's never felt before, not like this, not as if their telepathic connection has somehow been enhanced, allowing him to truly feel Brian's pleas for *more* and *harder*. Has this ability to read Brian's thoughts in sharper detail always been there and he simply hasn't used it? No matter, his senses are picking up Brian's desires loud and clear—so much static-laden lustful noise, its crackles and vibrations trip his nerves like clumsy feet crossing a minefield.

"You're hurting me," Brian says.

Kyle curls his fingernails into the vulnerable skin of Brian's lower back, just above the body-heated glow of his leather belt, hard enough to make him feel the threat of potentially damaged skin. His breath hitches.

"Should I stop?" Kyle asks.

The response, when it comes, is nonverbal, and Kyle isn't even sure if it's an intentional response—he may simply be delving that much deeper into Brian's subconscious.

Should but I don't oh God don't stop make me bleed take it want you to never enough never never so messed up you don't even know how far I can go push me push me please.

Kyle inhales sharply. He's never swum that hard against the current of Brian's mind, never encountered thoughts so raw. They were unlike Brian—conscious Brian, anyway. He's frightened. He's aware of his power, but he's only begun to understand its limits. He has a better grasp on how to use it to protect, rarely, or please, often, Brian, but this is neither of those things. This is different. Darker. Stranger. Less human.

They can't communicate effectively here—it's too loud to talk, and telepathy is unreliable when feelings and hormones are out of control.

Before he can decide what to do, Brian takes him by the waist and walks them off the dance floor and out the back exit. The alley behind the club is cold and full of people, some drunk and some not, walking, talking, laughing and mingling. Not a single head turns when Brian pushes Kyle against the side of the building and spears Kyle's mouth open with his tongue.

Doing things like this in public is rare for them, especially recently—between school, work, the leftover stress from the wedding and this potential blood tampering situation, they are both consistently overworked and frazzled, and making out in public, especially with an audience, is the last thing on their "this would be fun" list.

Maybe that's why Brian wants to. Maybe it's a release for him. Kyle can feel how tightly wound he is, can feel the desperate desire in him to let go, to breathe freely, to give over to something or someone else so that he can exist in peace for a while. But there's nothing peaceful about his hands surging up the front of Kyle's shirt or the rock of his hips against Kyle's. His mind is a skittering mess of jagged-edged lust Kyle can't hold on to.

"Here?" he asks, between kisses so hard they make his lips hurt. "Are—oh, god, are you su—"

Brian's face gives off so much heat Kyle doesn't need to see it to know how red it is. He grinds his cock against Kyle's leg, and when, in the course of steadying him, Kyle's fingers wrap around the curves of his ass, his body jolts.

"Fuck me," he says, filthy and desperate, against Kyle's jaw. "Fuck me and drink from me."

What his mind provides at the same time:

Want everyone to know what you do to me how you do it to me the way you smell right now can't even think can't just need it what's different it's been different I don't know I can't I just need it need my ass full need to be dizzy from losing blood want you to use me just you just you use me use me use me.

"Not here. We can't," Kyle says.

His mind, however, is no match for the sentiment. He wants to do exactly as Brian asks—push Brian belly-first into the gritty, dirty wall behind them, shove his pants and underwear down, and fuck him until they both hurt. Or maybe lift him with his back against the wall, drape his legs over Kyle's elbows, and watch him take it. Kyle wants every passerby to witness his excruciating pleasure, to hear his moans and know exactly who is responsible for them.

He almost does it. But the closest bottle of lubricant is—shit; they didn't take the car tonight. Failing a trip to a convenience store that neither of them is in any condition to make, or lucking out with a sample at one of the surrounding bars or clubs, the only possibility of a private location with supplies nearby is the facility. There's a dormitory in its lower levels.

"Follow me," Kyle says. It's a command, and he knows that his powers have something to do with how easily Brian falls into step behind him. It's only a few blocks, but he blurs them half the way, cradling Brian behind him against the rush.

He uses his security pass to enter the building, and then gets them past the retinal scan with ease. They pass coworkers and friends but don't stop, taking the stairs instead of the elevator down in order to avoid further conversation. He chooses the farthest room from the only other one currently occupied, and throws the lock so hard he almost breaks it—which says a lot, considering that the lock is designed to withstand a vampire's strength.

He's on Brian in a heartbeat, blurring across the room and pushing him down on the bed and onto his hands and knees at the same time. The medical kit in the bedside drawer has everything they need, and Brian has the top popped and the lubricant bottle out in record time. Kyle tears his belt and zipper open, and when he reaches for Brian, finds that Brian has done the same. He rolls Brian's pants and underwear down, letting them catch under his balls. He fills his palm with lubricant and slicks his cock and Brian's crack. His movements are graceless, but he couldn't care less. Brian is pliant beneath him, his ass tipped up and his knuckles white around handfuls of the bed-spread. Kyle holds him by his hips and pushes into his body, slowly but without yielding.

Yes yes yes yes yes

He plants his knees, grasps the metal frame of the bed's headboard, and grinds his cock as deeply as it can go. Brian cries out. He fucks Brian relentlessly into the mattress, pinning him in place to take every thrust.

Yours yours yours dick feels so good fuck fuck fuck

Kyle falls headlong into the soup of Brian's uncharacteristically explicit euphoria—it's not so much drowning as it is being smothered on all sides; he can't breathe or think clearly. Brian's ass and hips and waist become the canvas for a map of glorious bruises and scratches. He bends over Brian's back, fists one hand in his hair and pulls to expose his neck—his trembling, vein-laced, sweaty, so *alive*, human neck.

"I would have fucked and drained you in front of that whole club, if we could've gotten away with it." Kyle drags the blunt front of his fangs down Brian's shoulder blade. "Shown them all who you belong to." He thrusts forward roughly, and Brian makes a noise. "Mine." Again and again, until Brian is whimpering. "*Mine*. Say it."

"I'm y-yours," Brian sobs, finally allowing himself to speak the words. "I'm yours." He bites down on a pillow and then lets it go, spit-soaked, when Kyle's fangs sink into his neck without warning. "Fuck!"

The shock of his pain is glorious, and only serves to make his blood run faster. Kyle makes him feel it—doesn't rush the bite or the first few swallows as he usually does. He drinks until Brian is wavering mentally and then stops gradually, waiting for some congealing before he lifts his mouth from Brian's neck. Brian is so close to coming. It won't take much more than the friction the bed provides to push him over the edge.

"Come on my cock," Kyle says, his voice a rasp as he slams mercilessly through muscle and lubricant and hazy blood-loss mind fog. "Come on. *Come on*."

"Make me." Brian spreads himself wide open. "Make me come, oh *fuck*."

Kyle wraps his lips around the sluggishly oozing wound and sucks, hard. Brian's mind goes white with pain, then starbursts into even brighter light. Kyle feels him come as if the orgasm were his own, cinching tight in his balls and then surging, crisp and sudden and everywhere. Brian sobs—actually sobs—his body bucking like a live wire. His satisfaction could light up the block.

"Come in me," Brian whimpers, "please, come inside of me." His hips beg backward in gentle undulations.

Kyle rolls him over onto his back, ignoring the whine of pain that results from his neck shifting, and pushes his legs against his chest, sliding back inside of him. Brian is a mess and flushed to his sternum, which is as thoroughly streaked with blood as the rest of him. His thighs are sweat-slick and splayed wide like wings on either side of his torso. His eyelashes slow the progression of tears that eventually have their way, dusting his cheeks and temples.

He is indescribably beautiful. Kyle kisses his trembling mouth to reassure him that he's going to get what he asked for.

"Never letting you go," he says, when he begins to come. "Never."

9

KYLE IS WALKING HOME AFTER an evening out with Lee, his arm threaded through hers, when they come across some Turn Back flunkies outside a vampire-owned business, where the fang logo glows brightly but discreetly in the bottom-right corner of the front window. The group is heckling customers, subtly enough to avoid being noticed by the police.

"Jesus," Kyle says. "It's a taqueria. It's not even like their primary clientele are vampires." He doesn't give it another thought—if he let bigots stop him in his tracks every time he came across them, he'd never get anywhere—until they're a block away and he realizes that part of the group has broken off and begun following them.

"Are they serious?" Lee asks, out of the corner of her mouth.

"Solidarity in damnation is still damnation, lovebirds!" one of them shouts. "But salvation is a choice!"

"Wow, that is an epic load of bullshit," she says.

"And they're vampires, too. Damn, how much do you have to hate yourself to join an organization *dedicated* to hating you?"

"Just keep walking."

Three blocks later, Kyle realizes that the vampires who are tailing them aren't going to give up until they respond in some way. He also realizes that unless he wants to lead them straight to his neighborhood and doorstep, he and Lee can't walk in this direction much longer.

"Come on. I'm not going to let these nut-jobs see where I live." He leads her down a side street and then takes a few short-cuts to loop them back in a full circle. This is shaping up to be a real pain in the ass.

"We could split up to confuse them," she says with a shrug.

"They'll get bored soon enough."

But they don't. In fact, with every dizzying turn Kyle leads them into, they creep closer. It finally strikes him that they may have to do something about this—something not passive.

"Are we going to have to threaten these assholes?" he asks Lee.

"Maybe."

She looks about ten times more ready for action than he is, but he has to admit that he's beginning to feel excited at the prospect of not having to turn the other cheek for once. He isn't sure why. He's not a confrontational or violent person, despite being a predator for the last quarter of his short life.

Lee turns to face them. "We're just going home, man. Get lost."

"Protecting your spawn?" another one of them asks with a sneer.

What bothers Kyle is none of them look any different than the people who he goes to school and works with every day. How do beings so similar end up on such opposite ends of the spectrum?

"Fuck off," Lee says, a little louder, more fiercely.

Kyle's eyes tick from vampire to vampire, and then settle on the male who's standing directly behind and to the right of the female leader. He looks young, but his place in the group is like a black hole, a vacuum drawing on the power around him. He's much older than he looks. When he steps forward and bares his fangs, a shiver of warning works its way down Kyle's spine. This situation is about to go to shit, and he and Lee realize this at almost the exact same moment. He squares his shoulders. Her body tenses up.

"Damn it," he says, into the yawn of silence the second before their leader drops her fangs and blurs at them at full speed.

This is no video game. They don't pair off to battle gracefully with moments of perilous, compelling pause. He can't tell whether the woman, who looks as if she weighs no more than a hundred pounds soaking wet, will attack him with two centuries' or two weeks' worth of vampiric strength, or if the vampire who was clearly turned in his sixties will be the one to surprise him. The group comes at him in unpredictable combinations—the only universal is that every single one of these vampires is strong, fast and determined.

It doesn't help that they're outnumbered four to two. What does help is that Lee, for reasons unknown to Kyle, seems to know what she's doing. The way she moves and *when* she moves saves his ass a dozen times over as he tries to memorize his assailants' faces and learn their weak spots. But in the end, it's only a blur of supernaturally fast bodies he desperately tries to fend off. He has little hope of injuring them, much less killing them, even in self-defense. It's all he can do to protect himself and try to assist Lee in the process.

They burn most of their power right out of the gate in order to intimidate each other. Kyle wonders what's going to happen when the fight is slower and therefore easier to follow and more dangerous for him, when he sees lights flickering wildly off of the buildings around them.

The skirmish has drawn the attention of a passing police car, which scares the Turn Back vampires a lot more than it does Kyle, who has credentials from the facility that excuse him from minor infractions such as this, as long as he isn't the instigator. The police officer who stays behind to question him asks for his name and identification, and then rolls her eyes when she sees the laminated facility card and tells him to go home. He's relieved when Lee doesn't ask questions.

They aren't badly hurt, but Kyle's adrenal response is still through the roof. He feels as if he's glowing, his muscles are burning and buzzing so strongly.

He's glad that Lee is sharing the aftermath with him. It occurs to him as they limp away from the scene that he can make up, at least in part, for his lame combat skills by taking them somewhere to get patched up discreetly and safely.

BRIAN IS CHOKING DOWN A granola bar when the emergency alarm goes off. This isn't uncommon, especially not on a Friday night, so he pages the assistant on duty and makes his way down two short hallways to the back of the building. This particular door is a recessed entry way. He adjusts his coat and checks for chemical spray in his pocket before looking at the security camera screen.

Oh, geez.

His heart racing, he opens the door without hesitation. "Are you okay?" he asks Kyle.

"I'm dandy, thanks for asking," Lee says.

"Sorry, I mean—are you *both* okay?"

He reaches for Kyle, and Kyle's arms slide around his waist. "We're fine."

Lee smirks and rolls her eyes.

Brian takes them inside and then into an examining room. He asks them clipped, professional questions about their injuries and what caused them, and remains stone-faced as they explain. He makes sure that their injuries are as superficial as they insist and applies a spray-on, vampire-adapted bandage to the wounds that haven't healed yet.

He's surprised by these events. Kyle has never been involved in a fight like this one before. Especially not with other vampires. Especially not with *Turn Back* vampires.

"Why didn't you call the police the moment they started following you?" he asks. "There was no need—"

"There was also no time," Kyle says. "They went from insults to *charge!* in about three seconds."

That is not, strictly speaking, true. Kyle said that they were followed for quite a while before the confrontation. Brian can't help but wonder where Kyle's head is. Lee stares at Kyle shrewdly, and again Brian has the feeling that he's missed something.

"We defended ourselves," she says, after a moment of hesitation. "End of story."

Brian frowns. "But that—that's not their style. Their MO is nonviolence, no engagement and legal protest."

"This group was one-hundred-percent vamp," Kyle says. "Maybe they got carried away?"

They can't discuss the facility in front of Lee, but Brian knows that Kyle knows the first thing he's going to do is report this to Elisa and see what she has to say about it, so he might as well stick around. Lee doesn't need a babysitter to get home, that's for sure.

"I've got work tomorrow," she says. "Get some sleep, Jackie Chan."

Kyle rolls his eyes. "I was waiting for that."

"The wait is over," she says. "I'm prepared to dish out at least a week of combat-related jokes and references."

He laughs. "Go away."

"I know, I know; you've got extra-special super-healing doctor kisses to claim."

Brian smiles. "That's strictly off the record."

Lee winks at Brian. "Nighty night, boys."

WHEN THEY'RE ALONE, KYLE HOPS up onto the examining table. He attempts a flirtatious smile. "I can tell you where it hurts."

Brian takes his hands. "That was the whole story?"

"Yep," Kyle says. "We tried to shake them off, but they were determined. I used my facility identification to get the cops to let us go and that was that." He smiles and laces their fingers. Brian looks so handsome in his scrubs and doctor's coat—he's a sight for sore eyes as well as muscles tonight. "How's your shift going?"

"Trying to explain to supposedly 'immortal' beings why their human weaknesses are suddenly manifesting without telling them that we still haven't found a way to help them? That's pretty much my shift every day now."

Kyle shrugs out of the remains of his bloodied shirt so that he can get closer without ruining Brian's clothes. He slides his hands beneath the material of Brian's coat, around his waist and up his back. "I'm sorry." He kisses the tip of Brian's nose. "Are you coming home after you finish up?"

"I was going to swing by the facility," Brian says. Kyle can feel the exhaustion in his mind, like a tidal wave hovering above him.

Kyle rubs Brian's back. "Come home. I'll heat up dinner and run you a bath."

Brian practically melts. "Okay. I won't be long. Maybe an hour."

* * *

IN MARCH, KYLE AND BRIAN visit Michael and Jenn to catch up and watch their honeymoon videos.

Their house is friendly chaos, a modest but well-decorated three-bedroom outside of the city. Jenn maintains a kennel off of the garage—now enhanced by Kyle and Brian's wedding present—for the animals she takes home. The recent addition of cat walks and door flaps has given them freedom to roam. The only limitation is Michael's office, which is locked at all times, off-limits to everyone regardless of their species.

Kyle loses his mind over the videos of Greece and the Mediterranean while Brian watches him instead, love filling his chest and not a small amount of planning unfolding in his head. He wants to take Kyle abroad so badly—wants to watch sunlight play over his skin, see his eyes widen at every new sight and sound, and listen to him wrap his beautiful tongue around other languages. He isn't sure when they'll have the time to get away, but thanks to the salaries they're earning working at the facility, they most definitely have the funds.

All in all, it's a lovely evening.

"How's tricks, brother?" Michael asks Brian when they're alone.

"Work is rough, but... we're keeping each other going." Brian smiles. "We're good. Really good."

Michael looks at him, his head tilted. "I'm pulling strings to try and help you guys out on the sly, but it's like trying to get blood from a stone."

"I know, I know. We're all doing our best." Brian takes a pull from his beer bottle and tries to relax. "What scares me the most is not knowing where to start. Whatever this thing is, it's nothing I've seen before. Or it's not there at all and we're wrong. I've never felt so professionally out of my depth." He exhales. "And we can only do so much reaching out. We're not sure who to trust anymore."

Michael nods. "Understandable."

Brian waits, and then smiles. "How's married life?"

"Not that different from engaged life." Michael makes a face. "Though we seem to have about twice as many cats." He laughs. "I don't think there's any connection, though."

"I can't say that I'm surprised."

"It's good," Michael adds, a bit more seriously. "We make a solid team, you know?"

Brian tips his beer bottle in Michael's direction. "Hear, hear."

They stay late, and when Jenn offers them the guest bedroom, they accept the offer. Brian feels beer-and-pizza lazy, and Kyle has been quiet since dinner. Brian would like to give him some attention, preferably of the kind that doesn't require one of them to be behind the wheel of a car.

He finds Kyle in a pantry-like room off of the kennel space, covered in a litter of kittens. He's lying on the floor on his stomach, laughing as the kittens crawl all over him.

"Why do I have the feeling that we're going to leave here with a cat?" Brian asks from the doorway.

Kyle holds a black kitten to his face and mimes chewing on it. "You call them cats. I call them fuzzy snack packs." The kitten mewls and presses its tiny claws into Kyle's cheek. "Feisty. I shall name him The Claw."

Brian laughs. "Love at first sight." He steps into the room and is immediately bombarded with curious kittens stumbling over his feet and trying to climb his pants. "You okay? You've been in here a while."

"Kitten therapy." Kyle puts his cheek on folded arms as a kitten climbs up his spine and another tumbles over his head to the floor.

Brian nods. "Come to bed?" he asks, with a hopeful extension of his right hand.

"Give me a minute to get these furballs back into their box and then, yep."

It's a pleasure to feel at ease in this house, which is as lovely as it is lived-in. Brian feels stirrings of home and family he only vaguely experienced as a child and never as an adult until he lived with Kyle. The faint noise of Michael and Jenn talking, at least two televisions playing and the distant vibrancy of dogs barking fill him with peace.

He takes a quick shower, pulls on a pair of clean boxer-briefs and climbs into bed. He enjoys the show he gets when Kyle joins him and undresses: the sight of clothing being peeled off piece by piece, deliberately slow, and the revelation of creamy, long limbs. When Kyle finishes washing up and finally comes to bed, Brian begins moving down his body before he even settles, mouthing his belly and hips and inward over the bulge in his underwear.

"Oh, okay," Kyle says.

"Sorry—too tired?"

"And the dumb question of the evening award goes to…"

Brian presses his teeth lightly into the still-soft shaft beneath his mouth. "Mean."

"Never too tired for this."

Brian enjoys ten glorious minutes of Kyle's cock sliding in and out of his mouth, Kyle's fingers on the back of his neck, and the softest, breathiest noises imaginable from Kyle's throat, until he comes with a strangled whine, flooding Brian's throat. Brian swallows with a hum, savoring the eager grip of Kyle's hand.

"Love you," Kyle says. "Gimme a second."

"Don't worry about me." He's only a little hard, and the urge for more is less than the weight of his eyelids. They fall asleep like that, Brian's cheek on Kyle's stomach and Kyle sprawled out on his back.

In the middle of the night, Brian wakes up agitated, unsure whether he's dreaming. His thoughts are heavy and slow. He senses Kyle's mind like fingers trailing across the surface of his own, seeking purchase but finding none. He turns into the sensation, opening up, always happy to let Kyle in. But tonight it's like welcoming brambles and fog. He flinches, hesitates, and is so wrapped up in this telepathic fumbling that he doesn't realize Kyle's fangs are already searching down his neck until they brush his skin too hard. They're near a spot that Kyle typically avoids—there are as many dangerous if not fatal places to bite as there are safe ones, and right now Kyle is too close to his jugular for his comfort.

Wake up, he projects mentally.

There's a response, but it's faint, as if Kyle is "speaking" to him from across a distance—at the same time, though, Kyle's mouth moves farther down and to the right, and that's a relief.

Kyle's mind is white hot, already whipped to a hungry frenzy, and Brian lets the current of this froth carry him. There is something wonderfully simple about Kyle taking over.

Hungry. Want you, Brian hears Kyle think.

It's only been about a day and a half since the last time, but he feels strong enough. Kyle rubs against his body. He's already desperate. Brian projects encouragement—Kyle is well-acquainted with his consent responses—and feels the urgency, the unashamed, predatory excitement of an incoming meal course through Kyle. It's so bound up with lust that the two can't be separated, and tonight Kyle's projection is as clear as it's ever been.

Smell so good no one smells like you mine mine mine going to take you so fucking hard don't know which is more beautiful your pleasure or your pain, god your pain is like a thousand hands on my body so perfect the way you give in to me the way you crave it.

Brian encourages Kyle's thigh between his legs and pushes at the back of Kyle's head, nudging Kyle's mouth against the flush of the bite mark. Kyle's hands run the length of his arms and then pin his wrists and body to the bed, hard and sure.

"Yeah," Brian moans.

Can't wait can't please no can't he wants it it's okay but even if he didn't even if he's ours ours ours.

Brian's heart skips a beat, but it's too late—Kyle bites down. He has no time to wonder what is different or what that thought meant or where it came from. Kyle drinks from him in long, unrelenting swallows that make him feel as if he's being turned inside out. It's almost too much—which would normally be perfect, except for that worrisome thought. He can tell when Kyle senses something is wrong and, as Kyle's hunger is satisfied, that realization grows until it finally prompts him to stop. Brian is hurting and dizzy and, even though he loves skirting that conscious/unconscious line, he is too concerned to enjoy it.

Kyle combs his fingers through Brian's hair, cradling him as he licks over the wound to make sure that it's congealed with blood and not any worse than usual. "Sorry," he whispers, his voice choked with lust and blood and the raspy revelation of the monster within. "Sorry, sorry, sorry." There's dampness all over Brian's hip, residue from Kyle's soaked underwear—he must have come rubbing against Brian while he fed. Brian isn't hard anymore; true fear saw to that.

Shaking, Brian turns on the bedside lamp. Kyle scrambles off of him to retrieve the medical kit. He sees to Brian's wound while Brian swallows a restorative, a booster and a painkiller.

"Talk to me," Brian says, his voice a broken rasp.

"I'm sorry. I was dreaming and then I—I'm sorry."

"Was that normal? Those thoughts?"

Kyle's eyes glaze over—shame, fear and embarrassment. "They're not so much *thoughts*. More like instincts? I don't consciously process that stuff, it's just—what the hunger wants." Kyle wipes at his eyes. "And I don't know why you're hearing it so clearly now."

"If anything changes—if you feel actively different—please tell me, okay?"

Brian is as terrified as he is intrigued. He's observed vampires going through power-related growth spurts as they age. Maybe that's all this is.

They manage to fall back asleep, but Brian's mind won't stop spinning in circles.

* * *

IT'S LIKE THE FOG IN the horror stories that Kyle read to himself as a child, seeking the thrill of danger within the safety of the written word, except now he lacks the perspective of the reader. He can't see the creep of its edges. He can't tell how quickly it's condensing around him, turning the world shades of blinding white and gray. He has no sense of where he is within it or how he can escape it.

It isn't always there—he manages, gets through school and facility assignments with much the same focus as before, but then there's evening: want clawing up from his belly into his throat, dropping his teeth and blacking his eyes against all common sense. There's Brian's sweet body and blood, like a religious experience that Kyle has never wanted or wondered about.

He often forces himself to wait, and the wait is torture.

Brian standing at the stove, shaking his butt to the music coming out of his laptop's speakers. Kyle kisses the back of his neck, holds onto his hips and shudders. Brian on the phone, laughing, chatting with Michael, Jenn, Clara, Erica—Kyle has no idea. Kyle draws a fingertip from between his shoulder blades to the small of his back and breathes out hot and heavy, trying to hide his fangs and changed eyes. Brian taking a shower; the smell of body wash and shampoo is pungent, carried by steam throughout the apartment. Kyle walks past, watches that beautiful olive-toned body move naked and wet from shower to sink, and has to reach down and adjust himself because he's already tenting his underwear, and Brian has no cause to think he might be standing there already waiting. Brian with a towel around his hips, bending over to snatch underwear from a drawer, his back glistening, his ass round and full, hugged by cotton.

Kyle crawls under the sheets and hopes against hope that Brian is in the mood, and that it isn't too soon to drink from a neat place—his inner arm or thigh, maybe. Brian doesn't like to do anything more than the easy cleanup acts after a shower— hand jobs, the occasional blow job and shallow, brief bites only; Kyle can't hope for more. He strokes Brian's leg, thrilling at the coarse hair there, all the way to the inside of his knee, where he circles and then turns back, petting over one of the spots he usually bites.

Brian's face is a hazy shape in the fog, but Kyle watches him smile and recline against the pillows, feels the sweet tug of his fingers through Kyle's hair. "Just a little, okay?"

Kyle's heart slams against his chest. He slides down the bed, already overwhelmed, his lungs hardly functioning and his head swimming. He suckles at the spot on Brian's inner thigh until Brian sprawls out, puts one hand over his clothed cock and begins stroking it as Kyle's fangs press against his skin.

"Feels good," Brian says, with a hum of appreciation.

Brian's heartbeat is all Kyle can hear when he bites down—and then it's the heartbeat and his blood, a seemingly endless rush of sustenance, making his body quake. He holds onto Brian's leg harder. He knows when he should stop, but he allows himself two or three swallows more—Brian is about to say something (he can feel the need coil in Brian's mind)—before he finally does. He waits, licks and swallows, trying not to spill any. It takes every ounce of his restraint to not latch back on like a leech.

Kyle doesn't hesitate to fish Brian out of his underwear and begin jerking him off.

He isn't sure if his mind supplied any strange thoughts for Brian to hear, but Brian doesn't seem to have experienced any and so he relaxes, able to trust himself for tonight at least, as Brian's gorgeous dick grows hard and rosy in his fist. The bedside lamp glows yellow, throwing shadows across Brian's face, across that lovely pleased smile, and it's all so familiar and reassuring that tears burn behind his eyes. He buries his face against Brian's balls to hide it, licking across them as his hand pumps.

Brian's belly and thighs tighten. "I'm gonna come."

Kyle slides his lips around Brian's cock in time to swallow, working the head and glans against his tongue and pursed lips as the shaft pulses and then softens. Blood and come mixed together is a familiar flavor.

Brian sinks into the mattress, his lips curled in satisfaction and his fingers brushing the hair off of Kyle's forehead. "Mmm. Thank you."

This is a good night.

What Brian doesn't know is that bad nights are becoming more common—nights when sips of blood don't make the fog go away, and waiting for Brian to recover enough to give more than that is like walking around with railroad spikes jammed into his skull. He's too scared to patronize the blood centers, so he's been taking clients at the club and going to the university's donor clinic, but it's never enough, and he doesn't trust strangers or himself with strangers, and even when he takes the risk, it doesn't satisfy him. He can only truly let go with Brian. The dependence is horrifying.

What is wrong with him? *Is* something wrong with him?

"If anything changes—if you feel actively different—please tell me, okay?"

The stress from trying to identify vampires who've ingested the altered blood outside of his patient pool is wearing on Brian, and yet he's still present for Kyle, making every effort to be a good boyfriend while Kyle is simply terrified, and in the most selfish way possible. Then again, what if he's overreacting? What if this is simply another stage of transition in becoming a vampire? What if it's nothing? He refuses to add to Brian's already impressive pile of worry over *nothing*.

He redirects his urges, frustrations and worries the only way he knows how—into sex with Brian. He lets go, wallows in frantic give and take and, for just a few hours, tricks his hunger into thinking that satisfaction is close at hand. He knows Brian is making playful references to this increased tempo to his friends when one too many phone calls end with sly smiles and flushed cheeks and him hanging up as soon as Kyle enters the room.

"Are we bragging, Doctor Preston?" Kyle asks one night.

"Are we assuming that there is something to brag about, Mr. Hayes?"

Kyle drags their bodies together by Brian's belt loops. "It's not an assumption if it's a fact." He nuzzles into Brian's neck.

"You've been very attentive lately," Brian says. He gives in, encouraging Kyle's hands to roam his ass and back.

"I love taking care of you." Kyle is shaking, already getting hard. "I love working you until you can't take it anymore. I love making you *come*." He growls, squeezing Brian's ass. He's insatiable—whether giving or receiving, he needs it. If he can't slake his thirst for blood, he can do this, and it hurts no one.

He loses track of the hours they spend having sex in the weeks that follow. He drops in on Brian constantly—they fuck at the facility, the clinic, the club and even a few times at friends' houses, which is unheard-of for them. Kyle feels as confident in his sexual abilities as he ever has—when he has Brian up against a door with Brian's legs around his waist, or Brian bent over a piece of furniture, or Brian's cock in his throat, it's the ultimate power trip. Earning that overwhelmed, gasping, laughing orgasm and seeing that beloved face beaming at him, makes him feel as if he could take on the world. And there's no fog there, no darkness, no worry—only joy.

But when the sex takes a turn for the too-much, when Brian's body is bruised, when he swats Kyle away from his oversensitive cock, or his ass is wrecked and it's beginning to hurt, Kyle shudders away from the lust so fast it gives him whiplash.

There are limits when one partner is a vampire and the other is human. He can't help but think, in those more challenging hours, if what Max said is true, about being able to let go completely with another vampire in ways that you never could with a human.

There's darkness in Kyle. He sees it now. And maybe it's always been there.

10

It's 1:38 a.m. when Kyle rolls Brian onto his belly and pushes back inside of him.

Brian marks the time exactly because the glowing numbers on their bedside clock are the first thing he sees when he comes awake at the sudden intrusion.

This is not uncommon for them, not at all off-limits, but the shock of lubricant slick on the back of his cheeks and Kyle's dick filling him up is a lot to take all at once. They fucked before going to sleep, so he's still loose and the penetration isn't uncomfortable, merely unexpected. What's strange is the reverberation that occurs when he tries to reach out to Kyle's mind; it's like shouting directly against a flat surface—his thoughts skitter over it, going in all directions. None of these lead to Kyle.

He holds onto the edge of the mattress and lets Kyle in regardless, mewling under his breath when all he receives in response is Kyle pounding into him relentlessly. The bed shakes, tapping the wall. Brian tries to breathe but it's so much, so fast, and his body can't catch up. He's still sore from their earlier session.

Slow down, baby, I'm all yours, he thinks.

There's nothing in response. Nothing.

Every one of Brian's red flags goes up. He reaches for the can of spray that lives in a pouch that hangs off of the side of the bed. He has the safety flipped when Kyle bites him without warning, somewhere near the meat of his shoulder—the pain is excruciating, turns the world behind Brian's eyelids into white and red light, but he's so used to pain by now that he holds it together long enough to roll onto his side while maintaining a grip on the can.

He shouts verbally and mentally, "*Kyle, stop!*," which earns him the moment of pause he needs to make sure Kyle's fangs have withdrawn from his body before he brings his elbow around, hard and fast, into the side of Kyle's face. There's a muffled noise and Brian twists, brings the can up to Kyle's face and presses the lever down. Kyle screams and flails, trying to get away from him. It's horrifying. Brian doesn't feel anything but the need to follow procedure in response to this kind of behavior. They grapple for a moment. Judging by the fact that Brian doesn't have a limb torn off, Kyle is succumbing to the effects of the spray.

It takes several minutes for him to pass out entirely, and by the time he does, Brian is a sobbing, broken mess, shaking so hard he can't hold his phone, and his eyes are so blurred by tears that he can't see its screen when he finally does. He has no idea who to call first because he can't think, can't be logical beyond *oh god oh god oh god what do I do what happened is he okay*. His training is abandoning him as quickly as it asserted itself. He can't even look at Kyle's limp body, can't see past it to the bloody mess that their bed has become.

That's when he realizes he's bleeding. He fumbles for the first aid kit, destroying most of it in the process of retrieving gauze to press against the wound while fumbling for synthetic coagulant with his free hand. It's a botched job, but Kyle didn't nick an artery and he is able to patch himself up.

Calmer, he hits the speed dial button for Erica.

"I'm injured," he says, when she answers, "and Kyle is out of it. Can you get Elisa or Clara and come to our place?"

She hits him with a barrage of questions as she gets dressed and into her car, but Brian can't answer most of them. His mind is lagging, and Kyle is so still. He's afraid. The chemical spray is not lethal in small doses, but the last time Kyle suffered its effects, he was tied up and his blood was stolen and oh, god, what *happened* tonight? Kyle has been insatiable as of late, but this is something else entirely.

Clara arrives first, blurring all the way up the stairs. She's wearing sweats and looks ruffled but powerful, her eyes blazing and her posture erect. She takes in the scene with a shrewd eye.

"What happened just before?" she asks.

"He came home. We had sex. Showered. Went to bed. He was completely normal. And then—" He pauses. "I woke up and he was fucking me again, except his mind was—completely inaccessible to me. Like he wasn't even there. I grabbed the spray. He bit me."

She makes sure that Kyle is under, tilts her head, scans the bed and the nightstand and then looks at him. "You reacted quickly. That was good."

"What's happening to him? What—what can I do?" He doesn't give a damn about anything else.

"I don't know." She lifts Kyle in her arms. "But first we observe protocol."

"Oh, god, okay." Brian breathes, and gets up shakily to pack a bag.

Facility protocol states that vampires who present a danger to themselves or others must be confined before their condition is evaluated. Brian refuses to balk. Clara is perfectly calm. He isn't going to fall apart when Kyle needs him most.

Erica is downstairs parked by the curb behind the wheel of a facility van. When Kyle is restrained in the back of the van, she swaps and herds Brian into the front cab to tend to his wound while Clara drives. He feels nothing, at least not until Kyle is chained up in a holding cell inside the facility. At the sight of him unconscious and bound to a wall, Brian's knees weaken. He turns his face against the glass, tears in his eyes.

Erica squeezes his shoulder. "You need stitches. Come on, hon. He's not going anywhere."

Elisa arrives not long after in a flurry of rapid-fire Spanish, but, instead of facing her, Brian slips away to hide in one of the storage rooms. He often works at this little desk, which is currently hosting one of his coffee mugs, a tablet with his name on a label on the back and a stack of samples he intended to log the day before—private projects, and nothing light- or temperature-sensitive. He sits down, puts his head on the cool plastic and closes his eyes.

When he opens them, the first thing he sees is the vacuum-sealed bag that holds Kyle's shirt from the night he and Lee took on the Turn Back vamps on the street. He isn't sure why he kept it, aside from a vague thought about potential experiments he could do with Kyle's blood, but here and now in the absence of calm, an idea strikes him, and before he can think twice, he's grabbing the bag and bolting into the elevator and from there on to the lab.

Clara sees him and shoots after him, Elisa and Erica in tow. "Where have you—"

"Kyle is infected," he says.

"What?" Erica asks.

"Is this disease called 'Mindlessly Biting Your Loved Ones'?" Elisa asks.

"The time window of our security issue matches his emerging symptoms." Ignoring Elisa's sarcasm, Brian struggles through decontamination. "It also matches the escalation of symptoms in my patients, and the surge in vampire violence rates in the city. It's all connected. It has to be."

"But he isn't sick," Clara says, mulling this over.

"Exactly."

Erica's eyes narrow. "Okay. You lost me."

"He isn't sick because he never was." Finally suited up and inside the lab, Brian frantically slices the plastic packet open. He prepares a sample of Kyle's blood with automatic, precise motions. "Whatever it is that's causing human diseases and viruses and weaknesses to come out of vampiric stasis is nothing we've ever seen before—it's essentially invisible to our detection methods. Which is perfect for its purpose, because all we can prove is that vampires are degrading, not *why* they're degrading. There are no fingerprints. No smoking gun. Just illness. No one can be blamed. And their assumption must be that most if not all vampires will have had some weakness, some illness, some disease before they were turned for this thing to latch on to." He looks up at them through the glass. "But what about the rare few who didn't? Maybe teenagers who were over childhood illnesses and had clean bills of health otherwise when they were turned. They would be incredibly uncommon, but they could exist. What happens when an invisible weapon can't find its target? Sometimes, by failing to do what it's programmed to do, it becomes exposed."

Clara's eyes widen. "It's having a different effect on him because it *can't* make him sick."

"It's weakening him, but not through infection or disease." Brian types notes as they talk. "It's—I'm not sure, but it seems to be affecting his ability to control his predatory urges. Lowering his inhibitions. Making the more feral aspects of his nature stronger. At first, I thought that maybe the changes in his behavior were increasing power levels he was having trouble adjusting to. I've seen identical situations before, but this is… this is not that."

Clara and Elisa speak in a hissed, clipped combination of English and Spanish only they understand and pace back and forth while Erica taps notes of her own onto her tablet.

"And it's accelerated lately at an alarming rate." Brian's face goes blank with horror. "I—I should have known." Is Kyle's current state his fault? Could he have prevented this somehow?

"Bullshit," Elisa says. "This is not the time for a pity party." She bends closer to the microphone. "I want results. Scientifically verifiable results. How many lab monkeys do you need?"

Clara puts a hand on Elisa's hip. "He *needs* to recover." She turns toward the microphone. "Make as many notes as you can, and I'll pull a team together. But I don't want to see you in the lab for at least twelve hours. Go down to the dorms. Got it?"

Everything inside of him screams *no, I have to solve this*, but he won't be able to keep his eyes open for long, much less make his brain jump through hoops. He doesn't argue when Erica walks him downstairs and makes him swallow a handful of pills that will undoubtedly knock him on his ass. He'll rest now so he can fight tomorrow.

* * *

BRIAN FEELS ONLY SLIGHTLY BETTER the following day, but a shower and a hot meal do much to improve on that. Erica changes his dressing and declares him medically stable, so he immediately heads to the lab, where Clara has been working through the night in shifts with the more competent—and available—members of his lab staff. They won't let him visit Kyle, who is still not himself, but he's willing to give up that fight as long as they let him get to work.

Clara takes him aside. "This thing is incredible. Scary as hell, but incredible. A virus that only affects vampires, and a nearly invisible one at that. It mutates the body in ways that a virus shouldn't be able to. Kyle's blood is the first and only sample we've seen it in, and only because we knew we'd find something."

"We can use that to locate it in others," Brian says, or almost asks, hopefully.

She exhales. "That's where we're stuck. This thing isn't maintaining a normal pattern. I'm not sure if it *will* be detectable, even with what Kyle's blood can teach us."

"It's perfect except for when it has no flaw to latch on to." He jabs repeatedly at a key on his laptop. "Who would produce a virus like that?"

"I'll admit it is curious. But my main concern right now is wide-scale identification and, of course, how to neutralize it."

"The likelihood of full reversal is slim to none." The image of Kyle over Brian, mindless and violent, flashes before his eyes. Is that their future? Will Kyle ever be fully himself again, even if they find a treatment? Brian's chest contracts with pain.

"But we can invoke stasis again. Stop it before it gets worse. I'm sure of that. It's not a perfect solution, but it may be our best-case scenario," Clara says.

He chews his right thumbnail. "I have an idea about mass treatment without risk of further damage, if we aren't going to be able to flat-out identify the presence of the virus."

"Go ahead."

"We do have a bead on this thing's failure pattern. If we reverse engineer that structure, we can treat the infected vampires with the same method these people used to infect them, except we can avoid their failure—so that our treatment takes only if the virus is present—visible or not—and if it isn't, acts like a placebo and is simply absorbed."

"A good theory, but without full knowledge of their research process, our chances of synthesizing a successful treatment are not good."

Brian runs a hand through his hair. She's right.

"It's a place to start, at least," he says.

She nods. "It is. A good one." She sits on the edge of the desk, emptying her lungs noisily. "There's no point in keeping it from you that Kyle's condition is not improving. He's—in there somewhere, but he's delirious and not communicating. We've decided to keep him sedated and restrained to prevent him from hurting himself. But we don't know what the virus is actually physically doing to him."

It's like being stabbed and punched in the chest at the same time. Brian tries to stay calm. There are questions he could ask—medical, scientific, detached questions—but what he chooses to do here and now is control his breathing and make his face into a mask.

She touches his arm. "Brian. I need to know that you understand."

"This thing could kill him."

Her hand tightens around his arm. "We'll do everything we can to keep him alive. I promise you that."

Brian stands and gathers his papers. "I have to work. I have to do something."

She stands beside him, and nods. "Let's get rolling."

* * *

THREE DAYS LATER, BRIAN COMES out of a work stupor and realizes that he has mundane life details to worry about, too. He calls Kyle's school and tells them Kyle has pneumonia. A doctor's note with a name other than his is easy enough for the facility to fabricate. He answers several of Kyle's friends' text messages and voice mails, but leaves responding to Kyle's closer friends' communications for when he's more composed. They'll be harder to fool and he's too overwrought to be convincing.

He attempts to sleep in three-hour shifts, but half of the time, he lies awake instead, figures and lab results and ideas whirling through his head in endless loops. He wants to find a pattern, a consistency, something they can use to grapple their way through this maze. His team is good—he has confidence in them—but this is personal, and he can't let go of it.

On the fifth day, Clara lets him go down to the detention level to see Kyle. He looks dreadful—sweaty and deathly pale, his eyelids fluttering over unseeing eyes, his mouth working around gibberish. He's wearing padded restraints that are chained to the far wall.

Feeling sick, Brian closes his mouth and turns away.

"We're feeding him once every twenty-four hours or so. He's getting nutrition, at least," Clara says.

"He wouldn't want anyone to see him like this." Brian's voice breaks. Even with that in mind, he can't stop himself from putting his hands on the clear cell wall as if he could reach through it and comfort Kyle with his touch. He cues the microphone and says, "I love you. I'm here."

Kyle snarls and thrashes, his face lined with despair as well as rage. Brian whimpers and looks away again.

He can't let this continue. He *won't*. Conviction burns like fire inside of him, obliterating every other feeling. He is going to solve this. He is going to bring Kyle back to himself, and he is not going to let any other vampire suffer needlessly, even if he has to break every rule in the book to find answers.

Clara slides her cool, hard hand into his. "We should get back upstairs."

The work continues. Brian loses himself in it in ways he never has before. There is nothing to go home to, no shift at the clinic—covered for him by Elisa's rearranging—and no partner to curl up in bed with. There is only the work, laptop keys blurring under his fingertips, microscopes and readouts and test results and an endless stream of lab techs and scientists-in-training doing what he says, when he says it. It's a well-oiled machine that's performing admirably but producing few results.

Two days later, he allows himself to take a break. He fills Michael in on what's going on. He checks Kyle's phone and email again—both are quieter, of course, except for well wishes, and a flood of messages from Lee, whom Brian was waiting to contact until he was more in control of himself. He feels badly about forgetting; Lee is one of Kyle's best friends and Brian should have called her days ago. He uses this as an excuse to get some fresh air, goes up to the street and buys himself lunch from a food truck. Lee answers on the first ring, which surprises him. He's still chewing on a mouthful of chicken.

"Oh, my god, you *asshole*, where have you *been?*"

"Hey, Lee, it's—" Brian swallows quickly, and coughs when the food sticks in his throat. "Brian, sorry. I'm sorry, really, Kyle is sick, and I've been trying to catch up with all his messages—"

"How sick?"

"Pretty sick. He's on bed rest, actually."

"He's not in the hospital, is he?"

"No, he isn't. It's not—" The lie goes down no easier than the chicken did. "Not that bad."

There's a moment of silence, and then Lee asks, "How long will he be stuck in bed?"

"It could be weeks, I—I'm sorry to say, he—he's really weak."

"I'd call bullshit, except vamps are getting sick all over the place, so..." Something in her tone is strange and suddenly evasive. Brian narrows his eyes. "Look, I don't suppose there's any way I could visit? Maybe just to drop off flowers or something? I've been really worried."

Shit, she's persistent. Normally, he'd be happy that a friend cared so much, but in this case, he only has so many ways to shut her down without being uncharacteristically rude, and he doesn't want to make her suspicious. The last thing they need is a smart, powerful vamp like her poking around drawing attention to their group.

When he doesn't respond right away, she says, "If not, could you meet me for coffee this afternoon?" She sounds nothing like she usually does. Brian is immediately on his guard, but a longer break might allow him a fresh perspective when he returns to work, and so he agrees to meet her at Equal Ground. He tells Clara where he's going, knowing it's the smart thing to do and that she'll be happy to have him out of her hair for a few hours.

Caffeine is miraculous, he reflects after his second mocha.

Lee arrives on time. She orders for herself and then joins Brian with a wave and a smile, shrugging her textbook-laden messenger bag down onto the empty chair at their table.

She sips her drink. "Hey, sorry for being pushy earlier. I was just worried about Kyle."

"Oh, geez, don't apologize. I get it."

She taps her phone—it looks almost like she's typing a text message—and then very subtly turns it on the tabletop so that Brian can read it. He doesn't understand at first, at least not until he lets the words sharpen in front of his eyes.

I have information. If you can get the lady bosses to meet with me, I'd like to share it with you all.

Brian blinks, and then says, "I'd appreciate it if you could get me a copy of your notes from the classes you and Kyle share. He's nervous about falling behind." He pauses, types a text on his phone in reply and presents it to her.

They're your bosses too, aren't they? Why do you need me to talk to them?

"Oh, sure!" She types:

You know what I mean. I know you have no reason to trust me, but this is important. I know that Kyle isn't just sick. I'm running out of time and resources and if I let them lock me down in interrogation, which they'll do if I approach them solo, I'll lose the ground that I've gained here.

"That's so awesome, thanks." Brian types:

Who do you work for?

"No problem." She types:

Secure location before we say anything else to each other. Even this is risky. After I leave the shop, I'll text you an address on a disposable phone. Show it to them. Go crazy scoping it out. I'm legit. Just keep your head down. And remember: I'm on your side.

Brian parts with her amicably and doesn't let so much as a flicker of trepidation cross his face until he's blocks away from the coffee shop.

What the hell, he thinks, and jogs faster.

"OH, THIS IS DELICIOUS," ELISA says as she scrolls through a Google Map on her triple-encrypted laptop.

"She loves this cloak and dagger stuff," Clara says with a sigh, though there's a pleased lilt to it, and she's stroking Elisa's bare thigh as if she can't help herself. Brian has a feeling they both enjoy the "cloak and dagger stuff."

"Does it look like a trap?" He is fully prepared to trip a trap if that's what it takes to get information that might lead them to a solution.

"Not necessarily," Elisa says, slowly. Her brown eyes sweep back and forth across the screen. "It's one of the facility's remote hubs. Built on the foundation of our first lab. No one would know that, not unless they were somehow in the loop."

"She could still be a spy or an enemy. Just a well-informed one."

"The choice is personal," Elisa says. "No one knows the history of that location. No one has ever been there except for Clara and me. In any case, it's enough to justify meeting her—I want to know what she knows. We'll do thorough recon beforehand. I have escape routes everywhere at this location and in the surrounding area, so even if things go to shit, I can book it."

"I'm going with you," Brian says.

"Like hell you are," Elisa replies.

"Lee reached out to me when she couldn't get to Kyle. I'm a part of this. And I don't want you sticking your neck out alone. We can't risk losing you. You're our leader."

Clara's hand slides down Elisa's leg and folds over her knee in a calming but possessive gesture. "I would rather you didn't go alone."

"What kind of backup is *he*?"

"Hey," Brian says.

"He's a familiar face," Clara says. "It wouldn't hurt to have him along. At worst, you'll have to get him to safety as well as yourself, and dragging a single human around isn't a challenge."

"Okay, that's not exactly flattering, but I'll take it," Brian says. He looks at them each in turn. "Kyle isn't recovering. If we hesitate too long, he may never. And all of those vampires out there suffering… they could end up the same way. I can't sit here and do nothing while that happens."

Clara smiles, the smallest upturn of her heart-shaped mouth, and kisses Elisa. "Be safe." She looks at Brian. "Both of you."

It takes only a few hours to arrange the meeting.

"Nighttime gear, full kit," Elisa says to him, when they touch base that evening. "I'll meet you in the garage in twenty." She stops at the door. "If you're going to visit him, be quick about it, Preston."

"Yes, ma'am."

Even though Brian went through basic combat training, he's never had to put any of it to use. He's more freaked out about that possible necessity than he lets on, but he's also significantly more determined than he is freaked out.

He visits Kyle after he suits up, feeling silly in the sleek but reassuringly protective black combat gear, the faceplate of the head mask pushed up, a gun and a knife and assorted vampire-repelling items tucked into his belt. Combat boots aren't his style, and he knows he looks ridiculous. Kyle isn't enough himself to criticize the look, and Brian wishes more than anything that he was.

"Lee claims that she has information for us," he says, despite the fact that Kyle shows no signs of understanding him. "I don't know why I feel like we can trust her. She's obviously been lying about herself, but—I'm desperate, honey. I want to make you well again so badly. So I'm going to try—or, at least pretend to try while Elisa scares the shit out of her and then does all the work." He puts a hand on the glass. Kyle is calmer today. His head is rolling from side to side, his skin glistens with sweat, but he's not violent. Brian isn't sure whether this is a good or bad thing. Is he calmer or just weaker? "I love you. I love you so much and I'm not going to stop trying."

For all that, Brian still feels like an empty husk, dry and shivering. He would do anything for Kyle, for his patients, for this community, but he's not sure how well-equipped he is to fight, not sure about his abilities outside of the lab and the examination room.

Knowing that doesn't stop him from walking straight down to the garage and climbing into an unmarked vehicle with Elisa behind the wheel. She looks dangerous and confident in her combat gear; her hair is pulled back tight, tucked neatly under a mask.

"Ready?" she asks.

"As I'll ever be."

They scout a two-mile perimeter around the building before approaching. Elisa senses nothing of consequence, but she is relentless about completing the sweep before they enter the building through an underground entrance.

"No need to give Lee the element of surprise," she says.

This proves unnecessary because Lee isn't hiding from them. She's standing in the public entrance of the building in plain sight, apparently alone.

"Well, shit," Elisa says. "She picks a mean digital lock."

Brian stays behind Elisa, off to her right, as Elisa approaches, one hand on her gun and the other on her throwing knife, with the can of chemical spray in between, just beside her belt buckle.

"Miss Walker," she says.

Lee is dressed similarly to Elisa, and it throws Brian off—he's never seen Lee dressed so severely. Even her hair is tamed, folded up beneath a large ski hat. From this angle, it looks like a crown. She's intimidating.

"Miss Martínez," Lee replies.

"If this is about your paycheck, you could have just texted."

Lee smiles. "True." She lifts her hand. "May I pass something to you?"

"Slowly, but yes."

When prompted by Elisa, Brian walks forward, meeting Lee halfway as she slides a metal object no larger than a silver dollar across the concrete floor. He turns it over in his gloved hand, finds it seemingly harmless, and then passes it to Elisa. It looks like a defaced coin, the head replaced with what resembles a crude version of the now-ubiquitous government-approved fang-and-blood-drop logo.

"Where did you get this?"

"Kel asked me to say, 'Consider it a tip.'"

"I could have you netted and sprayed in seconds," Elisa says. Her face is tight with anger.

Lee nods at Brian. "He believes me. And you do, too, or you wouldn't be here."

Brian has no idea what's going on, but Lee must have said something right because Elisa pockets the coin and stands up straighter. "Why are you here?"

"Kel is in charge of special ops out of New York City now," Lee says, "and she needed undercover agents." Lee spreads her hands. "I'm one of them."

"What?" Brian asks. "Who is Kel?"

"Kel is one of the vamps who disagreed with pretty much all of our methods when Clara and I were developing the Chicago organization. She flounced off to New York like a cranky baby when we wouldn't put her ideas into action."

"The New York facility put her through the wringer," Lee says. "She's come a long way."

"Assuming this little yarn is true, what's your assignment here?"

Lee breathes out tightly. "I'm here to gather hard intel on the anti-vampire organization Turn Back. Intel that could be used to publicly discredit them."

"All this time?" Brian asks. "You—is that why you got close to Kyle?"

"He was a convenient link to the blood club, which I of course knew was a front for the facility, but no—Kyle's friendship was just a perk." She takes a step forward. "I was under orders to operate independently of the Chicago facility, actually."

"Have you made any progress?" Elisa asks.

"Some. Mostly at the member level. Enrollment documents, inside paraphernalia, member lists, recruiter names. But I've never been able to get my hands on the important stuff: financial backers, network maps, policy makers—the stuff that I came here to find. Turn Back drives all of its public relations, media and recruiting out of Chicago, so it seemed to be the place to start." She flicks her fingers, and a slip of plastic appears between them.

"Last week, I lifted this off of one of their members. I'm not sure the guy even knew what he had, really, because aside from PDFs of fliers advertising membership drives, there's a hidden file that contains the name of a product they call 'the cure.' It's insane shit—they're trying to convince their members that they have a cure for vampirism. Can't say any of it surprised me, though. In fact, they've published propaganda like this before. But this time—it's too specific. It references blood, blood centers, and compares distributing the cure to putting fluoride in tap water. The documents' creation date matches up with consequent reports of sick and violent vampires. I'm sure there's a connection." She slides it over, the same way she did with the coin.

"But my resources have dried up. I can't go any deeper, not with my current cover story. Dismantling Turn Back is still my primary objective, but this 'cure' thing—it's way above my pay grade and outside of my mission parameters. I need your help." She smiles, both sheepishly and teasingly. "Kel and her superiors need your help. The document contains medical jargon, some addresses and the names of researchers—it's not the whole picture, but it's something. The New York facility has given me permission to bring you on board with full project disclosure."

"This is tasty, but it's hardly a meal," Elisa says. Brian knows their working relationship with the New York branch has always been active but tenuous, and that Elisa would love to know what they know and have access to their resources, even limited ones on a temporary basis, but her poker face is effortless.

"I have a mark who I think might be able to tell us more," Lee says. She's obviously getting to her punch line. "The guy I lifted this flash drive off of. He's a vamp, so I think we can get away with netting him for questioning. But I can't guarantee that on my own. He's a match for my power, and I don't want to risk allowing him to bolt. He's difficult. I've tried to get him into tight spots for months now, but he keeps slipping through my fingers. Drives me crazy because before I knew he was Turn Back I had plenty of chances—and now that I know, he's become evasive." She exhales. "But you have a connection we can exploit."

Brian blinks. "We do?"

"His name is Max, and I think you know him pretty well."

"Oh, shit," Elisa says.

BRIAN SITS DOWN ON A nearby crate, even though it's probably against every protocol known to man and vampire and he looks like an idiot next to Elisa's battle-ready posture.

"How is that possible?" he asks.

"I found a membership packet under a pile of magazines in his apartment recently," she says. "That was all I found, but knowing his member name—he didn't sign up under his real name, of course—allowed me to look him up in their database and get the story he gave them."

"Which is?" Brian asks. He's barely keeping it together.

Max and Kyle have been in each other's pockets for a long time now, and all Brian can recall in this horrible moment is how Kyle used to patronize the center with Max like clockwork— Max must have known. Max led Kyle there, knowing full well what was in the blood. And how much of their relationship was based on genuine attraction and how much was Kyle's inhibitions being lowered and his nature being manipulated by the virus's effects? Anger makes Brian's vision go blurry. He tries to keep himself under control. Elisa senses his escalating reaction and shoots him a glare.

"He was turned against his will. He hated what he became. Turn Back loves vamps like that—they convince them that they can offer a way back to humanity or, at the very least, some form of redemption."

"Why would he know anything more about the organization than any other member?" Elisa asks.

"He worked on special projects for them, hence the flash drive. I think he was helping them design their new headquarters here. I have no idea how deep in he is, though."

"*This is Max Cumberland. He's an engineer.*"

Brian's chest rises and falls unevenly. His face is hot. He doesn't trust himself to be sensible at all right now, and so he says nothing. He's never felt the urge to hurt another living being as he does right now—it's like being invaded by an alien force, twisted up into black, ruinous knots that don't belong, that can't belong, except there they are.

Finally, when there's nothing left but mindless pain, he says, "I can get him to come to our apartment. Tell him that Kyle is sick and asked for him. He'll come; I've never given him any reason to suspect I know anything about him beyond what Kyle has told me."

"It could work," Lee says. She hesitates, and then adds, "He's definitely got a weak spot for Kyle."

Elisa paces. "Is it worth the risk of spooking him? And what if he runs to Turn Back after we let him go? We can't hold him permanently."

"Turn Back has no idea that when he isn't working for them he's enjoying all the pleasures of a 'hedonistic vampire lifestyle,'" Lee says. "I can threaten to expose his behavior to them. I have documented proof of it. That should be enough to keep him quiet."

"We would have to sedate Kyle and plant him in the apartment," Elisa says, looking at Brian. "Max would be able to sense if he wasn't actually there."

Brian flinches. "There's no other way?"

"We've been experimenting with scent mimicking, but nothing that would stand up to a field test if you were dealing with someone who had intimate knowledge of the source."

"But he—"

"He has intimate knowledge," Lee says. She looks almost apologetic. "You know that, Brian."

Brian tries not to let the rage build up again. "I'm not sure Kyle is strong enough to be put under without risking complication, and I don't have time to experiment with dosage or to observe him…"

"All we need is for him to be docile long enough to get Max through your front door," Elisa says.

Brian doesn't know how to feel about this. His whole being aches—throbs like an open wound around the worry, jealousy and fear that have taken up residence inside him.

"I might need a day or two to set this up," Lee says.

"No—that's too heavy-handed," Elisa says. "I assume you follow each other on social media?" Lee nods. "Okay. Wait twenty-four hours and then put out a status update or tweet or blog post or whatever about Kyle being sick. Make it sound like he's been sick for a while, but you only just got the news. After that, we'll make the call—it has to be Brian. He's close enough to Kyle for it to make sense, but far enough from your social circle that it won't look suspicious. I'll have undercover muscle cover all the exit and entry points at and around the apartment—at a sensible distance, of course, so the vampire concentration doesn't send his red flags up. Kyle will be sedated and restrained in the bedroom. Brian—it'll be up to you to open the door and get Max to step inside. We can rig the netting in the doorway easily. Once he's incapacitated, we'll take him to the facility for questioning." She looks at them each in turn. "I'm not a fan of kidnapping and interrogating my own kind, but if this kid can lead us to the science behind what's fucking with my people, I will grill him."

"I can bring in heat if you need it," Lee says.

"Darlin'," Elisa says, "*that* I've got in spades."

11

KYLE DOESN'T REMEMBER WHAT HIS parents looked like. He supposes that there were pictures of them in his aunt and uncle's house, jammed in amongst his childhood things, even if they were nothing more than drawings—stick figures with wisps of felt hair, a colorful beard or smear of make-up, a construction paper skirt or pair of pants. He was eight when they were killed in a car crash, old enough to have memories of their faces. But he doesn't.

The thing is—visuals aren't strictly necessary in the fog. He doesn't know why his parents are here, but he thinks he might be dead. This is awful for a variety of reasons that he can't list right now. If he is dead, though, he has no idea why his aunt and uncle are here with him. They aren't dead, are they? He doesn't know. Either way, the fog is currently a full house of people whose presence he can't understand or doesn't want. Besides family, there are people from high school—Jeffrey Simmons included—some teachers, a guidance counselor, the disgruntled community college student who worked the front desk at Mansford's blood distribution center and his cousin

Paul. All of them, in one way or another, have become players in the theater of his memory.

He's eight and a half and his cousin is visiting. They're playing in the backyard when his cousin asks about Kyle's parents. Kyle has no memory of what he says but he remembers crying, loudly and for so long that his aunt actually bothers to notice, to come and separate them, to shout at Paul. Kyle spends the afternoon clinging to her, but feeling no comfort.

He's fifteen and he's just auditioned for the school musical and lost the part to a freshman with a smaller vocal range and a diva complex. The worst thing is that no one even teases him about it; that's how far below the radar the things he cares about—even fleetingly—fall. He's no one and nothing.

He's ten when he realizes that he's gay. They put on a play in English class and at one point his character has to hold hands with his brother, and he spends the entire first act shaking and sweating and wondering why it feels so good to hold another boy's hand. He wants to go on feeling this way forever, wants to keep this moment like a firefly in a jar, feeding it until it glows, just for him.

He's sixteen the first and only time his uncle hits him. He makes a snide comment about being trapped under their roof and his uncle's hand comes up and across his face before he can prepare himself for it. He guesses his uncle justifies doing it because he thinks Kyle being a vampire will negate the hurt in some way. His aunt screams, drags his uncle away, and it never happens again. He's not sure that he ever feels the appropriate response.

He's also sixteen the first time that he drinks human blood. He ignores his hunger for weeks after being forcibly turned, unable to cope with the idea. But the need becomes too much, and he digs out the business card his guidance counselor gave him with the distribution center's address and phone number on it. He laughs when he finds the place and it's in a strip mall between a convenience store and a Chipotle. Creatures of the night. Sure. He shows them his identification card. They give him a packet of blood and leave him alone in a room the size of a closet. He drinks, and then spends a half of an hour clutching the hard plastic chair beneath him while the world spins in Technicolor all around him. It's the most intense thing he's ever felt, up to and including masturbation, which has been high on his list of "Yes, please" for quite some time now. He never bothers to put off the trip again.

He's six and his parents clap as he puts on shows for them after Sunday dinner. When he tells them that the kids at school never like his shows as much as they do and how much he loves them, he's too young to understand the pain in their eyes. He's just happy because he has the best parents ever, and they laugh when he does the voices and his mother doesn't mind when he ransacks her closet for costumes and his dad tells him that he's the best actor in the world.

He's nineteen when Jeffrey Simmons knocks him out and ties him to a chair with bungee cords, slices his wrists open and takes his blood. He doesn't hear Jeffrey's frantic, broken words of explanation: "Once I'm strong, we can be together," "You'll understand," "Played hard to get for so long but it's okay, I forgive you." He wakes up and fights for his life with a tenacity that he never thought he could feel, much less act upon. It turns out he does want to live rather badly.

He's nineteen when he walks into Chicago's downtown blood distribution center and looks into Brian Preston's beautiful brown eyes.

But Brian isn't there in the fog, and Kyle is lost.

* * *

BRIAN HANDLES THE PHONE CALL to Max with an ease born purely of performance necessity, adding the right amount of awkwardness, chagrin and worry that it requires. He panics afterward, though, sitting alone in what feels like the empty shell of their life—the apartment is stagnant without Kyle's presence—with his hands clasped and his muscles trembling. Everything feels unreal around him, but he has to perk up.

Eyes on the prize, Preston.

He meets with Elisa's operatives and Lee several times in the days that follow, learning who will be where and when. This is child's play to them, but to Brian it's like moving through a nightmare with Kyle at the center, growing more unreachable every day. Brian wants to be with him as often as possible, but time spent with him is time not spent working on a solution. Brian has never felt so torn. All he can do is continue working and breathing, forcing food and water down his throat when he's dizzy and sleeping when his eyes won't stay open.

In keeping with the general theme of things going spectacularly off of the rails, Max is late for their visit. The team adjusts accordingly, but by the time he's spotted coming down the block, Brian's nerves are twice-frazzled. He regroups as best as he can, trying not to pay attention to the blank hum of Kyle's mind coming from the bedroom. This is not the way that he imagined Kyle to come home.

When the knock finally comes, Brian's heart leaps into his throat, but he's beyond fear.

Seeing Max reminds him of the times they've met before, of feeling Max's desire for Kyle and knowing that Kyle felt a draw in return. He couldn't be mad about something neither of them had control over, but he *hated* it all the same—hated that this good-looking vampire turned his boyfriend's head. A part of him still hates it. He goes with that feeling.

"Max, hey," he says, at the open door.

All Max has to do is take two steps forward.

He doesn't.

"Uh, hey," he says. "Look, is it okay with you if I come back another time? I've had the whole walk to think about it, and I'm not sure I want to talk to Kyle like this, when he's so sick, I mean, we have a lot to say to each other, and—"

Shit, fuck.

"Oh." Brian does his best to look distressed. "He's been asking for you all morning. It would really upset him if you left." Max seems prepared to offer another protest, so Brian hastily adds, "I think just seeing you would be okay, even if you aren't in the mood to talk. And I could draw you some blood?"

Two steps two steps it's just two steps, come on.

Brian isn't prepared for it when it happens, it's so fast. The open doorway shimmers with crackling energy from top to bottom, freezing Max in place. His body goes rigid, jolting with the rush, and his face contorts with anger.

Right before his jaw goes still, he manages to spit out, "I knew you guys were gonna pull this shit."

Brian has no idea what that means, but he's too relieved to care. The net is holding.

He could say and do anything to Max in that moment, but he chooses to walk into the kitchen and call Elisa. Within minutes, the apartment is full of people: Elisa and Clara and their team, all with individual assignments. Most are responsible for transporting Max safely and securely to the facility. Some are there to medically assess Kyle and transport him back. Some are watching the street, building, windows and doors to make sure that Max has no backup.

Brian feels useless and then intrigued when he spots Lee. Max glares at her.

"Chill out, Maxy," she says. "We'll catch up later."

"How are you holding up?" she asks Brian, when she notices him watching her. She's wearing street clothes, so she must have been one of the distance operatives.

"I want to punch him in the face. A lot."

She smiles. "Honest answer." Her eyes drift over to Elisa and Clara. "Good job holding it together. I didn't expect him to balk at the door."

Neither did I, Brian thinks.

Elisa slinks over and puts her hands on his shoulders. "Look at you, all Mr. Adaptable Field Operative. Nice work. We'll make a ninja out of you yet, *pequeño*."

Lee tries not to smile, but Brian indulges himself. He'll take them where he can get them today. "Thanks. What's next?"

"You have earned some time with Kyle, I think," she says. "Go ahead with his transport team. We'll let Max stew until tomorrow. A little bit of hunger might soften him up."

"But you heard what he said over the wire," Brian says. "He knew he was walking into a trap. He hesitated but he still tripped it."

Clara comes up behind Elsa. "All the more reason to apply some pressure. If he was looking to get to us, he must have something we want."

"I want to be there when you talk to him."

"Of course," Clara says.

Lee buttons up her coat. "Thanks for the assist, ladies, Brian. I'll see you at the facility?"

"With an escort," Elisa says, her left eyebrow rising.

Lee smiles. "Sure thing, boss."

When Lee is gone, Clara smiles and says, out of the corner of her mouth, "She's hot."

Elisa's other eyebrow goes up.

Brian snorts. "And with that, I will see you two later."

The conversation relaxed him, and by the time he's settled with a cuffed, sleeping Kyle in the back of the van, he is significantly recovered from the capture ordeal. The team drives them around for a while to make sure they aren't being followed before they select one of the facility's many unmarked entrances.

Kyle is as gray as the sky before a storm. His eyelids flutter and his body twitches as if he's having nightmares. Brian prefers a reaction to nothing, but seeing Kyle like this hurts. He allows himself to stroke Kyle's slick hair back, again and again, and tells himself that he's doing something here he can't do in the lab.

Kyle's state allows Brian to convince the medical team that bathing him would not present a risk to Brian's safety. He takes his time using a massive sponge and the industrial sink down the hall from the cells, loving every stroke across Kyle's clammy skin because each one reminds him that Kyle is still alive and fighting somewhere in there. He goes through waves of emotion—anger at the situation, helpless love of Kyle and despair that he hasn't found a solution. At one point he gives in, bends over Kyle's body, clutches him despite the danger and cries until he can't cry anymore.

By the time he has dressed Kyle and returned him to his cell and restraints, he's drained and starving, so he stops to eat and drink. Sandwich and water bottle in hand, he finds Elisa having a cigarette in one of the common areas.

She exhales smoke. "How is he?"

"Stable but suffering." He sits down across from her. "From what, I couldn't tell you. Physiologically, it makes no sense."

The smoke dances around her face. "Not everything we are makes sense."

"It wouldn't be fun if there were no mystery, I guess."

She points at him with her cigarette. "*Sí*. You're learning." She grinds the cigarette butt into an ashtray. "You look like shit."

"Then the outside matches the inside."

Elisa watches him with unwavering focus. "You're a good man. You're good for him. He's good for you. You just need to learn to make that work as time goes by."

"I think we are. At least I thought we were, before all this."

Her mouth twitches into a vague approximation of a smile. "He's young, but his heart is as weathered as any vampire's. And he's given it to you. Who better to keep it safe than a doctor, hmmm?"

Brian's face goes warm. Her words make him feel better, stronger.

"Now," she says, rising, "let's take care of some business."

BRIAN, LEE, ELISA AND CLARA are the only facility members present. Max is restrained at his wrists, ankles and torso to a chair that's bolted to the floor. He's uncomfortable, hungry and furious, though not nearly as badly as they expected him to be. This shouldn't be much of a surprise, since Max knew he was being lured.

"Rumors of our hospitality have been greatly exaggerated," Elisa says into the microphone.

Max's sweat-soaked chest heaves. "The same could be said about your intuition."

Elisa tilts her head. Clara blinks at Max slowly, unperturbed. Brian has no doubt they could sit here all night waiting for him to talk.

"That was an impressively cinematic opening volley, but your follow-up leaves something to be desired," Clara says.

"You idiots," Max says, "I only showed up to that pathetically predictable party because I was *turning myself over to you*. How dumb do you think I am?"

"You almost ran," Brian says.

"Okay—cold fucking feet, I was scared shitless. Sue me."

Elisa cues the microphone again. "What are you offering us?"

For the first time, there is a flicker of fear in Max's eyes. "You know who I work for. Well, I want out. But I can't just walk. I need protection. Relocation. Whatever you can give me."

"Well, aren't you just precious?" Elisa asks. "Unfortunately for you, *amigo*, I ain't Santa Claus."

"You're a traitor to our kind," Clara says. "Why should we do anything for you?"

Max's eyes blaze. "I can give you everything you'll need to raze Turn Back to the ground. But most importantly, I know what the 'cure' is."

"Is that all?" Elisa asks. With a heavy sigh, she sits down and then cues the microphone again. "Okay, kid. Seems to me that you're dying to spill, so consider me Oprah and don't skimp on the personal details." Max surveys the group. Elisa pounces on his hesitation. "This is your audience, unless you want to embark on an involuntary hunger strike."

Lee's face is a mask, but Brian can feel her dread.

"I never lied to you about my history." Max stares up at the ceiling lights. "One summer when I was home on break visiting my folks, I got targeted by a vampire gang whose initiation ritual involved picking random humans to turn. I didn't know them. They didn't want to know me. After I was turned, they did what they always do—offered me a spot in the group if I did to someone else what they did to me."

"This happened all the time?" Brian asks.

"Most of the time, people did it, yeah. They didn't know what else to do or where to go. They had no clue how to live as vampires, so they stuck around others who might teach them something." His expression darkens. "But I didn't. I killed the gang's leaders. I didn't know what to do after that, though. The gang fell apart. I knew if I hung around I'd become a target for whoever stepped into the power vacuum the leaders' deaths created. So I went back to my family and pretended nothing had happened. I managed to fool them long enough to go back to college like normal."

"How did you become involved with Turn Back?" Elisa asks.

"I saw them on the news. Checked them out online. Found out there was a chapter in Chicago, at my school. They seemed perfect at first. You didn't have to be a religious wacko to join, though a lot of their members are. I could just hang out with the secular kids and hate myself in peace."

"They must have loved you." Clara's mouth twists with disgust.

"They realized how smart I was. Found out what I was majoring in at school and started asking me for help with projects. Mostly related to building design and security. I'm good at that. They gave me access to blueprints for some properties they'd acquired. And access to their systems, to a certain clearance level, so I could work on them. They had no idea just how tech-savvy I was, though—I got deeper into their systems than they ever realized. I figured it couldn't hurt to have some leverage on them, so I started saving documents. Communication. Ledgers. It wasn't that exciting, until this year. Before that, it was just names and numbers and vague lingo—everything you'd expect of an organization like that. Every now and then, sure, there were names of notable public figures, and money coming in from sources that were obviously covers for big, well-known companies, international backers and so on—but none of that shocked me."

"What did shock you?" Brian asks.

"The 'cure' project. When information about it started circulating, my focus shifted. I had a feeling they were gearing up to try something new. The official documents and the internal propaganda took on a new tone. I started digging and eventually hit pay dirt. The 'cure' project is New York-based, so I had to find new routes into the system to get access to the information. Their research and development is based out of one small, discreet location—of course, they don't advertise it."

"Define 'pay dirt', kid," Elisa says. "Whatever you're getting at, it better live up to the hype you're spinning."

Max's eyes narrow. "Each project Turn Back has on their books an assigned list of backers and underwriters, you know, to make them look legit on paper when they need to be, and none of the names or details or even the project names themselves are real. But the documents that are top-of-the-line secret, the ones that only the people who run the organization see, have, once you get past basic encryption, the real-deal information. Ultimately, there has to be an accurate record somewhere. They just never knew that I'd be able to find it."

Brian clutches the edge of the table in front of him. His heart slams against his chest.

"The 'cure' is biological warfare—a virus only vampires can carry, that reactivates human weakness in order to lead a vampire to an early death. It's completely undetectable by modern science, so there's no proof that the cause of death is anything other than 'natural.' It can be inserted into human blood for mass distribution. Because Turn Back has such an active social network in Chicago, it was decided to run the first 'trial' here, through the downtown distribution center. It's easy to pull up the names of those who get blood there, easy to track who gets sick and with what and how badly, either through official records or checking in with them where they live or work."

"And Turn Back members were okay with this?" Brian asks.

"It's sold to them as a way to turn vampires back into humans—as much as they can be, anyway. It's explained so vaguely that no one really knows what it is. They just want to believe. So they do." He exhales. "Finding out this stuff made me realize how fucked-up it all was. I'm not a saint, but—living here, going to school here, making friends with people like—like you, like Kyle—I realized not all vampires are predators looking for a meal."

"Tell that to the vampires you've killed," Elisa says, cool and disgusted.

Max tenses, pulls against his restraints. "They were turning humans against their will every day! I only killed the leaders, the ones who enforced the ritual. It was the only way to stop them and escape…"

"Which is what you're looking to do now. Again."

"You're damned right I am. Look, I'm not defending myself, and I know it won't even the score, but I am trying to give something back before I get out of this mess. I understand now how fucked-up Turn Back is, how fucked-up I am." He shudders. "Being close to Kyle—" Brian tenses. "It changed everything. Every time I dragged him to the center and watched him swallow the blood… I wanted to stop him." Brian's fingernails dig into the table. He doesn't feel the pain. "I am sorry for what I've done. I mean that. But yeah, I do want to save myself. I do want to get away from Turn Back before they realize I've been breaking their rules and stealing their documents."

Lee is vibrating with anger. "You realize that it isn't that simple?"

Max stares at her. "You've been spying on me. Are you with them, then?"

Clara turns off the microphone and touches Lee's arm. "Don't let him work you up. He knows who we are but he may not realize who *you* are, and that can only work in our favor."

When Elisa cues the microphone again, she makes it clear she's heard enough. "Here's the deal. You give us everything—and I mean everything—and if we're satisfied with what you supply, I can guarantee you protection and freedom from Turn Back. No more, no less."

"I need money and transportation, preferably out of the country."

"I can get you to a coast, free and clear," she says, "and that's my final offer."

He hesitates—his desperation is palpable—but doesn't take much longer than that. "I accept."

"Sit tight," Elisa replies and then leads the group out into the hallway.

"You can't be serious," Brian says. "You can't let him go!"

"I didn't say that, did I? I said I'd get him to a coast." Elisa looks at Lee. "Brian is right. We can't let him go. So if you want me to continue working this assignment with you, you'll take that demon back to New York. Keep him at your facility. Put him to work. Make him *earn* redemption—lord knows the human justice system wouldn't."

"Elisa," Lee says, "I don't know if—"

"Make it happen. I don't want him in my city. I want him to be educated and I want him to suffer a little. I want him under Kel's fucking combat boots."

Lee nods stiffly, and Elisa turns to Brian and Clara. "You two, with me." She turns back to Lee. "Keep an eye on him." When they're behind a closed door, just the three of them, Elisa pushes the air out of her lungs and collapses into the chair behind her desk. "Thoughts?"

"Do the facilities regularly mete out justice like this?" Brian asks. He knows the human system is even worse, but at least it's the devil that they know.

"The capture of our own kind is rare," Elisa says. "Max is a pretty unique combination of 'done wrong' and 'has useful information.' We desperately need what he's got, but he's also trespassed badly enough for me to hesitate about letting him run free, especially with funds and anonymity. He's in my territory. I don't trust him. I have to make the call. Polling the other facilities for advice or assistance would make me look weak." Her mouth twitches. "We aren't going to waterboard him, if that's what's got your boy shorts in a twist." She glances at Clara. "Are we in agreement, love?"

Clara perches her peach-colored sundress-covered backside on the arm of the sofa that sits parallel to Elisa's desk. "For the most part, yes. Rock, hard place, et cetera." She shrugs. "I would also suggest letting Lee work with him personally. They have an established relationship; it's not much of a stretch. Max is seriously troubled, but he could be useful, if he matures and adapts."

"As long as he's useful in New York," Elisa says.

For reasons both selfish and otherwise, Brian agrees completely.

* * *

IN THE FOLLOWING DAYS, BRIAN abandons all pretense that he isn't living at the facility.

The data Max has provided them is a massive collection that requires extensive sorting and more than a few pairs of eyes. Max wasn't kidding about the "dirt" aspect; there's enough here to create serious public relations issues for Turn Back.

The science is not as specific as Brian would have liked, but it confirms many things he's suspected about the virus. It also offers a lot of gap-filling information—an explanation of how the virus piggy-backs on refrigerated human blood cells and then goes from there to being active in a vampire's blood stream, for example. There are no references to what the virus does in a case like Kyle's, which validates Brian's suspicion that whoever created this did not plan a failure contingency. Nor is there any information about detection or immunization—when Brian tells Elisa this, she isn't pleased.

"Can I change my stance on waterboarding from 'absolutely not' to 'maybe just this time?'" she asks, with a growl.

"He never said he had that information." Brian tries to hide his fears that maybe the answer to that question is that there simply is no immunization. Developing antiviral treatments from scratch at this stage would be insufficient and time-consuming, but they may have no other choice. Experimental antiviral medication may be their only recourse. Suggesting this now would be premature, though. They have plenty of new information to sort through.

When the scientific data is arranged to the best of his ability, Brian assists with the other categories. It's brainless, repetitive work that allows him to take his mind off of things for hours at a time. When the room is dark except for desk lamps and computer screens and he can't keep his eyes open, he stuffs a protein bar in his mouth and then sits wrapped up in a blanket outside Kyle's cell, dozing with his head against the stone wall beside its glass front.

After he's managed enough rest to ensure he can continue to function, he trudges back upstairs to the office space they're using to work on the general data—a long meeting table lined with two rows of laptops ringing a nest of wires and hard drives. He puts on his reading glasses—he can't be bothered with contacts right now—and picks up where he left off.

His eyelids begin to droop after several hours, and he's about to drag himself away from the table to go in search of coffee when he sees his last name on the screen in front of him. He sits up, adjusts his glasses and squints. His name isn't uncommon, but it's only natural that when he comes across it, it catches his attention. This time, though, when he sees the first name attached to "Preston," with the title of "attorney" in the next column, he's out of his chair so quickly he has no memory of standing. He bypasses Elisa's office and goes directly down to the cell Max is being held in, which is isolated on the other side of the building.

He runs the whole way, breathing rapidly; his peripheral vision is blank with urgency.

Max is reclined on the cot in his cell. Brian slams one hand against the microphone button.

"Did you know?" he asks. "Did you *know*?"

Max sits up, squints at the glass, and replies, "Look, if this is about Kyle—"

"Did you know that my father is on Turn Back's fucking *payroll*?" Even as Brian asks this, he knows that Max didn't know—if he did, it would have been one of the first things he trotted out, if only to get a rise out of Brian.

"No, I didn't. But if you tell me his name and I know something about his function in the organization, I'll share it with you."

"How can you not know my father is Edwin Preston?"

"Oh, fuck. Are you serious?"

Brian reaches down and turns on the recording software. "Start talking." Max scowls at him. "Look, you've already received the maximum allotment of Elisa's generosity. This is for me. For what you did to Kyle." His voice shakes. "For flirting with him and putting your hands on him and making sure he got sick."

"I am sorry. About the blood." Max's throat bobs. "But that other stuff—it was his choice. That's not on me."

"It was, and he and I need to figure that out—but how much of that was him and how much was 'the cure'? We'll never know, and you had a goddamned nerve moving in on him when you knew he had a partner. You didn't have to hit on him to get him to take the blood."

"He turned me down," Max says, as if that's all that matters. Maybe it is. Maybe it isn't. Brian hasn't decided yet. "Yeah, we pushed the line. But we didn't fuck, and even when we got close to the possibility—man, you were the only thing on his mind. He *cared*. He felt guilty for responding to me. That has to count for something."

Brian swallows and turns away for a moment to force himself back on track. "Tell me what you know about my father's involvement in Turn Back."

"Edwin started out consulting. Completely behind the scenes. Maybe two years ago? He's climbed the ranks since, though. I'd say he's more or less running the legal team now." It's impossible to find that surprising, but it still hurts. "He—that New York address I gave you? He is definitely, physically there on a weekly basis." A pause, and then, "I'm pretty sure he knows everything about the cure project. There's a short list of senior members who do, and he's on it."

"His is the only name I recognized."

Max shrugs. "Likely. Not many well-known figures sign up for this kind of gig. And he uses pseudonyms on the public docs like everyone else."

Brian sits down all at once. Spots float in front of his eyes. His father is more deeply, more specifically, involved than he could have ever imagined. He isn't shocked, but he's disgusted and so profoundly disappointed it's all he can do to not vomit. He puts his head between his knees and breathes.

What to do next?

Even though every inch of him screams *take the address and get on a plane and solve this*, he brings the information to Elisa and Clara. For a moment they are flabbergasted—that it's hitting this close to home, that the connection is so fraught, that a father could continue to prove himself to be such a monster. When their disbelief passes, he prepares himself for a speech warning him not to meddle, not to take risks and to leave the work to the professionals—namely them—all of which he would understand and, beyond gut instinct, not question.

But then Elisa looks at him as if the world has begun to rotate in the opposite direction and says, her eyes glazed over, "What can you do?"

Brian's heart slams once, twice, and again. "What?"

"If you were able to speak with him, alone, with evidence of what we have on him and Turn Back, what do you think you could do?"

"Are you—are you asking me to fly to New York and confront him?"

Clara pins him in place with her eyes. "No. We're giving you permission to fly to New York and confront him."

"What about Lee and her facility? I'd be going right into their territory, won't they—"

"We'll brief them once you're on the ground," Elisa says. "We're the wronged party, and so I'm going to handle this my way. They can back us or not, but either way it's happening—if you're willing."

Not quite trusting his voice, Brian says, "I am more than willing."

After that, everything is a blur of packing, debriefing and making copies of the most damning information with which to threaten Edwin. Through it all Brian feels the same withering inadequacy and dread that his father always inspires in him, but that feeling is no longer forefront. It's buried under loathing and panic and fear and not a small sliver of hatred, pure and simple, that people like his father not only exist but are allowed to wield the power that they do.

This particular plot has to end, and maybe ending it will put off attempts like it, at least for a while. If nothing else, taking action will prove they are paying attention and capable of self-defense.

Brian is booked on a flight to JFK International, and by the time he's packed and dressed, he only has about an hour to spend with Kyle. They agree to let him into the cell as long as Kyle's wrists are bound, and he acquiesces because he's out of time and Kyle is beyond basic discomfort. He's physically stable but mentally unreachable. Whatever the virus is doing to him, it's interacting with parts of his vampire nature science has yet to categorize.

He doesn't waste his voice trying to string words together. He pulls Kyle into his arms and holds him and breathes in the smell of him, which no amount of industrial soap can change, feeling the tumble of emotions inside of himself like an orderly avalanche, piece after piece slotting into place, the shape of his life—*their* life—so clearly defined it's like a vision of both present and future overlaid end to end. It has taken him this long, and maybe the suffering of these events, to arrive here, to know without a doubt that *this is it*—Kyle is it.

Instead of saying that, he thinks it, projecting it like a wave. It feels as if it's coming from his heart instead of his head.

I love you. I love you, and everything is going to be okay.

12

THE TURN BACK OFFICE IS in Queens. It makes sense that it has remained unidentified—no one would think an organization like Turn Back would have a base of operations in this neighborhood. The office is nondescript and small and shabby, blends into its backdrop seamlessly and is flanked not by other offices but jammed between a grocer and a nail salon.

How it must torture his father to have to walk in and out of it regularly. Brian allows himself a twisted smile at that mental image—he's earned the luxury.

He landed six hours ago, and since then he's been bombarded with long distance communications from Elisa, mostly regarding the fact that the New York facility is furious but has no plans to interrupt his operation. She supplies him with a layout of the office building, an entry and exit strategy and instructions on how to cut the power after sealing the exterior door and window locks so he can guarantee that once his father is inside, he won't be leaving until Brian releases him.

It's all very James Bond, except that Brian has never wanted to be James Bond, cutting wires makes him incredibly nervous and he really has to pee.

To add insult to injury, three days go by before his father, looking harried and cold in an ankle-length coat, deigns to show up, late in the evening when Brian is beginning to feel the drag of a day's worth of surveillance. Brian has been waiting so long that this seems like a strange fever dream finally reaching its conclusion. Under the cover of relative darkness, he slips into the building behind his father, using the codes and security pass the facility provided him.

His father's office is on the third floor. He creeps up the stairs like someone doing a passable impression of a cat, sensitive to every footfall, every breath in his lungs and every knock of his heart. *I'm a fraud. I'm a parody of a comic book character.* He's trying to calm himself down with humor, but near-hysterical laughter is threatening, and that is not something he can afford right now.

This giddy nervousness evaporates when he arrives at his destination. Light shines from under the door of his father's office. He hears keyboard clacks.

He uses a digital remote to cut off primary power to the building—the backup generator he sabotaged is nonfunctional and so, according to plan, the lights go out. The windows in his father's office are barred and screened for security purposes, so there's no exit aside from the entry door. Brian has successfully sprung the trap.

He shuffles down the hall to the silence that falls when his father stops typing, puts his hand on the doorknob, and—he's out of time. This is it. He's here, and this is going to go down right now. The usual bowel-quivering fear his father induces in him dissolves.

Without waiting for his father to realize he isn't alone, he opens the door, slams it shut behind him and slaps a digital seal over the door and its jamb. Brian looks up. Edwin goes still. His expression is blank, and then his mouth curls in disgust.

"I can't say that I'm surprised."

"Funny. I was about to say the same thing."

Edwin circles his desk. "Well. You're here, so I suppose you're informed."

"Don't move, and keep your hands where I can see them."

Edwin freezes and then laughs. "My, my, aren't we the little vigilante? I knew those comic books would give you twisted notions." His lips twitch. "You always were different."

Brian can't feel shame. He can't feel anything. All he can see is his father's face floating in semidarkness, distorted by shadow and stretched like a grotesque carnival fun house visage.

"This building is secure," Brian says, measuring his words carefully, "and we aren't leaving any time soon." He nods toward a chair next to the door. "Take off your coat and throw it to me, and then sit down." His father complies. He tosses the coat out of reach and, when his father is seated, takes the Taser from his pocket and approaches him. "I'm going to check you for concealed items. Please don't make me use this."

He finds a small hand gun strapped to his father's ankle and a can of chemical spray in one of his pockets and removes both items. Otherwise, Edwin lacks anything that might be used as a weapon. When there are a few feet between them again, Brian takes a tablet from his pocket and puts it on his father's desk.

"Like you said, I'm here, and I'm informed. But maybe you don't realize just how informed I am." He looks at his father. "I know about 'the cure.'"

"Many do. So one of our loose-lipped members talked. So what? The project isn't a secret. And in fact, we have several experimental treatments in the works that have shown promising signs of being able to undo the vampire infection, many of which are a matter of public record—"

Brian's mouth twists. "No." He crouches down, bringing his father and himself eye to eye. "No, Dad. That's not what I mean. I know what it *actually* is. I not only know, but I have every scrap of data your organization has on it. I know it's a virus. I know it's making vampires sick. I know its purpose is to kill its hosts. I know you unleashed it into an urban population center."

A muscle in Edwin's jaw ticks. "You're bluffing."

Brian turns the tablet toward his father, where he has a document already open that shows a briefing on the virus, one of the ones created to disclose details to a group of researchers that Turn Back hired to work on it.

"This is just the tip of the iceberg," he says, savoring the rage on his father's face. "We have a year of data and information on every branch of Turn Back, from science to public relations to finances." His throat swells, but he forces the words out. "Your name, wherever it publicly graces the page—and every single document's source is verifiable. This is what happens when you put your signature to institutionalized bigotry and attempted murder, Dad. Eventually, your dirty laundry airs itself."

He shakes so hard the tablet wobbles. He puts it down before his father notices.

"There is only one way out of this for you. We're going to dismantle Turn Back no matter what you do or say. But it may take time for your role in the organization to be exposed. I will give you that time, and you can use it to run or hide as you see fit." Brian swallows heavily. "In the end, you're just one of many sick, twisted people behind this—and, to be frank, we have our sights set higher. But if you want that time, you'll give me the immunization and the antiviral data, right now. I know this building has a basement that Turn Back installed here to store their lab and the research for the cure. It's here, and you're going to show it to me. And then I'm going to send the data to my people, and, if what we synthesize is viable, you're free to go."

"Who the hell have you gotten mixed up with, Brian?" Edwin's expression is as cold as ice. "Fucking them is one thing, but just how deeply have you gotten yourself into this nonsense?" When that earns him nothing but silence he adds, in a rasp, "They aren't *people*, son. You do realize that? They're mutations."

Brian's eyes fill with tears, but they aren't of shame. He whispers, brokenly, "Michael is a vampire. The people you see every day—many of them are vampires. There are even vampires *in your organization*—"

"All of whom understand that they need *help*—"

"Do you actually believe the bullshit you're spouting?"

"Don't use that tone with me, young man." Brian's throat closes up. "And what in the world makes you think there's a way to undo what the cure does?"

"Because when science goes down that road, there are risks involved, and people who create weapons always create ways to protect themselves against them." Brian narrows his eyes. "Now. Enough stalling. I have backup. Resources. I can stay here indefinitely if I need to. But you don't—can't. So take me downstairs and show me what you have."

Edwin looks Brian up and down. "I had no idea how involved you were. I don't know whether to be impressed—or disappointed, as I usually am by you."

Brian's throat works around the softball-sized lump inside of it. "The love of my life is lying unconscious in a cell in restraints because of what Turn Back and you have done. He may never recover. My patients grow weaker with every visit." Tears slip down his cheeks. He can't hold them back. "If you think I'm going to let your abuse affect me more than their reality, you don't know me at all." He gets close, the Taser between them, his eyes wet and his vision cloudy. "We're going downstairs and we'll stay there until I'm satisfied. And only then do you get the head start you don't deserve out of this shitstorm. *Move.*"

THE LAB IS SMALLER THAN he expected, but Brian has no room left in him for curiosity. He's running on adrenaline and emotional fumes with a Taser aimed at his father.

He handcuffs his father to a table that's bolted to the floor. "My team is going to pick this place clean, but if you lead me to the specific information I need, you'll get out of here faster. A few hours could make all the difference for you right now—don't waste them."

"Are you enjoying threatening me?" Edwin asks. "Ah, but I suppose I can't blame you." When Brian doesn't answer, his glare grows more unforgiving. "If I capitulate, you'll have the power to destroy me, no matter what I choose to do after the fact. It could be the end of my career and definitely the end of my work with Turn Back."

"If you don't cooperate, I'll have your name on the front page of every major news publication tomorrow morning. That's the alternative."

"We will never speak to or see each other again. And the same goes for your brother. Neither of you will ever meet your sister." Brian feels this like a dagger in his belly, but he doesn't react. He doesn't cry. He doesn't Tase his father in the fucking face. He just lets the pain wrack him like an electric current snapping through water. "Very well. There's a cold storage room behind that shelving. In the case closest to the right wall, you'll find the samples you're looking for. Each experimental stage of the virus as well as the immunization and the bacteria that will re-invoke vampiric stasis. The treatments have the same distribution method as the virus, and are harmless if given to an individual who isn't infected." His face is a mask of hatred.

"You've had them all along?"

"As you said, we had to take precautions."

He wants to say so many things. "You're going to pay for this," is so cliché he doesn't consider verbalizing it. "I will never understand the ruthlessness inside of you," is better, but even that he can't bring himself to say.

Brian takes his phone from his pocket and makes a call. "I need two agents. We're in."

Elisa has connections in New York that the city's facility isn't aware of, and Brian is going to need someone to secure the building and his father while he gathers data and packs samples for transport. He can't believe their luck—with raw data only, it might have taken them years to develop viable antiviral medication, much less an immunization, even with their access to advanced research and equipment and the more or less unlimited funding of the federal government.

He doesn't waste time bantering with his father after the operatives arrive. They're two vampires, one male, one female, who descend like Navy seals and don't speak a word outside of confirming Brian's commands and calling him "sir" at the end of every sentence. When he's deep enough into the lab to speak without his father overhearing him, he calls Elisa again.

With her, he allows his voice to shake. "I'm alone. And you aren't going to believe this."

"Hit me."

"They have treatment methods. And stasis reinstatement. And immunity."

"Fuck me, you are fucking *kidding*."

"I need the full team to help me get these things out, but after that, I'm coming back here. I'm going to hold him until we know this stuff works. You have my notes, and my lab team knows what to do—we'll start with Kyle and then move on to the patients I've selected. We'll be able to judge viability within a few days, but Kyle should show more immediate signs of recovery."

He hopes.

"I can send more people. You don't have to stay there."

"No. It has to be me. I have to do this." He swallows. "He's my father. This is my cross to bear."

"You probably can't tell, but I am actually vomiting right now." She pauses, and then says, "Look. Lee is coming to your location. I couldn't keep her here once she found out what we were doing. Let her boss around the operatives. Stay a day, stay two—but the *second* Kyle responds, I want you on a plane. Don't wait for the other patients to respond. Do that for me?"

Her offer is tempting. Maybe it would be better to leave this to the professionals. And why let his father keep him from going home to Kyle? "Okay." He can almost feel her relief over the phone. "Okay. But only—only when Kyle—how, how is he?"

"Ask me that again tomorrow night."

Lee arrives with her game face on, and Brian is more than happy to step aside.

It takes him two hard drives, one U-Haul, and a vampire assistant to empty the office. He knows there are probably duplicate and triplicate and even digital files tucked away in other places. That doesn't matter—what matters is they have copies. How the information will be used is up to Elisa and Clara. He only asks for what he needs to treat his patients.

Exhausted, he barely feels the morning sun on his face when he leaves the building the following day. He chokes down a granola bar and a coffee the size of his head and is practically carried into a taxi. He forgets to thank Lee for being amazing at her job. He says nothing to his father.

He finds a motel and pays in advance for one night. He won't even be there all night, but he doesn't think they'll care as long as it's paid for. He intends to call Elisa, but falls asleep the second he lies down on the bed. He sleeps straight through to the afternoon and, when he wakes up, walks to the nearest pizza joint he can find and eats four slices of pepperoni pizza without stopping to breathe. His phone against his ear, he crams a cannoli in his mouth on his way out.

"How's that New York pizza?" Elisa asks.

"You put a tail on me?"

"It would be a shame if anything happened to that ass."

"How is he?"

"Calmer. He regained consciousness briefly. He's responding to stimuli."

Brian stops in midstride, gets told off by the person walking behind him and bursts into silent, shoulder-shaking tears right there on the sidewalk. He has to hold on to a mailbox to keep himself upright. Elisa says nothing for a long while. He wants to tell her he loves her.

"C-can I t-talk to him-m?"

"He isn't that awake, doc. But get on a plane. You're the first person he's going to want to see."

Adrenaline leaves Brian bug-eyed for the time it takes to gather his things and call a cab—Elisa booked his plane ticket before they spoke—but when the car is humming beneath him, his eyes drift shut. He sleeps through the cab ride as well as his flight. Everything is catching up with him, and not in a conscious *I can power through this* way. His body just shuts down.

In their neighborhood, he wakes up well enough to take stock of himself and decides to swing by the apartment to shower and change—Kyle would appreciate the effort, and once he's at the facility, he has no intention of leaving until Kyle leaves with him, so he might as well begin his stay clean and looking decent. He puts on his nicest jeans and the shirt that drives Kyle nuts—with the sleeves that cut into his biceps—and laughs and cries at the same time at the ridiculousness of checking himself out in the mirror to make sure he looks good for his unconscious boyfriend.

He isn't even past security when Elisa and Clara rush to meet him. He's quickly surrounded by very strong hands and arms, and when they take turns kissing him right on the mouth, he isn't at all surprised. He laughs, overwhelmed and happy, because this is home. These women and what they've created and his work here are familiar and so *good*. He's almost bloated with gratitude—that they came into his life, that Kyle turned his whole world in their direction.

"The initial samples look good." Clara holds one of his arms and Elisa the other as they walk down into the facility proper. "That lab had *everything*. We'll have no trouble mass-distributing now, though categorizing individual cases will take time—"

Elisa smiles. "Darling. Let him go."

"Oh." Clara brushes his arm off. "Of course. Later."

Brian kisses them both on the cheek and jogs off.

"He's in the hospital wing!" Clara calls.

Brian changes direction.

His journey lacks the cinematic conclusion of finding Kyle awake and waiting for him. Kyle looks clean and comfortable, though, restrained only by his wrists to a recovery bed. Brian touches his beautiful face, just once, feeling as if his own heart is about to explode, and then reads his chart and checks his vitals and the machinery he's attached to.

A nurse comes in, and Brian asks him when Kyle was fed last.

"He's due for blood in a couple of hours," the nurse replies.

"I want it to be mine. Is that all right?"

"Of course, Doctor Preston."

The nurse draws his blood, and when that's done, Brian sits beside Kyle's bed with his bandaged arm on the mattress and his hand folded around Kyle's forearm. Kyle feels warm and his skin isn't clammy, and he's too relieved to cry. He puts his head down on the edge of the bed—close enough to smell Kyle's skin—and falls asleep.

He wakes up to fingers in his hair and senses Kyle's conscious mind before he realizes Kyle is touching him. The mental brush is like a wave of sunlight creeping across the side of his face through the blinds in the morning.

You're here.

Oh.

I'm not dead.

Kyle.

Brian? BrianBrianBrianBrian

Brian opens his eyes. Kyle's is trying to reach for him. He turns his face into Kyle's open palm, knowing now there is no danger—and wondering if he'd care even if there were—and kisses that soft skin over and over again, saying nothing. His tears soak Kyle's hand.

Kyle's lovely eyes are open, slitted and twitching but open, and he's looking at Brian and he knows him and everything is right with the world.

"H-hey," he says, all rasp and dry throat. Brian sobs into his forearm.

Kyle looks around briefly, but his eyes close not long after. His nurse comes in and urges Brian's blood down his throat—it brings a flush to his cheeks. He goes in and out for hours. Brian disengages once, long enough to use the bathroom and chug a cup of coffee. The nurse tells him he didn't miss any lucid moments.

It takes half of the night for Kyle to come around for longer periods of time. He's still out of it when he does, but eventually there's a five-minute stretch when he seems to realize he's in a hospital bed. To Brian, his thoughts are disjointed and incoherent, mostly confusion and surprise and relief that Brian is present and he is not dead. After a lot of griping on Brian's part, his restraints are declared unnecessary.

In the middle of the night, Brian wakes suddenly when Kyle sits up and clutches the rails of his bed, making them rattle. "Honey?" Brian asks.

Kyle frowns. "Gonna be late for class."

Brian has to smile at that. He puts a hand on Kyle's leg. "Can you focus for me, Kyle? Look at me, okay?"

Kyle's hair sticks up in four different directions. His eyes are puffy and red-rimmed. He has a few days' of scruff on his face, and his lips are chapped.

He's the most beautiful thing Brian has ever seen.

Brian cups Kyle's face. He doesn't have any more tears to shed, but his eyes burn all the same as Kyle tucks his cheek into the central groove of his palm.

Kyle blinks slowly. "I'm sick. I should have—told you sooner."

"You were sick. But you're getting better." He isn't sure how much Kyle is going to retain at the moment, but he goes on. "You had the virus. Only you didn't have any human weaknesses for it to prey on, so instead it made you wild. Lowered your inhibitions and allowed your powers to assert themselves too often."

"Oh." Kyle's eyes glaze over. "I hurt you, didn't I?"

"Not very badly. Don't worry about that now."

"Tired."

"I know, baby. Go to sleep."

Brian gradually ups Kyle's blood ration. Kyle improves dramatically, and by the third day, he's waking up for longer stretches of time, lucid and able to understand and retain the things Brian says.

He tells Kyle about the virus and Lee and Max's roles in the scheme of things. Kyle isn't surprised to hear that Lee is an operative—though he isn't crazy about the deception—but the news about Max hits him hard. He's revolted by how determined Max was to get him infected, and disappointed that Max was, in many ways, the opposite of what he professed to be.

At one point, Kyle convinces Brian to get in the bed with him and Brian gets to hold him for the first time, under the dim glow of hospital lighting and the beeping of machines. Everything smells like sweaty linen and sour disinfectant.

"I was infected for a while, wasn't I?" Kyle asks.

"I think so, but it's difficult to say."

"I—I was attracted to Max from the minute we met," Kyle says. Brian's chest hurts. "I don't want you to think it was just my inhibitions being lowered. I mean, yeah, when I drank, and I constantly was around Max—god, it's so obvious now, he was always insisting we go to the center—it was worse, but..." He exhales. "We danced in clubs. We got close. Touched. And then that night, I drank from him. I was wrapped around him and—I almost came rubbing off on him. I wanted him. I did. His power and his ability to work me up was overwhelming—I just, I need you to know I fucked up, that it was my choice, no matter what happened later. It was a mistake, and I am so, so sorry."

"I know." Brian turns his face against Kyle's throat. "And I was mad. And jealous as hell. Max—Max told me that when you two were together, I was always on your mind, but—he didn't need to. I know you." He swallows around the lump in his throat. "I'm not angry at you anymore."

"I feel like I should have known he was lying to me, but how could I have?"

"He was a good actor."

"So you captured him and he gave everything up?"

"Yep. He walked right into it knowing something was up."

"And he led you to the office in New York and your father." Brian nods and curls up tighter around Kyle's body. "I'm sorry. That must have been a nightmare."

"I don't think it's hit me yet," Brian says, barely above a whisper. "And I—I have to tell Michael, and I don't know whether I want him to be angry that I did what I did without consulting him or not." He closes his eyes. "But what matters is that I didn't let Dad get to me. It felt good to rise above it, to get what I needed without giving him satisfaction. And I didn't even see him afterwards. I didn't say goodbye. There was nothing to say goodbye to. No loss. We could never be a family again."

"You have a family here." Kyle kisses his hair. "The facility and the club and the clinic and Michael and Jenn—and me. We're your family."

Brian lifts his weary head and smiles. He stares at Kyle's face, and then bites his lip. "Of course you are."

Kyle's cheeks go pink. "You haven't kissed me, you know."

"I wanted you as conscious as possible for that."

"Does my current state work for you?"

"I'd say so." Brian threads his fingers through the hair at the nape of Kyle's neck and tugs. Their lips touch. Brian makes a noise—or Kyle does, he isn't sure—and Kyle holds him with surprising strength, licking into his mouth. They tangle up together on their sides, their legs slotting together, their breath coming faster.

"You're here," Kyle says in between kisses. "I was so scared. I thought I was dead, and the nightmares were—"

Brian leaves a warm trail of kisses down Kyle's neck. "None of it was real. It's over. It's over, honey." He can feel Kyle's tears on his cheeks when they stop to breathe.

"Are your patients getting better?"

"We don't know yet for sure, but Clara says the signs are good."

"How long do I have to stay here?"

He strokes his hand up and down Kyle's back. "At least a few days. I want to observe your condition and run some tests." He smiles. "Elisa straightened things out with your school over the weekend. You can make up what you missed over the summer."

"I hadn't even thought of that! Shit."

"Once we've verified that the information I took from New York is good, Lee is going to let my father go and come back to Chicago herself. It's up to you if and when you talk to her—and Max, before she takes him into custody."

Kyle nods. "I want to see her. I'm just not sure about Max."

"He's pretty insistent about turning over a new leaf, but he has an attitude, and when he finds out Lee's taking him to the New York facility instead of letting him go…"

Kyle's expression hardens. "If he wants to redeem himself, he has to prove it. I agree with Elisa. He should pay for his crimes by doing something good for his kind."

This must be a vampire thing because Brian still isn't sure if he's comfortable with the idea—but it isn't his call to make. The only thing he's truly invested in right now is Kyle's and his patients' recovery. Kyle's marked improvement is giving them high hopes.

* * *

KYLE DOESN'T TELL BRIAN ABOUT the foggy place his mind was in or that his memories of what happened the night he lost control of himself have returned, mostly because Brian has been through enough. He does spill to Lee, though, when she returns. She comes to his room in the middle of the night, looking tired but hopeful. She puts a tentative hand on his bed. He opens his arms, and she rushes to hug him.

She smiles. "I wasn't sure if you'd want to see me."

"I wish we'd met under different circumstances, but you didn't become friends with me because you had to, so."

She sits beside his bed. He tells her about remembering biting Brian against his will. He tells her about the nightmares of his childhood. He tells her about thinking he was dead and in some kind of purgatory—he doesn't believe in that stuff, but it felt so much like the crap he was told by his aunt and uncle growing up that he wasn't able to avoid making the comparison. He tells her he doesn't know what to do about Max.

"I think it would be good for me if I talked to him and put it to rest," he says, "but I'm terrified of how he makes me feel, and I'm *angry* on top of that… "

"If he capitulates, he'll be working at the New York facility. You'll probably see him again. So maybe talking to him now is a good idea. He's an ass, but I'd rather have him in my sights than running free. If we can change his attitude, maybe he'll even become a useful operative. He wouldn't be the first criminal vampire to walk that path." She shrugs. "But I want you to know—I feel awful about introducing you two. I had no idea what was going on at the time."

Kyle reaches for her hand. "None of us did. So, you aren't really a student, then?"

"No, I am. In fact, I'd love to finish school while I work." She smiles. "After all, I did spend almost two years undercover as a student. And everything I told you about my past was true."

Later, Lee speaks briefly with Elisa and Clara in the hallway outside of his room. When they're finished, Elisa and Clara flank his bed like anxious parents. Kyle sits up straighter.

Elisa smiles. "Hospital couture looks good on you, *gato.*"

"I try."

"You look healthier," Clara says.

He takes a breath. "I want to see Max before I go home." He's being discharged tomorrow, so now is the time.

Clara tilts her head. "Are you sure?"

"I think I need to."

"Okay," Elisa says. "If you're okay with us being there. We're recording everything he says."

Kyle is fine with that. They help him into slippers and a robe and stay by his side for the walk downstairs. He can't believe how unsteady he is—he hasn't felt this weak since he was human—but he's mentally sound, and that's what matters.

Max is in a holding cell. He looks disheveled and angry. Kyle has never seen him like this.

Max stands and approaches the glass as Elisa turns on the recording software and shows Kyle where the microphone is. "You're okay."

Kyle's jaw tenses. "Was it fun? Getting me to take the bait, fucking with me the whole time?"

"No." Max flinches. "No, it wasn't like that. How I felt about you—that was real. It killed me, what I did to you."

A sizable portion of what Kyle feels for Max now is pity. Other complicated emotions still lurk inside him—anger on behalf of the vampires who suffered because of Turn Back, most of all—but he can't bear the weight of them alone, not even here in relative safety and support. He has to set them aside if he intends to move ahead.

Max is as much a pawn as a solider. He was brought into this life against his will, and a small part of Kyle sympathizes with him.

"I'm sorry," Max says, when Kyle doesn't speak again.

"Then you'll be happy to prove that," Elisa says, as Lee steps into the room behind them. Elisa gestures to her. "Your one-way ticket to a coast, as promised."

Max's eyes flash, and then go dark. "You lied to me."

Elisa smiles meanly. "No; I misled you."

"It's a second chance, Max," Lee says, her chin raised. "Put your money where your mouth is and prove to everyone that you can be a better person." She tilts her head. "You'll have a roof over your head, blood in your belly, a job and protection from Turn Back. Where else are you going to find that kind of a deal now?"

Max lowers his head, and then nods stiffly. Kyle feels a rush of relief so keen it stings. He'll be able to relax knowing Max will not only be gone from Chicago, but will be doing something productive under strict supervision.

"Good luck. I hope—I hope you find a place there."

Max tries to smile, but fails. "Feel better. Be happy."

Kyle leaves without looking back, his heart slamming against his chest.

* * *

BRIAN SHOWS UP ON MICHAEL and Jenn's doorstep with an expensive floral arrangement, a crystal flask of blood, a bottle of wine and a desperately chipper smile.

"What did you do?" Michael asks, by way of hello, and Brian deflates. "Oh geez. It's the stepped-on-a-puppy look. Come in."

After pleasantries, Brian uncorks the wine and pours Jenn a glass. "Can you give us a second?" He wants to tell her the story, but he needs to share it with Michael first, mostly because he isn't sure how Michael is going to take it and he doesn't think Michael would want to overreact in front of Jenn and upset her.

She nods, smiles, kisses his cheek and leaves them alone in Michael's office.

Michael sips from his shot glass of blood. "It's Dad, isn't it?" Brian blinks. "I've heard some rumblings, nothing specific, but…"

So much for the subtle approach.

"We got a lead, and I followed it." Brian sits beside his brother. "It was Turn Back's New York research base. Dad had an office there. He's their lead attorney." Michael puts his head down. "All of the research on the virus was there. It was something they created and let loose here. An experimental biological weapon.

We confiscated everything in exchange for allowing Dad a head start out of town. He—he said if I went through with it, he wouldn't speak to either of us or our families again. That he wouldn't let us meet his daughter."

"Ah," Michael forces out. He sniffs loudly, a sheen over his eyes. "Well. Shit."

Brian reaches for his arms. "I'm sorry I did this without asking you first. But everything was moving so fast—vampires were dying, *Kyle* was dying—and I had to act." Michael wraps his arms around Brian. His brother is both taller and wider than he is, and it's a relief to lose himself in that big, strong, almost paternal embrace.

"This hurts," Michael says, his voice thick with tears, "but— he was—he was awful, wasn't he? And there was no changing him." He huffs out a breath. "You—fuck, little brother, you did it. You really did it. I'm proud of you." He whimpers and then cries into Brian's hair for a moment.

"I was a part of it. Elisa, Clara and Lee did most of the work."

"That's good, though." Michael puts him at arm's length. It's strange to see Michael cry—he hardly shed a tear at his own wedding. "You work with some powerful people. This city's vampire population is in good hands with those women in charge."

"Amen to that."

"Can I bring Jenn into this?"

"Of course."

Michael obviously tells her in the brief window of time during which he disappears, because she comes back to the office with wet eyes and a black kitten in her arms, which she holds out to him.

"Take this," she says. "It isn't safe to go alone."

He laughs and then tears up, taking the kitten, which he recognizes as the one Kyle fell in love with not long ago—the one he dubbed "The Claw."

"I guess I don't have a say, here?"

She hugs him. "Not really. Congratulations. You're a father." She squeezes him and says, to him alone, "And you're already a better one than the one you got saddled with. Love you."

Tears blur his vision. "I love you, too."

Michael wraps his arms around them. "Can you stay over? I don't want to jump the gun here, but I think I'm up for some couch time with my two favorite people in the world."

Jenn bats her eyelashes. "Can I be in the middle?"

Brian turns red. "Oh, god."

Jenn leads them both by the hand out of the office. "You Prestons have such dirty minds."

Brian isn't sure what he expected coming here tonight to deliver terrible news, but it certainly wasn't for Michael to see to the heart of the matter the way he himself has come to. He's learning that this is what family is and does, though, whether it's biological or found or a blend of both. It forgives and loves and moves forward, even when all of the above seems impossible.

* * *

KYLE IS ELBOW-DEEP IN PAINT samples when Brian comes home from his overnight stay at Michael and Jenn's. He figured that a decorating spree was as good as any method of distracting himself from his nervousness about their reaction to the news, but it hasn't done much except make visions of credit card bills with too many digits dance through his head.

Still—this apartment could use some love, and Brian would agree.

Things between them have been settled and sweet since they resumed their version of a normal day-to-day life. Brian has been spending more time at the clinic than the facility, treating patients who have the virus—so far, most of them have responded well to treatment. Empowered by the ability to actually *help*, he is a lot more like the vibrant, excitable man Kyle fell in love with, though new lines around his eyes and a shadowy maturity behind every smile tell a sad story.

But they're both better for having survived the ordeal. Kyle has learned a lot about trust, attraction and what makes him tick. He's realized that now, more than ever, social work is his future, and that he wouldn't turn down a night job as Elisa's apprentice any day of the week. He's that much surer of both the vampire and the man he's becoming.

He smells Brian coming, but there's an additional note he can't identify. Brian stumbles through the door with a cardboard box in one hand and a plastic shopping bag in the other, and Kyle realizes what the scent is.

"Oh, my god!" he squeaks, blurring upright and over to Brian in a heartbeat.

Brian pants. "I put a ribbon on this little demon, but he destroyed it and my hand on the way home."

Kyle coos. "I *love* him." Directly out of the box, the kitten purrs and claws its way up Kyle's arm to nuzzle into the space below his jaw. "Whossacutewiddlebabyesss?" He hugs Brian with his free arm. "I completely forgot about him! Thank you."

Brian smiles and kisses him. "I couldn't say no."

"I'll take that as confirmation that things went well? I don't think Jenn dispenses kittens as a way of saying 'get the fuck out.'"

Brian shrugs off his jacket. "It was rough. Michael was—I mean, he was upset, but he understood. He knew from the way Dad was at the wedding that there was no fixing things."

"I'm glad you went alone." Kyle takes the shopping bag of cat supplies from Brian. He sits down on the living room floor, then switches the kitten from one hand to the other. "I think he needed to focus on you and what you were saying. There are times when he actually *doesn't* want an audience."

Brian laughs. "Rare but notable moments."

Kyle gives the kitten a thorough scratching and then sets him down. He scurries, and then steps more cautiously, deciding to explore the carpet under the coffee table.

Kyle makes a tormented face. "He's so cute."

"Are we still going with 'The Claw'?"

"Nah," Kyle says, "I like yours better." He smiles. "Demon."

"Not sure if that's an improvement."

"Maybe not, but it's accurate."

Demon is busily climbing the back of the sofa. The tufts of white fur above his eyes and the pale whiskers that stand out from his face like horns quiver with every determined grab.

"Can't argue with that," Brian says.

13

BRIAN IS, PERHAPS, OVERLY CAUTIOUS in the weeks that follow.

He isn't sure what Kyle is ready for. More than once, he's wondered if Kyle is still holding on to that night and the hazy weeks leading up to it, when neither of them were themselves—Kyle under the influence of the virus, and Brian responding to his needs as only a donor who is also a partner could have done. Their dynamic has been off since Kyle was cured—they've been unable to find their way back to the easy sexual intimacy they shared before.

Kyle has yet to go back to school, which only contributes to the anticipation—he is home more often than not, reading or surfing the Internet or playing with Demon or painting the walls or rearranging furniture. They're seeing a lot more of each other, and the urge to reach for him and make him feel good is becoming overwhelming. Why are they hesitating?

One evening, Brian comes home to find Kyle napping with his headphones on—it sounds as if he's listening to the original Broadway recording of *The Phantom of the Opera*. He undresses and slides beneath the covers, not surprised when Kyle's mouth twitches.

"I can smell you from a block away, you know that, right?"

"Common courtesy, you." Without opening his eyes, Kyle takes his headphones off and then pulls Brian down on top of him. Brian discovers that he's delightfully naked. He wraps his legs around Brian's waist and kisses his neck. "Michael Crawford really gets you going, huh?"

Kyle laughs into his shoulder. "You're the worst."

Brian trails one hand from Kyle's hip, along the outside of his thigh, all the way to the back of his knee where he's warm and a little sweaty. Brian's cock throbs, filling against his belly. Kyle feels incredible and smells even better. Brian's mouth goes wet at the taste of the salty skin of Kyle's collarbone. He inches downward from there, nipping and kissing, desire cramping in his balls and at the base of his cock. Kyle's fingers thread through his hair. He leaves a trail of kisses across the length of Kyle's torso, savoring the concave dip of his belly.

Kyle twitches upward and whimpers. "Fuck, please." His cock is hardening, already flushed at the slit.

Brian drags his tongue up the shaft and then wraps his lips around the head, drawing on it once or twice before letting it go with a wet pop. "I want to eat you out," he says, licking, licking, licking at Kyle's cock, making it tighten and fill, "and fuck you. Okay?"

Kyle is red to his collarbone and his eyes are a striking shade of dark blue. His body yields to Brian: his legs fold up and back, his spine arches. He's grasping at himself and holding his cheeks apart well before Brian's mouth travels over the soft spill of his balls.

"Brian," he moans. "Please don't tease me, it's been so long, I need—"

"Get the lube, sweetheart." Brian kisses his cheeks on either side. "Were you touching yourself earlier?"

His lip bitten in, Kyle nods. "Just dry, though, I—wanted to wait."

Brian kisses his pink, jagged perineum. "I'm glad."

"*Please—*"

"Put your legs over my shoulders."

Brian loves Kyle wrapped around him like this, open and desperate—loves those unforgiving vampiric fingers pulling his hair, loves the whining breaths Kyle exhales when he digs in, holds Kyle open and sucks tongue-filled kisses against Kyle's rim and hole. The flavor is familiar—it feels like forever since he tasted it last—and he moans as it spreads across his tongue.

When he presses his tongue inside, the small of Kyle's back rises off of the bed. Kyle puffs air in and out of his lungs, whimpering whenever Brian slows down or goes faster. Brian can't resist reaching up to pinch those lovely, pink, pebbled nipples. The pinches morph into twists, and he has to stop to make himself breathe when the resulting pain causes Kyle's fangs to drop. Kyle licks out over them, clearly hungry in more ways than one.

Brian's cock bobs heavy and full between his legs. "So gorgeous."

Kyle clicks the lubricant tube open with an eager glance at Brian's cock. "Come here." Brian lies down on top of Kyle, putting his weight on his elbows, and inhales sharply when lubricant spills sloppy and cool between their bellies. Kyle angles a handful down, and slicks his crack and then Brian's cock, wrapping his fist around it. "Fuck, want you." He pushes his heels against Brian's ass. "Want you in me, fuck, please." Brian reaches down to line them up, letting Kyle's hips swivel until the angle is better, and then pushes forward, digging his knees into the bed. The clasp of Kyle's legs does the rest. "Oh, fuck, oh, my *god*, yeah."

Brian bottoms out and grinds forward, edges back out to the head of his cock, and then sinks deep again, his eyes rolling back. "God—"

Kyle's legs twine around Brian's torso. "Come on, come on."

Brian wraps his arms around Kyle's shoulders from underneath, hooking his fingers around their slopes as he bites down on the curve of Kyle's neck. "I know, just, let me, oh, god." He forgot how good this feels: the tight, elastic, grip of it; Kyle's overspills of vampiric strength making every thrust that much more intense; and the moment when his ass relaxes and starts to not only take it but try to keep it, milking Brian's cock like a fist.

He opens his eyes to stare at Kyle's fangs and trembling mouth and is caught in Kyle's gaze instead. He finds pleasure there but also affection, and an attachment so complete it makes his heart leap in his throat. The animal rhythm of his cock driving Kyle open, *making* him feel every inch of where they're connected, is too much on top of the love in his eyes. Brian stops to avoid coming so soon; his hot skin prickles with fresh sweat.

Kyle's body rolls, sending his ass down around Brian's cock. "Just you. Just you, you know that, right? I never—I never—"

Brian begins to rock again, driving himself in and out. "Shhh, don't. I know. I know."

Kyle's hand moves jerkily up and down his own cock. "I'm gonna come." He grips Brian's ass with his free hand. "Oh, fuck, make me come, fuck, *fuck*—"

Brian thrusts into him blindly. When they kiss, he feels the dangerous jab of his fangs. He tastes blood and moans, opening his mouth to swallow down every noise and bit of profanity Kyle offers up. Shaking and panting, he follows Kyle over the edge a moment later.

When he can move again, he savors the sight and feel of Kyle's body under his—Kyle's face turned to the side, his throat heaving, his skin flushed a deep, flattering pink, and his forehead glistening with sweat. His ass is still fluttering around Brian's softening cock.

Kyle's fingertips slide up his sweaty back. "God, that felt good."

Brian bends low to lick a stripe of come off of Kyle's ribs. "We waited too long."

"You weren't—I mean, the last time we—I hurt you."

Brian licks again, lower. "No. It didn't even come to mind. Was it an issue for you?"

"No. Not at all. That person wasn't me."

"I'm glad." Brian kisses Kyle's stiff nipples. "You've been through enough. I don't want what we have to get screwed up for you, too."

"It isn't. Don't worry." He smiles. "Although I will have to tease you from time to time about punching me in the face."

"Technically, I elbowed you in the face."

"And sprayed me!"

"And sprayed you."

Kyle's mouth twists. "You took me out. I'm kind of proud."

Brian rolls his eyes. "I don't think I've arrived at the humor place yet."

"Awww, okay. I'm sorry. I just wanted to make you smile."

Brian gently guides two fingers back inside of Kyle, through the tacky mess of drying lubricant and come. "Well. I can think of a few ways you might accomplish that."

Kyle breathes rapidly through awed surprise. "Again?"

Brian smiles, kisses him and, instead of answering, simply hauls his legs around his waist.

* * *

THEY'VE NEVER USED THIS MEETING room. Then again, they've also never needed a bug-free, soundproofed meeting room with a single entry point before—but, as Elisa told Kyle when she brought him into the fold of the facility, times are changing.

Elisa went so far as to schedule this meeting, so it must finally be time to discuss the fallout of recent events. The time off has been lovely, but Kyle doesn't want to sit on the sidelines forever. He's eager to know what their next move is going to be.

Clara and Elisa enter the room.

"Uh-oh," Kyle says, "they're on time. That can't be good."

Elisa ruffles his flawless hair with a smirk. "The peanut gallery will be silent."

He pouts and fusses. "Okay, okay."

Clara sits at the head of the table. "We really need to remember to cater these things." She shuffles a stack of folders and then hands one to Kyle and one to Brian. "The information Brian brought back from New York, as well as what we got from Lee and Max, has proven to be very useful. Figuring out what is real and what is not in terms of the identities of individuals and organizations involved with Turn Back has been challenging, but we're getting there. The Chicago data in particular has been game-changing—with it, we've managed to weed out leaks in a variety of locations."

"What kinds of leaks?" Brian asks.

"A security guard at the club," Elisa says, "a janitor at the facility, and your clinic office manager, Beth, I'm sorry to say. They were all spying for Turn Back."

"Beth?" Brian's face goes red. "Are you sure?"

"Yep. She spilled the beans as soon as we started questioning her. She's been funneling patient records to them for months."

Kyle squeezes Brian's hand.

"Identifying patterns in their documents has allowed us to pin down suspicious activity much faster," Elisa says. "We now know what to look for. Beyond that, there are a lot of names and places to research. But what we do have, locked down and definite, is enough to begin discrediting them in public—of course, we need to be strategic about how we do it, and we can't allow the activity to be traced back to us. In the meantime, we'll put our agents in their path, in businesses and at locations they have no idea we know about. We can infiltrate their ranks, member by member, until we reach the board level, and then we'll see just how quickly rats desert a sinking ship."

"Do we know anything about the board?" Brian asks.

"Well, your father was on his way to becoming a member, but he never quite made it—and he's the only legitimate name we've found so far. Regardless, he's lost to us for the time being." She shrugs. "My guess is the board is a mix of big business interests and politically funded conservative organizations. The paper trail reminds me of the contracts we worked out with the feds back in the day. The language and formatting is eerily similar." She exhales. "I think this goes up much higher than we originally thought. I think someone in our government is green-lighting Turn Back, biological weapons and all."

A wave of dread goes through Kyle, but he isn't shocked. He's always thought Turn Back was too successful in its media campaign and geographical sprawl to be a simple grassroots organization. Development of biological weapons doesn't come cheap.

"Are they breaking the contract?" he asks, when silence falls. He looks at Elisa, Clara, and Brian in turn. "Is the peace over? Are they the enemy?"

Elisa's eyes darken with approval. "*Gato* has brains as well as claws."

"We can't prove it," Clara says.

"We don't need to prove it," Elisa says. "You and I both know this isn't about Turn Back. They're just a weapon that's being pointed at us."

"What do we do?" Brian asks.

Kyle's mouth twists upward. *My handsome problem-solver.*

Elisa stands, arranges the black dress she's wearing over her wide hips and puts her fingertips on the table. "The word of the day is 'alliance.'"

Kyle perks up. "With whom?"

"After Lee went home with her new charity case in tow and her mission suspended for the time being, I got a call from her boss and her boss's boss."

"Kel?" Brian asks.

"In one, doc." She smiles. "She gave me hell about our New York operation, but she was glad to have Lee back, and she seemed eager to crush Max into a new shape. I gotta say, we bonded over that. She's not as bad as she was."

A flush runs down the back of Kyle's neck. He's still embarrassed about what happened with Max.

"It's time for the Chicago and New York facilities to work together instead of side by side," Clara says. "Their operation is roughly the same size as ours but they cover a wider area—they have a broader network of field operatives and their interests are more diversified, whereas we have a more developed science division." She nods at Brian. "An alliance will benefit us both. Our recent experience with Turn Back blew the lid off the idea that the powers that be are still playing nice in exchange for our cooperation."

Kyle's heart slams in his throat. This change in the status quo is disorienting, like stepping out onto what seems like solid ground only to have it buckle under his feet. Maybe it was inevitable—the plotting, the mistrust, the creation of weapons on both sides, *just in case*—but it's unsettling to watch it unfold.

"An alliance makes sense," he says. "And if you need us—"

Elisa tilts her head. "At this point, that should go without saying." She looks at Clara and then back at them. "In order to kick this off, we need face time. Clara and I want you two to come with us to New York—get the full tour, meet everyone, be a part of the alliance negotiations. Brian, you'll represent our science division, and Kyle, you'll be presented as the head operative of our social interfacing efforts. Fancy ways of saying you're VIPs. Nothing you do or say while we're there should contradict that. But don't be fucking modest, either. You won't be the only agents we bring, but you will be the most informed and involved, and we expect you to own that."

They share a look. Kyle sees trepidation in Brian's eyes and wonders what kind of face he himself is making right now. Beneath the table, he squeezes Brian's thigh.

New York is good. I like New York, he thinks.

Me too.

"When do we leave?" Brian asks.

Elisa smiles.

BRIAN LEADS KYLE DOWNSTAIRS TO the storage room where he often hides, to the desk where he had the idea that Kyle's blood might be worth testing for traces of the virus. It's been weeks since he's come down here. He wants to collect his coffee mug and sweater and the good pen he left next to the computer. Now that they have a viable treatment for his patients, he'll be spending more time at his clinic than the facility in the months to come.

"You okay?" he asks Kyle, who has been quiet since their meeting ended.

"Actually, I am." Kyle leans against the desk. "This alliance with New York feels right. And I'm excited about working with Lee and getting to know her better."

"*I'm* excited to see New York with you. We've never been together. Remember that time I went for a conference there and came home to you waiting outside my apartment?"

Kyle smiles. "I pounced you." His cheeks go pink. "I couldn't believe how much I missed you. It was like the world went gray as soon as you left."

Brian laughs. "And they say I'm the romantic."

Kyle is quiet for a moment, and then his expression softens. "We kind of got lost this year, didn't we?"

"I felt so distant from you. From our whole life. And I know my workaholic streak had something to do with it. I'm sorry."

"I know, honey. And I—I'm so sorry about Max. I'm just glad it's over; I can't even tell you how much."

Brian smiles. "You're allowed to find other men attractive. We're dating, not dead below the waist. But I'll admit—I'm glad you didn't sleep with him."

"Me too." Kyle inches closer until his knee touches Brian's arm. "I don't think I'm the sleep-with-someone-just-to-get-off type. It's not a morality thing. More power to people who love sex that way, but I like knowing the person I'm getting intimate with. Is that weird?"

"Not at all," Brian says. "I've always been that way, too. When all that's on offer is an orgasm, it feels pointless later."

Kyle nudges Brian's arm. "For the record, though? You give pretty amazing orgasms."

Brian smiles. "You're not so bad yourself."

"And you are a wonderful boyfriend. I don't tell you often enough."

"I love you." Brian kisses him. "New York isn't going to know what hit it."

"I am so ready." Kyle tugs Brian onto his feet. "Are you ready?"

"With you around? Always."

THE END

☾

Acknowledgments

I WOULD LIKE TO GIVE a heartfelt thank you to the team at Interlude Press for their unwavering commitment to the art of LGBTQ storytelling, and for the opportunity to grow Brian and Kyle's small but fascinating world into a universe.

As always, my love goes out to the people who cheer me on every day: my husband Brad, my best friend Johnna, and the adopted mom and sister I lucked into finding in middle school, Donna and Erika. I wouldn't be a published author today if you all hadn't encouraged, loved and bugged the crap out of me. Thank you for being you.

☾

Questions for Discussion

1. Compare Clara and Elisa's story with Kyle and Brian's. What similarities are there?

2. What does Kyle get from working at the youth shelter that was missing in his life?

3. How do Kyle and Brian's relationship troubles contribute to Max's plan?

4. How do Kyle and Brian's communication problems get worse throughout the story? How would dealing with them earlier have changed their trajectory as the story goes along?

5. In what way do Kyle and Brian use sex to communicate? Does that help their other issues or make them worse? Why?

6. How does the way Brian and Michael deal with the relationship with their father affect the outcome of the story?

7. What are the advantages and disadvantages of human/vampire relationships versus vampire/vampire or human/human? If you were a character in this story, which would you pick and why?

8. Prejudice against vampires runs rampant in the world Graves created. Relate that to prejudice we still see in ours. What else can be done to make prejudice disappear?

9. After the wedding, Brian and Kyle made a conscious decision not to talk about what happened with Brian's dad. Was that the right decision? Why or why not?

10. Kyle's deterioration began long before it was noticed by the people that love him. Track his symptoms and discuss why it was so easy to explain them away, until all of a sudden it wasn't.

11. Brian has two confrontations with his father, one at the wedding and one in New York. How were they similar? How were they different?

12. Brian and Kyle are off to another adventure in a new city. What do you think comes next for them?

About the Author

A VETERAN WRITER OF FAN FICTION with thousands of followers, Melissa Graves wrote her first story at age thirteen, and by age sixteen had met her future husband in an online vampire fiction chat room. A fan of science fiction and fantasy, she has a degree in anthropology and a passion for good chocolate, amateur erotica and fan worlds that celebrate diversity. She is mother to two cats.

Bleeding Heart, book one of the *Mi Corazón Sangrante* series, was her debut novel for Interlude Press.

☾

Also from Melissa **Graves**

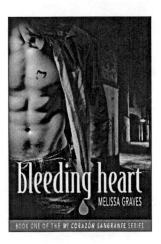

Bleeding Heart by Melissa Graves

While the public struggles to live side by side with vampires, medical student Brian Preston has dedicated himself to their care and study by working in a government-run clinic that monitors and feeds the resident vampire population. He has learned to expect the unexpected in his job, but life takes a surprising turn late one night when a young, mysterious vampire named Kyle stumbles into his clinic and into his heart.

As they draw closer, can Brian come to grips with loving the elusive vampire and can Kyle find the strength to share the secret that can separate them forever? Bleeding Heart is the story of love, blood and the secrets that can spell the difference between life and death.

ISBN 978-1-941530-01-6

Coming Soon

Kyle and Brian follow the trail of intrigue and betrayal to New York City, in the conclusion to the *Mi Corazón Sangrante* series.

One **story** can change **everything**.

www.interlude**press**.com

Now available from

interlude  press™

The Sidhe by Charlotte Ashe

Brieden Lethiscir has always admired The Sidhe, the beautiful and magical beings native to the Faerie world outside his homeland of Villalu. Though he grew up in a culture accepting of Sidhe enslavement by Villalu's elite, Brieden finds that he can no longer tolerate the practice when he becomes a steward to a vicious prince who is abusive of his sidhe slave Sehrys. Captivated by the handsome, mysterious slave, Brieden vows to free and return Sehrys to his homeland.

As they escape and navigate a treacherous path to the border, Breiden and Sehrys grow close. Breiden soon learns both the true power of The Sidhe, and that the world that he once knew is not what it seemed. If they survive to reach the border, he will have to make a choice: the love of his life, or the fate of his world.

ISBN 978-1-941530-33-7

Hush by Jude Sierra

Published by Consent, an imprint of Interlude Press

Wren is one of "the gifted"—a man with the power to compel others' feelings and desires. He uses his power as a game of sexual consent until Cameron, a naïve college student, enters his life. As Cameron begins to understand his sexuality and gain confidence under Wren's tutelage, Wren grows to recognize new and unexpected things about himself. Can their game become a relationship as the power shifts from teacher to student?

ISBN 978-1-941530-27-6

Love Starved by Kate Fierro

Micah Geller considers himself lucky: at 27, he has more money than he needs, a job he loves, a debut book coming out, and a brilliant career in information security before him. What he doesn't have is a partner to share it with—a fact that's never bothered him much.

But the romantic in him isn't entirely dead. When a moment of weakness finds him with a contact to a high-class escort specializing in fulfilling fantasies, Micah asks for only one thing: *Show me what it's like to feel loved.*

ISBN 978-1-941530-32-0

Platonic by Kate Paddington

Mark Savoy and Daniel O'Shea were high school sweethearts who had planned their forevers together. But when Mark goes to college in California rather than following Daniel to New York, he embarks on a decade-long search for independence, sexual confidence and love. When Mark lands a job in New York and crosses Daniel's path, they slowly rebuild their fractured friendship through texts and emails. If they finally agree to see each other, will they be able to keep it platonic? Or will the spark of a long-lost love reignite just as Daniel accepts a job overseas?

ISBN 978-1-941530-02-3

One **story** can change **everything**.

www.interlude**press**.com

CPSIA information can be obtained
at www.ICGtesting.com
Printed in the USA
FFOW04n1219281015
18107FF